SPIKEY'S POINTS!

Four Musical Sequels:

Welcome Spikey's Points
Catch A Friend
Spikey's Cool School
Happily Ever After!

Spikey Trademark copyright © 1993

Joy Winter-Schmidt

authorHOUSE®

AuthorHouse™
1663 Liberty Drive
Bloomington, IN 47403
www.authorhouse.com
Phone: 1 (800) 839-8640

Published by AuthorHouse   04/27/2016

ISBN: 978-1-5049-5170-8 (sc)
ISBN: 978-1-5049-5169-2 (e)

Library of Congress Control Number: 2015915651

Print information available on the last page.

Table of Contents

THE BEST POINTS...

The Best Points start from kindness within.

A smile from your heart, is a win, win.

When others see it on your face,

they feel peace, as tension, you erase.

What we do for ourselves dies fast.

What we do for others, lives on and lasts.

No one has the right to judge or criticize.

We haven't walked their walk...

or looked through their eyes.

Having a heart to help, is the best point of all.

Listen to hear your call...

Preface

'Spikey' was written for more reasons than to 'make and prove a point,' or ask "What's the Point?" Joy first experienced the power of humiliation and bullying when she was in Gr. 1. A classmate, the prettiest and most popular girl in the class, told Joy she "had to give her money if she wanted to be in her group of friends." In Gr. 2, she watched a girl cry uncontrollably in front of the class, because she'd been made fun of for doing her homework wrong. Gr. 3 became a very significant year. Joy moved to a farm and attended a one room school house. The horse she and her brother rode to school was kept in the "student stable." Joy read her first newspaper article that fall, posted on the bulletin board, with the headline "Assassination of President JFK." After she found out from her teacher, what it meant, Joy stood in a state of shock, reading it continuously. She asked her teacher, "Why? What did he do wrong to deserve that?" Her teacher replied, "There was no reason, maybe just because he was the President." Later, she recalls watching a young boy sitting in the corner wearing a dunce hat. She wondered, "What's the point?" As others laughed, she noticed his trembling lip and a tear rolling down his cheek. She does not remember what he did wrong, but she remembers the cruel laughter, the pain in his eyes, and how he must have felt. These moments empowered her for life. Why do people do mean things to others? What point does humiliation prove? Gr. 4 was Joy's fourth school and a difficult year. She told herself "to make a friend, you have to be one." She struggled, but was supported by her incredible teacher, who told Joy 'she could ring her home doorbell anytime.' Joy didn't go to her place, but knew she'd be welcomed if the need arose. Joy was fortunate to have caring teachers. This book is for them!

Joy continued to question why bad things happen to good people. Later in life, Joy became unpopular when she tried to stand up for the underdogs. Always small, nicknamed "skinflint" and last picked to join sports teams, she became upset with those judged by their appearance. In later years, Joy stopped bullying actions and words, when she saw others passing around germs or starting "clubs," opposing innocent students. When the "germs" got to her, they ended with her! Spikey evolved from her experiences! Spikey is about showing empathy, helping others in their journey and offering a smile and a helping hand. The purpose of writing the four sequels, is delivered through Spikey, as he speaks universally of how we're all different and yet all the same. Spikey is grateful for being cared for by Grammy. He is grateful for kindness received and shows his appreciation by helping others to get back up! 'Spikey' is a 'tribute' to Joy, Dave and Andrew's beloved 'adopted' dog Haley, of 17 years.

THE SPIKEY FABLE: Spikey conveys several morals and comes full circle. He begins as an orphan with an uncertain future, to a desire for an education, job and caring for others. The Spikey sequels are a collective of four scripts, pertaining to obstacles, friendships, bullying and life experiences. Attitude is a choice. There are several storylines, with adults and Spikey teaching lessons, sharing good points regarding being the best you can be, and setting positive examples. Spikey is naïve, but many see an ambiguous, puzzling character, an 'enigma.' The introduction of a female and baby porcupine, create an even larger world of disbelief and lack of acceptance! Spikey makes a point by remaining soft spoken and kind in spite of physical and verbal attacks. Although often misunderstood, his point is to make the world a kinder place by being helpful, emphatic and maintaining his optimism and gentle spirit. Spikey's primary focus is on ANTI-BULLYING, inclusion, acceptance, not judging by appearance, and accepting that life can be unfair, but don't allow negative circumstances to destroy you. Make a positive point, wherever you are.

THE SPIKEY ANALOGY: The 'park' is the world as the 'world' is a stage. The metaphors depict the park as Spikey's forum of diversity and acceptance. Spikey is the 'sunshine.' In spite of cynics, Spikey makes changes with his attitude of genuine compassion and a mature, turn the other cheek approach. Spikey teaches us not to 'underestimate' ourselves or others, and proves an 'endangered species' can become a leader. Joy is proud to be a Canadian, and sees Canada as the picnic table in the park. Our great neighbor, the USA is on the other side. Together we are stronger. The park benches are open to other countries and new neighbours. The centre rock is symbolic of a 'sounding stone' and solid community,' supporting others. All are welcome. Spikey is about 'giving back,' not about ego. He has a tolerance for suffering and doesn't get flustered. He makes a point to get up and keep moving. He focuses on team building and working together to unify. His strength comes from his family, Grammy and friends. He's a mentor with 'positive points,' setting a strong moral example.

COMPASSION WINS: *In 1972 Joy was 16, in Grade 11, and very interested in politics, psychology and diplomacy. She succumbed to 'Trudeaumania' and ran through a crowd of fans to meet Prime Minister Pierre Trudeau. Some were angry protestors and/or farmers, hurling tomatoes and eggs at him. As he was being 'bullied,' she (at 5' 2") tenaciously made her way to the resilient, popular Trudeau; trying to stop the mean words and senseless throwing. She'll never forget his smile when she finally approached him with pen and paper, requesting his autograph. He took the time to sign, as they stood in the midst of chaos. She felt his confidence, as peace and calmness fenced them in. One of her deepest regrets much later, was allowing the teasing/bullying of others, to pressure her into throwing his signature away. They convinced her it was "worthless and stupid." She met Prime Ministers, Trudeau and Mulroney many years later when she worked at The Brandon Sun newspaper. She shook the hands of these national, gracious icons, (but did not ask for autographs). She admired the competent PM Harper but in October 2015, she, her husband and son voted for Justin Trudeau. His clean, proficient, 'no bullying' campaign won with dignity and class. His 'no hate but hope' style proved compassion, a kind heart and optimism is empowering; an integral way to leave a legacy. Engraved in her memory is PM Harper's son graciously putting his arm around his hard working, defeated dad. 'Spikey,' strong leaders and many team players, have resonated with the people. They have all taught, whether it's a victory or a loss ... 'in the end - kindness and caring always wins!'*

ABOUT THE SEQUELS

GRAMMY inspires SPIKEY to get up and move on, following the loss of his parents. She nurtured and cared for him. Grammy helps Spikey understand how overwhelming a loss can be, but we can be strong and get through it. A loss is tough, but her positive points have influenced and strengthened Spikey. Grammy gave him time to cry, encouragement to keep moving, and not stay down. She ensured, he can handle situations and that we all feel alone at some point. In spite of fear, bullying, trying and failing, Spikey becomes educated and makes it with a little help from his friends! Grammy and Spikey inspire others, so they too, can move on with their lives. The characters interact in the common setting of 'the park,' and have a 'together we can make it,' philosophy! Friendship and the power of love is unconditional. The characters in the script believe everyone has the potential to help and inspire others!

Sequel 1 – WELCOME SPIKEY'S POINTS:

Spikey, the loveable porcupine with many fine, soft points, is found hurt by the side of the road, and adopted by Grammy. They celebrate one year together, plus plan a tribute to Spikey's parents. Spikey has learned to count, read, speak in rhyme and sing! He meets the new girl Keri, plus a few not so happy parents. All meet to help clean up the park. The ending is a special surprise. Spikey, as all of us, has mostly 'good points.' Spikey is about love, acceptance, understanding and peace. It's about doing our best, to make the world a better place, by cleaning up and having a positive attitude.

Sequels 2 – CATCH A FRIEND:

Spikey joins a ball team and Keri wants to join the dance team. They both want and need to 'catch a friend.' Keri and her mom, a teacher; have moved and are starting a new school year together. Someone has poked holes in the roof of Mr. T's (Keri's Grandpa) convertible. Who could it be? Will someone innocent be accused? Will Jessica allow Keri to join her 'after school dance team?'

Sequel 3 – SPIKEY'S COOL SCHOOL:

Spikey realizes he has so much to learn and wishes to go to school. Will he be accepted? Will porcupines ever be allowed in a school? The new Vice Principal, Ms. Radcliffe, is concerned about safety in school. But Spikey has a dream. Could it come true? A sequel full of sparkling surprises!

Sequel 4 – HAPPILY EVER AFTER:

Spikey attends the opening of the new alternative school, Porcupine Community School; with Grammy and friends! Spikey gets bullied and hit in the eye. He needs more than an ice pack to make him feel better. His friends help him get back on his feet. He's excited about attending a double wedding. Life is about relationships and respecting others. We can make a choice to be happy. Together we can make this world a better place.

DEDICATION

In Memory of Joy's Beloved Father and Mentor

Hugh Oliver Winter
Peaceful, Selfless Hero

July 15, 1932- January 26, 2010
"Faith is the mortar that holds us together." Romans 8:38

Hugh was born in Oxdrift Ontario. He's Resting in Peace at
Windsor Cemetary, Tuelon Manitoba, Canada

The inspiration for Joy's creation of Spikey, was instilled by her loving, hard-working, non-judgemental father. He never raised his voice. He opened her world and made her feel she could "follow her dreams." He loved his family and all of humanity, unconditionally! He was brilliant, profound and dearly loved and respected by all who knew him. At 77, he walked briskly with upright posture. He was honest and had class without arrogance. He enjoyed farming, restoring vehicles, mechanical, electrical and carpentry work. He encouraged his five children to make the best of any situation and not complain. He was generous, never rude and always helped others. He instilled a "your home is as big as your heart," philosophy. He was fearless in his endeavours. When he sold the farm, he creatively designed and built a new home. He later became a Reflexologist and taught it at Red River Community College in Winnipeg for five years, with his wife, Jo. His "healing hands," were held in daily prayer. He was very spiritual with a strong faith.

He loved to read. He read his bible cover to cover, six times. He loved nature, and was drawn to water. A few years before he passed away, he discovered his Metis heritage on his Scottish mother's side. His father, an American from Michigan USA, was a minister, turned farmer. Joy's dad didn't preach Godliness, he lived it. He spoke quietly and listened intently. He was humble, calm and never critical. He died unknowing of how much he was truly loved and admired. When he lost his niece to cancer, he told Joy over the phone, "I wish it was me instead of her." She replied, "Dad, I love you; please don't say that again." He didn't. Four hours later, he passed away. He was Joy's mentor, but she didn't tell him. She wishes she had.

The pain of losing this integral man, with a sudden, unexpected heart attack, left his family with holes in their souls. They cling to his memory. He was a strong Christian who never lost his faith. His common sense, charm, continuous twinkle in his puppy dog eyes and infectious laugh, were magnetic. He had a constant flame in his heart. The fire may have gone out, but his memory lives on. He was their mortar with a noble quiet strength. It made all feel secure. He was inspired by his grandmother, and asked to be buried beside her. His wife will be buried beside him. Hugh, middle child of 9 children, was also very close to his mother.

Joy questioned her father's final thoughts and how he felt before he passed. She realizes we may not get over pain, but we CAN get through it. Her father taught her, "if you try, you appreciate life so much more, and you have more to give others. A loss is the worst feeling ever, but it makes you remember life's lessons and try to be a better person." Joy's wish is to become half the person her father was, full of purity, passion and depth. His warmth and sincerity made him one of a kind, with a fun sense of humour. Joy loved him. He set an excellent, moral example. He lives through Spikey with his empowering points! Joy thanks him for 'being himself," with a dimple in his chin and a warm smile in his heart.

He was a master of forgiveness and an inspiration to all who knew and loved him. He was not wealthy but rich in spirit. He taught his children to believe in themselves, set a positive example and not take anything for granted. He was an early riser who gently taught that opinions differ, but all deserve tolerance and respect. He read nightly bible stories to his family, concluding in prayer. He lived his journey of life, in peace, harmony and love.

Acknowledgements

Joy gives a Special Thanks to her amazing musician men, husband Dave and son Andrew, plus supportive mom Josephine! They've stood by her and faithfully supported her 'theatrical' dreams, non-profit Spikey Productions and other charity/volunteer work, Joy gets involved in! They believed in her and encouraged the publishing of Spikey. She thanks her son for taking the author photo, Sept. 2015. She thanks her Grandmother, all aunts, (Hazel, Ruth, Adele, etc.) mom and especially her Great Grand-mother Esther Morrison, who became her image of 'Grammy.' Joy's father, husband and son inspired the 'innocent, boyish, loving, selfless and uncomplicated,' image of 'Spikey.'

Special Thanks to her fabulous friends and proof readers: Suzanne Mouflier, Marilyn Gault, Heidi Dixon and Shelly Gurr. Thanks to her family and theatre friends, especially Harry Rintoul for his writing workshops. She thanks Jim Forsythe, BU Drama Prof, teachers Jim D., John S. and many others for their support in creating a non-profit theatre company. She also thanks Terry & Cathy, Bob & Wanda, Sandy, Ted, Derek, Pat/Jenni & family, Karen & Rick, Karen & Len, Simon, Debbie, Katherine, Mark H, Kelley, B. Pat Burns, Ardis, Tammy, Rebecca, Erin, Anne & Doug, Diane N, Stephanie B & family, Mark E & family, George, a few Daves, Jeff and more, plus all past, present and future Spikey cast and crew!! Thanks to Krista for the custom made Spikey pins/pendants. Thanks to those who made costumes, props, programs, posters, banners, Spikey t-shirts, souvenirs, etc.

Thanks to Pastor Doug Wiebe, Lucas, and several churches, schools, halls, theatres and Coralie from Glenwood Community Centre for rehearsal and performance space. For music arranging, a special thanks goes to Paulo and Dave, plus Roberta MacLean, Somer Kenny and Marianne Crittenden. Thanks to Paulo, for his fun latin, salsa music, as it continues to inspire the cast, crew, and audiences of all ages! Many mentors have empowered her to continue creative projects, including English Prof John Blaikie who gave her first public Directing review and Steven Schipper (Artistic Director from Winnipeg's MTC Theatre, for teaching her Directing fundamentals!) The study of theatre gave her a writing template, as both are studies of life!" It led to scripts '86 - '96 (e.g.'Spell Success' for Literacy Awareness ,"Accrual Family,' mafia murder mystery for prov'l CGA conference, and "Shades of Grey') plus her first movie 'Brothers Bond.'

Thanks to all who've believed and trusted in her and inspired her to follow her dreams! Joy is truly grateful to all who've had faith in her 'projects,' plus Laura Devlin and sponsor Riverside Lions Club of Winnipeg Manitoba. Proceeds from the productions support the community and live community theatre. Character Coach Bob, was inspired by her smiling Uncle Mike, a great person, musician and ball player. The baby porcupine "Punky" is dedicated to Joy & Dave's only son, Andrew, the first to play the role. Thanks to Andrew for sharing his nickname "Punky," and playing Punky, Ben and Mark. She thanks her husband & son for their patience during her focus on 'Spikey.'

Joy thanks her RN sister, Eveleen, and her Reflexologist mom, for their incredible 'TLC' in getting her health back! They were by her side constantly, along with her husband and son. She also thanks ALL her encouraging hospital visitors and others for their cards and emails. She credits her father-in-law for his 'visit from heaven,' to regain feeling in her body from toes to chin. She felt his presence. The care from so many, inspired her to 'complete and publish Spikey's Points!'

Joy thanks all who came to see the SPIKEY Stage Musical Productions, and all the actors who brought it to life! She sends 'Best Wishes' to future actors, producers, directors, choral directors and choreographers! She says, 'Words are words. It's actors, singers and dancers that bring the script and song writing to life! Your support gave her a foundation! It's an honour for her to have her first book, "Spikey's Points," be published by Authorhouse USA. Special Appreciation & Thanks from Joy; starting with Jon Lopez to Nancy Summers/Jessica? from Authorhouse, for their support in getting 'Spikey' published!! Joy thanks Professional Artist Francis for encouraging her to study Art; but especially to Inspirational Charge Nurse Tina Ferris, who taught 17/18 year old Joy, the power of love and acceptance, and how everyone has feelings and a heart, regardless of disability and appearance! Joy thanks all those who purchase "Spikey's Points," book of scripts, just to read! She thanks those, including Lori and Teresa who allowed her to "not over think and let her 'inner child' flow." She thanks Wilna, Takashi, Graeme, Tara, Lynn, Paige, Raymond, Matthew, Dan & Michelle, Roger, Choreographers, Sewers, Production Assistants and all artists, friends and family who have supported and inspired her.

She thanks her teachers for public performance opportunities with speaking, theatre, gymnastics, etc. She's grateful to fellow worker, Brandon Sun reporter Gord, for asking her to design a community theatre logo in 1985. He became a catalyst for her addiction and passion to theatre, as he later got her involved in set design, acting and directing. She gives thanks to Winnipeg's Louis Riel School Division, including Lisa, Susan and more; but especially to Principal mentors George Gartrell, (Samuel Burland School) and Phil Trottier, who opened her classroom doors. She's forever grateful to George and Superintendent Lynda, who instilled confidence in her, by hiring her within minutes of the interview. George later told Joy "you're a natural teacher," and suggested she work as an EA while pursuing an Education degree. She loved working with George, VP Irene, teachers Kathy, Judi and more, plus assisting in Resource. George introduced Joy to Principal Phil Trottier. Phil accepted her at Windsor School without an interview, for a two year position, heading the Precision Reading and ESL programs, under administration supervision. Joy appreciated the opportunities and also as a volunteer to conduct Gr. 7-9 lunch hour Drama classes, in the same large room. She thanks Phil, VP's Ken Bartel and Marlene Murray for their guidance and room decorating support. She thanks teachers including Betty, Jane and Chris for believing in, and supporting her. Before Phil retired, he surprised Joy at an Art show by presenting her with a watercolour book. (Team Marlene, Ken and Joy transferred schools). She thanks principals at Glenwood, hard working Claire and Carla, for their anti bullying/drama support; and to Barry, Rick, Brian and supportive teachers, Jason, Jacquie, Lia and more! Joy worked with K-9 students, later working with a Behavioural therapy team. She continued her noon hour drama program, Gr. 3 and up, until her retirement. She thanks teachers who acted in, or directed SPIKEY, including Lia, Charlie, Deb, Janice, Chris, Jennifer, Dean and Stephanie. The school setting offered a writing template for "Spikey's Points!" Joy thanks supportive students, parents plus EA friends including Manette, Cindy, Marie and Emilie who believed in her. Her school years since 2000 kept her pen flowing. Her night table notepads were overwhelming with a plethora of 'points, and jokes' from her thoughts plus those of students and teachers. She thanks Justin, Director/owner of Dramatic Theatre, and others who "LOVED reading the Spikey scripts."

She thanks Pat Gouldie and Community Living Brandon for approaching her to write a play for their special needs students in 1993; and for being the first organization to produce and present Spikey's Points, with the premier performance at the Westman Centennial Auditorium for Brandon School Division students K - Gr. 6. Thanks to Debby Dandy from CL Brandon, for its school return in 2014, for K- Gr. 5 students. She thanks all Winnipeg venues, especially the Exchange Community Church, Deaf Centre, Fringe venues, Samuel Cohen Auditorium, Ellice Theatre and to Nick and all at the Gas Station Arts Centre for the four consecutive (2014-18) videotaped Spikey sequel performances! Joy thanks Cody and Samantha for videotaping and to all listed on the back, order page. She apologises to any she may have inadvertently missed. With an appreciation for all acts of kindness and encouragement, she cherishes people and memories. She concludes with "Thanks to all for your support and friendship and Thanks be to God." She thanks her siblings, the Blight kids and all she babysat; for listening to her made-up bedtime stories, when books were scarce or over-read. You inspired her to be creative, by requesting her stories! Thanks to All at Authorhouse USA, Jon Lopez to Heather Carter.

About The Author

Joy was born in Dryden Ontario, Canada on July 16, 1956; to a Russian, Ukrainian, Austrian mother and an English, Scottish, Metis father. She's a farmer's daughter, and eldest of five. When she first moved to the farm, after Grade two, she felt lonely. She created a little park and called it "People's Park," for herself and siblings. Her Dad added tire swings. It became her oasis of peace, and 'happy' place, following chores and homework. The 'park' became the foundational setting for all the Spikey sequels!

Joy was a former cheer leader, and after taking a little Jazz dance, she became a certified YMCA aerobic dance and fitness instructor/leader. Her background and training was in Psychology, Commercial/Graphic Arts, Fitness, Theatre, and Business. She retired following 40 years of employment; first in Graphic Arts, working for a newspaper, printing/sign companies and a second career with the school division. She continues to sub within the schools and volunteers to produce Spikey, within a non-profit organization. She also sings in church choir.

Joy's employment, as an Educational Assistant from K - Gr. 12, introduced her to a 'palette of personalities!' Many teachers, students and parents she met, painted her writing brush! Joy enjoyed writing the Spikey sequels and it became her passion and creative outlet, involving both the script and the stage! She appreciates the similarities between acting/directing and writing. The parallels are similar as the fields, stage and paper, create and 'layer' characters. Likewise with painting, she feels you can create strong images, with subtle lines. Joy is an artist, author, songwriter, director, producer and actor. She's been involved as a co-ordinator, writer and choreographer for provincial, national and international sporting events. She was often inspired to write around 3:00 am!

Her acting includes "Margo" in 'The Diary of Anne Frank' and leads as 'Molly' in 'The Mousetrap,' 'Izzy' in 'Crossing Delancey, and 'The Snow Queen.' She played both the aunt and mother of the bride in the musical 'Tony & Tina's Wedding.' Directing includes 'Spikey,' and other commissioned plays, several Neil Simon comedies, 'The Marriage Proposal,' 'Cactus Flower,' 'Noises Off,' 'Driving Miss Daisy,' 'Lend Me a Tenor,' 'Crimes Of The Heart,' 'Steel Magnolias,' and 'The Wisdom Of Eve.'

Her teaching Sunday school and school drama classes; directing Christmas concerts and five summers at theatre school, gave her a respect of actors, scripts and all involved with productions. Joy and her musician husband were recipients of a Mayor's Arts & Culture Award for their Community Volunteer service. Her involvement included theatre, choreography, songwriting and coordinating events for Manitoba Winter/Summer Games, Scott Tournament of Hearts, World Youth Baseball and World Curling. She was a Creative Memories Consultant, and a painter who founded a non-profit art gallery, "Keepsakes Gallery of Winnipeg Inc., 2006." Several stars visited, (some played the piano). A few months after opening, she had surgery to remove a large cyst. July 2011, Joy was diagnosed with cancer, CLL/SLL, choosing several surgeries over chemo. She retired from school, June 2013. Two months later, she spent 33 days in the hospital with double pneumonia, ARDS and a near death experience. Her imperfect life includes a divorce (amicable) plus snide comments and coldness from a few; and regrets for her words and actions, or lack of them. She apologizes to any she may have hurt or offended. As a cancer survivor, she enjoys yoga, bike riding, skiing, travelling and walking. Her survival instilled a strong desire to publish 'Spikey!' She's been on many volunteer charity and non-profit boards, presently 'Uniquely Manitoba' arts board since 2011.' She has designed logos for, and became involved with, The Association Of Community Theatres (ACT Manitoba) and the Brandon Jazz Festival. She has appeared in several films plus taken and conducted many theatre workshops.

Her Volunteer work includes fund raising for several charities, including the Canadian Cancer Society, Library Arts Council Board and as Vice President for The Canadian Mental Health Association. Her many years of Calligraphy included certificates and deceased member pages for the Elks 'Order of the Royal Purple' Book of Memories; Schools and the Canada Summer/Winter Games. Her future plans are to tour with 'Spikey', as a 'puppet show,' through schools, children's hospitals, etc.

Joy and her Juno award husband, married since 1988, reside in Winnipeg, Manitoba, Canada. They have a loved and cherished musician son Andrew, born in 1995. Her passion was writing, directing and producing 'Spikey.' Joy hopes you enjoy reading and performing "Spikey's Points!" She believes everyone is an artist, just may express it differently. She encourages all to follow their dreams, and their heart!

Joy: photo by son Andrew, Sept. '15.   *Family Photo: Grace Kokoschke, Dec. 2015*

Joy's MANITOBA Schools: 1962 - Grad '74. Gr. 1-2: Two schools in Thompson. Gr. 3: one room country school in Pine Creek.

Gr. 4-8, Austin Elementary, Gr. 9 Austin H.S., Gr. 10 MacGregor Collegiate, Gr. 11-12 Arthur Meighen HS, Portage la Prairie.

Her school days, post secondary education, former teachers/employers/staff; work as a Nurse/Psychologist's Aid, Artist, Home Day Care when her son was two, and school division work - helped to create/inspire her characters!

Thanks to all for purchasing this Book of Scripts!

History Of Spikey

The idea and concept of "Spikey," the porcupine with good points, was conceived in 1989. In 1993, Joy was commissioned by the "Brandon Association Of Community Living" to write a play incorporating special needs of their students. With the character "Spikey," in mind, the lead stage role of Spikey was born and created! A brown furry costume with spongy spikey quills was made. Additional characters were cast for "Spikey's Points." Her husband Dave composed music to her lyrics and they created the theme song, "Together We Can Make It," a Spikey trademark. She contacted friend Debbie Wilkinson to assist with writing/editing. Some of the cast had special needs. A 25-30 minute 'Spikey pilot' was brought to life on June 3, 1993 for a sold out school and public performance at the Westman Centennial Auditorium. Joy secured the "Spikey" character, to survive the original script. The present role of "Keri," went through name changes. The original mother was 'nameless.' Most of the cast played animals in costume. The setting was a forest. Within it lived the antagonist, a panther. Spikey the protagonist, remained dormant for 7 years, as Joy became Artistic Director of a Community Theatre Company.

Joy moved to Winnipeg Manitoba, in 1999. She worked with students at Maple Leaf School, Kids Korner. In 2000, she taught a volunteer noon hour drama program at Victor Wyatt School. She wrote a play for students with special needs. Following a successful school matinee and evening performance, the students felt inspired to perform again. Joy re-wrote her school play, entitled "Catch A Friend," by adding Spikey. Fortunately, her non-profit theatre group was selected to perform in the Winnipeg Fringe Festival, 2001. She recast the role of "Spikey," re-added the theme song plus more music, creating a Fringe Festival Musical, with cast from the two schools. Spikey was 'revived' and "made a point" during the Winnipeg Fringe Festival, for six years! Live musicians included her husband on piano and cousin Rick on drums. Spikey toured through schools, churches and senior homes. Although a script and some lyrics, music and characters are no longer used, the 'Fringe' Spikey experience introduced budding actors to live performances. It gave behind the scenes talent, an opportunity to stage manage or be involved as production crew. Derek, Shannon, Lori, Jennifer, Donna, Carrie, Tracie, Dillon, Steph and others had opportunities to write, direct and produce. Joy helped them and they assisted her! Although the Fringe scripts are no longer used, many composed music and designed choreography for earlier productions, with cast up to 31! Music continued to be added and recorded. Joy was cast in the musical theatre, "Tony & Tina's Wedding" and met stage musician, Paulo Bergantim. The Spikey scripts, music and choreography changed again!

Joy commissioned Paulo to write more music for her new 'Spikey Lyrics.' For the last two sequels, Paulo had professionally arranged and recorded Spikey music, to be used on a continuous basis. After the Winnipeg Fringe, and sellout shows, more sequels were written. The 5 productions from 2001 - 2006, had been rewritten and revised into 4 consecutive musical sequels, with a 'core' cast. The lead girl is now, Keri, with mother

'Sarah.' The cast and dancers have been reduced. The pre-quel, Sequel #1, "Welcome Spikey's Points," was the final script to be written. All sequels have been on tour and continue through schools and for public non-profit groups. Joy's inspiration for lines came mostly from students, parents, teachers, friends and the cast! She carried a notepad and pen constantly! Although there's cheesy and cliché lines, the morals and "good points" are solid. Keri and Jessica's dialogue mirrors Joy's own frustrations and Gr. 7 girls, students she worked with. The new music for all sequels, composed by Paulo Bergantim, 2005 – 07, has become Spikey's trademark music! Erin J. McCallum's Choreography (2013), also a Spikey trademark, is featured on the DVD's. The two additional porcupines, 'Misty,' and baby 'Punky' found in the park, show 'Spikey' is all about community and team building. Spikey's goal is to erase jealousy, meanness, prejudice, judging and bullying in 'the park' or 'any place.' The kind-hearted Spikey sets a 'share and care' example. His peace within, instills a peaceful park, and healthy environment. Spikey, as her dad and husband - live on as the quintessential peacemakers!'

Photos used by permission from Dillon Spicer, Somer Kenny & Andrew Schmidt

Photo used by permission from Dylan Hatcher

Spikey Musical Cast of Characters:

SPIKEY: The LEAD. He's Energetic, Positive and Naïve. *(triple threat, age 15-25, approx.. 6.' Spikey wears a dark brown furry costume, with sewn on, painted, soft spongy quills. It includes separate 'paws' 'head cap' and 'feet.' If Spikey is a tap dancer, he could wear furry foot covers, so the bottoms of his shoes are exposed. He can be of any ethnic race or height, but should be boyish, naïve, innocent and charming).*

GRAMMY: A middle aged 'very spunky,' non-judgemental 'grandmotherly' woman. She's a retired nurse, never married and devotes her time as Spikey's adopted 'mom.' *(She volunteers at the hospital and within the community. Her knitting bag is with her at all times. She could be wearing a funky hat with flowers and dressed matronly. She smiles, laughs exuberantly, and is always kind).*

KERI: Strong Lead Girl - dramatic stage presence. (Approx.10, *in sequel # 1. She is moving away from her old school and friends. She begins the series, upset and at times, temperamental. Her age and maturity progresses during the sequels. She'd be 14 in Sequel #4. Keri, as ALL kids on stage, is dressed in casual SUMMER CLOTHING).*

SARAH BELL: Keri's divorced mother. She's employed as an elementary school teacher. *(She's nervous, a perfectionist and always tries to do the right thing. Keri is her only child. Dress: business casual...skirt, blazer, pant suit).*

MR. T: Sarah's father and Keri's 'grumpy' widowed grandfather, with a warm heart. *(He is totally devoted to his daughter and grand-daughter. He's thrilled they've moved back home to be near him. Dress: t-shirt, or plaid shirt with sleeves rolled up, suspenders, shorts, socks, sandals).*

LARRY LAW: A hard working, anxious, widowed lawyer; raising boys who dislike his cooking. Dress: conservative - dress shoes, pants, tie, short sleeved shirt.

BEN: Larry's youngest son. He's bold and strong willed, energetic and fun loving.

MARK: The oldest son of Larry. He's well mannered, mature and polite.

SALLY: A sweet girl next door, about Keri's age, who tries to become a friend to her.

TIA: Sally's little sister, who adores her big sister. She wants to be involved with the 'big girls.' *(If there is no 'Tia,' Sally would take her lines).*

LISA: (Sequel 1 only. Age 9 -13**)** Smiling, kind, happy. Could be ethnic minority girl.

STAR: (Sequel 1 only, male or female). Star sings feature song, "Celebrate Life," or their choice of a popular cover tune. They could also choose to perform their own composition. *(Star is dressed in character to their song/style).*

COACH BOB: (Sequels 2–4). A construction worker, who plays and coaches ball. He's Spikey's and Larry's friend. *(Dress: golf shirt, shorts, runners, baseball cap, construction hat).*

JESSICA: (Sequel 2 only) A generally kind, well-dressed leader of the after school dance team. She's upset, as she has to move mid-way through school, due to her dad's transfer. She reacts by being a 'bully.' She transitions when she's aware of the kindness around her.

MISTY: Bubbly, positive female porcupine and Spikey's new friend. *(She's dressed in caramel coloured fur with peach and caramel painted sponge quills, peach fabric bow, peach lips/blush).*

MS RADCLIFFE: The Vice Principal, some students see as cold and hard. She proves she has a soft side and later doubles as a JP *(Justice of the Peace)* for the weddings in Sequel #4. *(Dress: grey/taupe skirt/business suit, pumps, hair in bun/french roll).*

ROBYN: The "model" leader/student who feels uncomfortable being the "VP's daughter."

PUNKY: A male or female 'baby' porcupine. *(Small child 5-8 years old. Costume: ivory fur with separate feet, mitts and head piece. Painted 'funky' head quills are green, purple, orange, etc.)*

CHORUS: *All sequels could feature dancers and singers, 'hanging out' in the park, until a song starts! They could be reading the "Community Quill," a book, playing cards, sitting at the small picnic table, or on the ground.*

WELCOME SPIKEY'S POINTS!

Spikey's Points: Sequel 1 of four sequels 75 *min. (Script. Approx. 45 min. Music: 30 min. 11 songs)*

LIGHTS UP ON SET: *(Set never changes. Same set for ALL 4 Sequels!) Morning BEFORE school. Projected park scene on screen. Set-* **trees,** *rock,(seats two) two park benches, seating 2 – 3 each. Options: (green lighting on floor, painted stepping/cobble stones CS, SR/SL. Spikey/cast could tap dance on them.) Metal garbage can SL behind bench. Recycleable and non-recycleable garbage in clusters SR/SL (Garbage should not interfere with dancing). (Recorded pre-show music or stage musician, flute, birds chirping. exit) (Grammy enters. Takes out knitting. Sits on SL bench) (Person on rock, reading "The Community Quill,") CHORUS: SR at Picnic table, SL on lawnchair or bench. In all 4 Sequels: ANY (kid's) hand greeting can be exchanged for a 'high-five.'* **Sound:** *Birds chirping, nature sounds...to fadeout...(cue for voice over to start., stage musician exits.*

Child VOICE CUE: *(Spoken Backstage or Recorded. Track #1) (Voiceover* **opens** *ALL sequels)* "Once Upon A time, not that long ago, lived a walking, talking, singing porcupine, with mostly good points. His name was Spikey. His parents didn't make it across the road. Spikey barely made it. He lay injured on the side of the road. A dear old lady everyone called Grammy, found him and nurtured him back to health. He became a friend to many because he always tried to do the best he could. He lived, he loved, he laughed, he became a great example to follow..."

MUSIC CUE: ***Together We Can Make It**Theme Song Intro Instrumental, track#2)*

*IF SPIKEY wears glasses...Add...***TIA** *or a VOICE FROM CHORUS: (Spikey enters SR)* **Wow, Spikey! I really like your new glasses!** SPIKEY: **Thank you! – That's kind of you!** TIA: **I've read that porcupines have poor eyesight!** CHORUS and 'TIA': **They Do! We've read that too!** *(Spikey immediately starts counting song)*

(OPTION: Kids can enter on a bike, skateboard, etc.)

SCENE 1

Music fades as Lisa and Sally enter SR, sit on eiher side of Grammy on bench. Spikey enters SL. Girls cheer.

SPIKEY: *(singing song to the tune of "Old McDonald") (stands in front of the rock)*
    1, 2, 3, 4, 5, 6, 7... 8, 9, 10, and 11...12, 13, 14, 15...

LISA: 16, 17...

SALLY: 18, 19...!

SPIKEY: Let's just end at 20! I think 20 is plen-ty! *(kneels on rock...all laugh)*

SALLY: Wow Spikey! You rhyme and count in the <u>hundreds!</u> What else has Grammy taught you?

SPIKEY: I can add, subtract, multiply and divide! I can spread my arms *(spreads arms)* this wide!

LISA: Great Spikey! And Sally and I taught you to dance! We helped Grammy teach you to sing.

SPIKEY: *(Stands, mimics Elvis)* Yes. Thank you. Thank you very much...*(shakes head, puts hand to head)* I'm singing that counting song even in bed.
I wish I could get that counting song out of my head. *(sits on rock)*

GRAMMY: It'll pass. My goodness Spikey, you're so smart. I wish I could get you in school.

LISA: You're a good teacher Grammy. You've taught him lots! Hey, *(gets up)* I've got some questions to see if you're ready for school, Spikey. Here's some. Name two things that contain milk?

SPIKEY: Well... not sows...I know - TWO COWS!

LISA: You're right, *(eye roll)* I guess. *(beat)* What's the formula for water?

SPIKEY: H, I, J, K, L, M, N, O... You know! H to O *(all laugh, Grammy continues to knit)*

SALLY: *(gets up)* My turn. What's the longest word you know?

SPIKEY: SMILES! *(all look confused)* In between the two s's, is a mile.

SALLY: *(smiles, rolls eyes)* Okay. *(beat)* What's the capital of Manitoba? *(replace Manitoba with other province or state - where production is performed).*

SPIKEY: Oh that's a gem? The answer is the letter M! *(change letter to location required)*

SALLY: *(shakes head)* It's Winnipeg...*(or name of location)* Okay. *(beat)* What are Grammy's best points?

SPIKEY: She <u>collects</u> points! *(Sally sits)* She buys gas and groceries! She saves lots on travel fees!

LISA: *(laughs)* I have one. I have went. That's wrong isn't it? *(Spikey looks confused)*

SALLY: It <u>is</u> wrong Spikey. <u>Why</u> is it wrong?

SPIKEY: Oh, now that's easy to get. Cuz you ain't went yet? *(stands behind Grammy)*

GRAMMY: *(pats Spikey's hand)* Oh we do have fun don't we! Lisa and Sally, you two have become such good friends with Spikey!

SALLY: Yeah, but we weren't at first.

LISA: We were scared of all those points! *(moves to stand behind rock, by Spikey. She touches his quills)*. Spikey's a prickly teddy bear!

SALLY: Spikey, *(stands, hand on bench)* remember when you told me you were like a pencil?

SPIKEY: Yes, I remember too. Now why, I ask you???

SALLY: Why? I remember. Because you're no good unless you've got a point.

LISA: *(all laugh)* Spikey has lots of good points! *(still standing behind bench)*

SPIKEY: I have a <u>few!</u> Yes I <u>do!</u>

GRAMMY: I have a point too. I'm making something for you girls. Because you like dancing in the park, and you offered to help clean it up this afternoon, for Spikey's party....well a few weeks ago, Spikey and I decided to sew some special outfits. I'm making a few extra. *(Sally stands by Grammy)*

SALLY: *(stands by Grammy)* Wow, I know they'll be beautiful!! Thanks Grammy!!! *(kneels on bench to hug Grammy)*

LISA: *(hugs Grammy)* *(stands by Lisa)* You're the best!!! Thank you Grammy! They'll be awesome, I know!!

GRAMMY: I think you will like the tops. I gave them to your parents. I'm making your pants last.

LISA: *(sits on bench SR)* My pants don't last. How do you make pants last?

GRAMMY: I put extra lining in the knees. *(Spikey ponders, as he moves to sit on rock)*

SPIKEY: *(standing)* I thought you make the tops first, to make the pants last. But it doesn't matter, cuz Grammy sews fast! *(all laugh, as he sits on rock)*

SALLY: *(standing)* Oh Spikey, you're so funny. And you're lucky. You have **ALL SEASON clothing,** with ALL that fur! *(touches Spikey's arm)* *(girls stand in front of bench)*

LISA: *(stands by Spikey)* Yeah, you don't need anything else! Besides you'd tear any clothes to shreds, if you put them over **all those spikey quills!** *(touches a quill, sits on arm of bench)*

SPIKEY: Different with my fur and quills, I am! But I'm kind and gentle as a lamb!

SALLY: We like you just the way you are Spikey! *(Girls knuckle greet Spikey) Sally sits)*

LISA: And Grammy too...just the way she is. Because you two, are kind to us, and everyone! *(stands behind bench, hugs Grammy who's sitting in front, on the bench)*

SALLY: Exactly! Thanks Grammy, for all you do for all of us! I love being with you and Spikey! *(aside)* Oh and you too Lisa! *(they smile and high-five)*

GRAMMY: Thank you. What kind words. What a beautiful day. The rain was supposed to fall.

SPIKEY: When the rain falls now and then, does it ever get up again?*(Spikey, CS)*

GRAMMY: In **'dew,'** time, Spikey...in 'due' time! *(All laugh)*

CUE MUSIC: ****<u>MAKING A POINT</u>**** *(Track 2) (Chorus could enter SL. Spikey is Centre Stage. Grammy on bench during first verse. Gets up on Chorus, stands by Spikey. Spikey could be tap dancing during instrumental. Grammy, Sally & Lisa and 'park dancer/chorus' sing/dance. Grammy joins in on Chorus. Stands by Spikey. Chorus/Extras exit or sit in the park reading a book or reading the "Community Quill" newspaper).*

SCENE 2

(Keri runs into park SR. Ben, with blue hair spikes, runs in park SL, carrying blue recycle bin. Spikey sees Ben. All three scream, as they meet CS. Ben puts down bin, SR by bench and runs to hide SL)

BEN: *(enters SL)* You're the scariest thing I've ever seen!! Stay away from me! *(Spikey hides behind rock. Ben hides behind metal garbage can SL).*

KERI: *(enters SR, screams when she sees Spikey)* Go away! Mom told me to stay away from strangers and strange looking animals! *(Spikey hides behind rock)*

LISA: *(Keri backs up)* Sorry Keri. I meant to tell you about Spikey – but Sally and I just kinda met you this weekend and I...*(Spikey sits on rock, then gets up)*

SPIKEY: *(runs behind Grammy)* I didn't even say Boo. *(sits on bench SR closest to rock)* Keri?! *(Keri makes an alarmed face, as she nods).* I didn't mean to scare you. A new friend is a treat. Where did you girls meet? *(Sally sits by Spikey).*

LISA: At the mall...*(sits on bench SR)*

KERI: He speaks! I think I'm going to faint! Yuck! *(Lisa pulls Keri to sit on bench)*

GRAMMY: Be nice – you can catch more flies with honey than vinegar.

SPIKEY: Grammy, I don't think we need any flies. *(moves behind rock)*
I just want to be friends with these girls and guys.

GRAMMY:*(Laughs, moves to comfort Ben)* It's okay Ben. *(Ben sits on bench, far SL)* Spikey is scared too. C'mon. Yes, it's SMART to be cautious. Look – you two scared Spikey. Now, now Spikey. It's okay! *(comforts Spikey)* You scared them and they scared you. Ben's got blue spiked hair and you've got brown spiked quills. *(To Keri)* What's your name dear? *(Spikey stands behind rock pretending to reach for and catch a fly).*

KERI: Hi... Umm, I'm Keri... Is he *(gets up as she points to Spikey)* is <u>this</u> really, for real? You look, dangerous. *(Looks at Spikey then Ben)* You both look scary! *(moves away from Spikey)*

SPIKEY: *(front of rock. To Keri)* Scary? Scary me? I'm as friendly as can be! Just like this fly above me.

KERI: *(backs up, shakes head)* You're not normal. You Speak?! You rhyme?!?*(Spikey sits)*

SPIKEY: *(on rock)* Wish I was a frog on a log, a cuddly puppy dog or a cute little hedgehog.

KERI: (*beat*) Awwhh. (*smiles*) But you seem, harmless... Sorry for being so mean Spikey. (*sits on rock, head down*)

SPIKEY: Thank <u>you.</u> I have feelings <u>too</u>. (*Spikey lifts his head up*)

GRAMMY: Thank you for apologizing. Spikey means no harm. He's a teenage porcupine... but he's like an overgrown pup. (*gets up...to Keri*) Are you okay, dear?

KERI: No...Nothing goes right for me!

SPIKEY: (*gets up*) Then GO LEFT, when nothing goes right. Keep trying with all your might! (*Keri gives Spikey an annoying look, gets up*). (*Spikey sits back on rock*).

KERI: What a strange place! What a messy place! (*kicks pizza box, can, etc., away*)

LISA: Keri...Spikey, Grammy, Sally and I are here to organize a park clean up this afternoon.

SALLY: You should have seen it before!

GRAMMY: Because we're having a party to celebrate Spikey being here with me for one year today... we're cleaning up!

KERI: Yeah, well, whatever... (*Keri sits in the centre of bench, SR*)

MARK: (*enters SL. Could carry a blue recycle bin*) (*to Ben*) I knew I'd find you here!

BEN: Keri, this is my brother Mark.

KERI: Hi Mark.

MARK: Hi, Keri, nice to meet you. Hi Grammy...

GRAMMY: Hi there Mark. Good to see you again!

MARK: Hey, hello Spikey! (*sits on rock by Spikey, between Spikey and Grammy*)

SPIKEY: Hi there Mark. Good to see you in the park.

MARK: Thanks, Spikey!

BEN: You knew about Spikey!!? Why didn't you tell me? (*Keri rolls her eyes, shakes her head*).

MARK: I was going to, when the time was right.

BEN: Yeah, right!! (*glares at Mark*).

MARK: *(To Ben)* Would you have believed me!? Anyway, Grammy, I'm here to help clean up!

BEN: Yeah - Me too. This park sure needs it!!

GRAMMY: Good for you boys! So how was your camping and fishing trip with your Dad?

BEN: It was awesome!!

GRAMMY: When is fishing not great!

BEN: When you're the <u>worm</u>!! *(Keri starts to laugh but stops when Spikey laughs heartily. It scares Ben and Keri. They hide behind the rock). (Mark Laughs)*

MARK: Dad taught us how to filet a fish! *(To Keri and Ben)* I just met Spikey last week. Look, Spikey is kind of like us, but just a...a porcupine.

GRAMMY: That's right Mark. *(to Spikey)* Spikey, Ben's okay. You've already met his brother Mark. *(Ben moves away) (To Keri)* I used to babysit these boys.

MARK: Hey, c'mon Ben...give Spikey a chance. *(Spikey tries to leave. Lisa pulls him back)*

SPIKEY: Grammy, I'm causing trouble. Maybe I should take off on the double.

GRAMMY: It's okay boys. Spikey, it's time for you to come out and meet the world. You've been wanting to meet people for a year. *(Ben and Keri come out from behind rock)*

LISA: Yeah, Spikey. You've met all of us, but you hide when anyone else comes by.

KERI: *(Stands arms crossed)* It's bad enough that he speaks but WHY does he have to speak in rhyme?

GRAMMY: Because he used to sit behind this park bench all day and listen to people read Dr. Seuss and Mother Goose stories.

SPIKEY: I like poetry and to sing and dance, too. It makes me feel, so brand new!

KERI: You talk!? You stand <u>up</u>right?! *(at side/arm of bench, near Lisa)*

BEN: Pleasssse. Don't sing! I should leave! *(He tries to leave but Mark holds him back.)*

KERI: I really wanted to hear Lady La La *(<u>name of current singer, ex. Justin Timberwood, Bruno Starrs</u>)* sing at the concert tonight! But I <u>don't</u> want to hear a porcupine sing!

SPIKEY: Okay, my singing may not please you. But, I'm glad you like <u>Lady La La</u> *(<u>Justin</u>)* too!

11

KERI: Who doesn't? Sure wish I could have gotten tickets to his (her) concert. My life sucks! Big time!

MARK: I wanted to go too!

BEN: Yeah, me too – but it was sold out months ago!

LISA: Sally and I tried to get tickets too.

SALLY: I soooo wanted to see him! (her!)

GRAMMY: And I like him (her) too! *(beat)* See Keri. Spikey's okay. He's sweet and a lot like you. He's harmless and has mostly good points! *(Keri & Sally sit by Grammy)*

MARK: Grammy, I still can't believe we're talking to a porcupine. I started to tell Dad a week ago and he said I needed sleep. What's the point! *(to Keri)* Are you, Mr. Taylor's granddaughter? *(she nods)* He told me you will be moving here.

KERI: Yes, he's my grandpa. But I'm <u>not</u> moving anywhere! I'm leaving! *(crosses arms, starts to leave)* *(Lisa pulls Keri back. Keri stands by Lisa SR)*

GRAMMY: *(touches Keri's arm)* Please talk to Spikey first. *(Keri crosses her arms tightly over her chest, as she walks away. Lisa pulls her back)* *(Keri stands by Lisa SR)*

MARK: *(Gives Spikey a high-five)* See, he's okay, Keri! I've never met a porcupine that sings and talks – and dances before either. See how lucky we are! Do you enjoy living around here, Spikey?

SPIKEY: Yes, I do. On the road by this park, Grammy found me. We come here, frequently. *(to Keri)* We live just behind this park here. Do you want to see? It's very near.

KERI: *(Keri and Ben move away)* Let me think … uhh. No! *(crunches box on ground, with her foot)*.

BEN: Maybe another time. *(Keri sits on bench, or arm of bench)*

KERI: Well, we sure picked a messy park to meet in. *(Sally picks up box, puts in recycle bin)*.

MARK: Because, we all live just a few blocks from here. We're close to Spikey.

BEN: He means, we <u>live</u> close to Spikey.

SPIKEY: It's a pleasure to meet all of you. But I'm a little nervous talking to you. Everything to me, is still, all so new!

SALLY: You've been shy like <u>me,</u> for so long Spikey, you <u>see</u>… *(mimics Spikey, Spikey laughs)*

LISA: Yeah, it's time to see the world!

MARK: *(stands)* Ahh, we're all okay kids.

BEN: No, we're all awesome kids!

KERI: Ummm, Mark. So, you might know my grandpa.... Joe Taylor? He said he comes here quite often to feed the birds.

MARK: Yeah, I've seen him around here. He looks kind of grumpy, but he's actually a nice guy – when you talk to him.

KERI: *(jumps up)* He's not grumpy! No one in our family is!

MARK: Sorry I didn't mean it that way.

KERI: He just looks grumpy to you, but he's <u>not</u>!

MARK: I guess I shouldn't judge things on how they seem to me. *(sits)*

BEN: Like me with my blue points.

KERI: Okay – or me, with Spikey... *(Spikey walks to Keri and high–fives with her)*

SPIKEY: *(to Ben)* Neither you nor I were born with a sharp point right? And now Ben – you look outta sight! *(feels Ben's spiked hair)*

SALLY: Yeah, you're right...he does!

LISA: What a mess this park is. Sure needs a good Clean Up!

KERI: Right! I'm surprised birds even come here! *(stands, kicks box)*

LISA: Would you like to help us clean up, Keri?! *(Keri shakes her head no)*

SALLY: We'll start soon!

SPIKEY: Yes, maybe you could help our crew. Together we could clean it to make it look new!

SALLY: Hey maybe later you could join us for dance rehearsals, Keri!

KERI: I just want to leave and go back home! *(girls pull Keri back. Keri sits on rock and pouts)*

MARK: Well, I better go. But we'll be back soon to clean. I just came by to get Ben. Ben we're meeting Dad at the ball diamond just behind here. *(to Grammy)* We're going to practice hitting and catching.

BEN: Yeah, before ball season starts again.

MARK: So, see you in a while. Oh Grammy, I forgot to tell you, my dad is going to help coach again this fall.

GRAMMY: That's wonderful, Mark.

MARK: We'll get you playing, Spikey. *(pats Spikey on the back)*

BEN: You play with a ball and a bat, Spikey. *(with sarcasm)*

SPIKEY: *(stands SL)* Wow! I'd like that. Me hit a ball with a bat.

MARK: I bet you'd be a great hitter! Well, we gotta go. *(Does a knuckle greeting with Spikey) (Taps Ben on shoulder. Ben and Mark exit)*

SPIKEY: Nice boy, Mark is. I like that attitude of his! *(sits on bench by Grammy)*

KERI: Yeah, he's kinda nice. Wish I had a brother or sister. Why am I telling you this? You're just a big scary porcupine. I need to **be** with someone that makes me happy.

SPIKEY: No – YOU **need to be** someone that makes you happy!
    It comes from inside, you see?
    You're afraid of something bigger than me.
    Could you possibly tell me what it might be?

KERI: Since when do porcupines care?

SPIKEY: I really do care. Your fear you can share.
    It's hard to be happy when you hang on to the past.
    Tomorrow's a new day. Choose happiness to last.

GRAMMY: You're so right Spikey. *(moves near rock to talk to Keri)* You can tell us – what's bothering you dear. It's good to talk about your feelings.

LISA: *(Lisa stands behind rock)* Yeah, feelings aren't toys. You don't just break them or throw them away. *(all nod)* Keri, we know you're angry. *(all nod)* But you can still be nice. Spikey cares, so please don't bully him.

KERI: Sorry...

LISA: All of us here, care! *(Keri forces a smile)* Share your points with us!

SPIKEY: *(To Keri)* I think your points will be good. I bet you're just misunderstood.

KERI: Thanks Spikey. *(pauses as she sits on the rock. Speaks to all)* Well, my Mom's a teacher. She wants to move here next year and I don't want to. I'll miss my friends and my home. And I <u>don't</u> want to go to a stupid new school where she will get a teaching job. I <u>hate</u> everything!

SPIKEY: A strong word, <u>hate</u> is. That word makes my tummy fizz!

LISA: Mine too, Spikey. But I'm sure going to a new school is tough.

SALLY: *(Gets up. Stands by rock beside Keri, who's still sitting on rock. Lisa stands on other side of Keri)* At least you've met Lisa and I. You can text your friends and go on Facebook,

LISA & SALLY: And Instagram...

SALLY: And Twitter. *(all nod)* Keep in touch with us, okay? *(Lisa, Spikey and Grammy nod.)* *(Sally gives Keri a knuckle greeting.)* *(To Keri)* <u>Send a selfie!!</u> *(All stand together facing audience, touch a shoulder to each other. Sally pretends to take a selfie of Grammy, Keri, Sally and Lisa)*

GRAMMY: Life can break us. Friendship can fix us!

SPIKEY: You'll make new friends, Keri.
Just wait and see! *(Keri still looks sad. She makes a face, as she enters CS for solo 'No Choices')*

SCENE 3

MUSIC CUE: **No Choices** *(Track 3) (Keri's Solo – Lisa, Sally join in on chorus) (Choreography / dancing during chorus) (Other park dancers could join in on chorus / dancing)*
Sally and Lisa pull pick up SL bench and place it in front of SR bench, to form a 'car.' Grammy and Lisa sit in front bench. Keri sits on 'back bench.' Spikey and Sally are standing behind. 'Kids chorus' joins.

KERI: Spikey, sorry I was mean to you. You scared me. You're just sooo, <u>different</u>...

SPIKEY: Different isn't dangerous - different isn't bad. You had to get to know me first. Just fear is what you had.

KERI: Good points! But I'm not afraid anymore. <u>Being different is cool.</u> Spikey, you're cool! *(play punches with Spikey).*

LISA: Oh, Keri - your mom's coming!

SPIKEY: I'll meet her another time.
This time is <u>not</u> fine. *(Spikey runs and hides behind the rock) (Sarah enters)*

KERI: Hi mom.

SARAH: Hi sweetie! Oh hi Lisa and Sally. *(they wave)* So this is it, Keri. What do you think of moving here? *(Keri turns away from her mom)* You've got almost a year to get used to the idea. *(to Grammy)* I see you've met another new friend, Keri. *(to Grammy)* Hello, I'm Keri's Mom, Sarah...*(starts to offer her hand, to shake Grammy's hand). (Spikey pokes his head up when Sarah is not looking).*

KERI: I don't want to move! Why do I have to? *(Sarah drops her hand) (Keri sits on park bench with Grammy, and moves closer to her).*

SARAH: Keri, Keri...

KERI: Mom, mom - and your point is?

GRAMMY: *(gets up)* Hi. I'm Mary. But just call me Grammy. *(shakes hands with Sarah)*

SARAH: *(SL)* Hi Grammy. I'm Sarah, Sarah Bell. Pleasure to meet you. *(embarrassed but calm)* Keri, we've gone through this before. Please honey. Neither of us can change the situation, just... how we <u>deal </u>with it. Look, I've got a chance to teach here next fall and it's a great school for you...

KERI: I don't care! I won't like it here. I'll miss my friends. I want to stay at my old school! *(moves quickly to SR)*

SARAH: Sorry Grammy. *(to Keri)* Look Honey, we can't afford to stay where we were. The apartments by Grandpa's will be okay for a while, until we find a little house. *(sighs)* This is a nice park. Come on, let's check out the school? *(Keri shakes her head no).* Well, look on the bright side. At least I won't be teaching you!

GRAMMY: *(to Keri)* Speaking of teaching - I can teach you how to knit whenever you're ready - and I can show you around town, whenever you'd like.

SARAH: Can you teach me, too!? Would it relax me!? *(Keri stands SR, arms crossed, pouting)*

GRAMMY: *(SL)* *(puts arm around Sarah)* Of course dear. Look, both of you. I know things are tough right now. But this is a wonderful caring little community. You'll be able to make a lot of new friends here. I'll make sure of it!

SARAH: Thank you. You're very kind, Grammy. I'll just check and see if the school's open yet. I'll be right back. You okay for a minute, Keri? *(Keri nods, but is still pouting)* *(Sarah exits SR)*

SPIKEY: *(gets up from hiding behind rock. Stands in front of rock CS)* Life isn't always fair. You'll be going to school here, and not there. *(Keri moves to bench SR, near Spikey)* You're mad and your mom is sad. We've just got to make the best of things. *(pauses as he looks at Keri)*
C'mon Keri, <u>laugh</u> - it's not every day you'll meet a porcupine that sings!

GRAMMY: Spikey, good for you. You'll be making friends with kids, before you know it. *(Spikey smiles at Grammy, then looks at Keri)*

SPIKEY: A new school and a new home sound scary, but your mom's with you.
She'll help, too.
You're afraid to fit in.
Just like me - we feel we can't win.
But a new school could be cool - wish I could go.
It could be exciting, Keri, you know!

GRAMMY: And like your mom says - You've got almost a year to get used to the idea...

SCENE 4

MUSIC CUE: ****Spikey**** *(Ballad) (Track 4) (FULL CHORUS with Grammy, Spikey and Keri) (Spikey sits on rock. He's upset. Grammy starts singing CS) When Keri sings SR. Grammy is SL.*

GRAMMY: Keri, you may have found yourself a friend in Spikey, and me.*(sits on bench SR, by rock)*

SPIKEY: Yes, Grammy, is a friend to you and me! *(sits on bench SR, by Grammy, close to rock)*

KERI: *(to Grammy)* Are you a Grandmother? *(sits by Grammy)*

GRAMMY: No. But I'm like a Grammy to many of the kids around here. I always wanted a child, and when I found Spikey on the side of the road and nursed him back to health, well - he became like a son to me.

KERI: You're lucky he can talk. It's weird... it's all in rhymes...

GRAMMY: He didn't talk much at first. He didn't even have a name. We discussed it and both agreed on Spikey. I think it suits him.

KERI: So do I. *(to Spikey)* Can you read?

SPIKEY: *(nods)* I started learning by stories Grammy read.
Then listening with a tape, I pointed and followed along in bed.

GRAMMY: He didn't like the stories I used to tell him! *(Spikey makes face, shakes head)*

SPIKEY: A witch tries to eat Hansel and Gretel!
A wolf tries to eat 3 little pigs! How awful!
A wolf climbs into Grandma's bed,
as a little girl walks in wearing red.
Then a baby going rock-a-by in the tree top falls to the ground!
I was glad with the happy stories, Grammy later found!

GRAMMY: Like the silly one about the peacock. *(snickers)*

SPIKEY: Yes, that book that came in the mail. *(laughs)*
That was a beautiful tale! *(Spikey and Grammy laugh)*

KERI: *(starts to laugh)* Spikey, you are so funny!

SARAH: *(runs in, SR)* School's locked *(screams)* Keri, what are you doing with that hideous looking creature?!! *(Keri gasps, mouth open. In shock seeing/responding to her mom)*

SPIKEY: *(from bench)* Oh no, **where!** *(he and Keri laugh)* Oh, don't <u>despair</u>. *(hand to his forehead)*
I'm just a silly porcupine. *(Keri laughs)* Keri and Grammy are friends of mine.

SARAH: Well, Keri is <u>not</u>!! Grammy, this thing! - it talks! like a ... a person!!!

KERI: *(stands near Sarah)* Well, yah... don't have to lose your temper!

SPIKEY: Maybe lose it way over there. Then I wouldn't care. *(Grammy gets up. Walks to Sarah)*

GRAMMY: Sarah, calm down. He's like my son. I've been caring for him, a year, <u>today.</u>

KERI: *(tugging Sarah's arm to get close to Spikey)* Look at him. He's a porcupine. He's kinda scary but he sings and talks and dances. He's very friendly and kinda funny.

SARAH: Keri, stay away from <u>it</u>! It might bite and give you some strange disease. *(pulls Keri SL)*

GRAMMY: He's been for a complete check-up and has had all his necessary shots. Look, Sarah. You don't know me either. We can't tell by how things look. But rest assured. I wouldn't let anything happen to Keri, and neither would Spikey.

SARAH: *(from SL, in extreme panic)* Oh, let's get out of here!!!... Ohhhhh, NO!!....

SPIKEY: *(on bench far side SR, leans away from Sarah)* Hi, Sarah. I'm Spikey. Grammy named me.
I don't bite - or sting like a bee.
My quills won't poke you.
But I have scared more than a few.
I don't see many people. It's a pleasure to meet Keri and you! *(puts hand out to Sarah)*

SARAH: *(rejects Spikey's hand)* *(he walks away)* Uhh, Keri. I think we should go... Grammy. It's nice to meet you. Spikey... Umm, look, I thought my Dad might be here. You may know him. the grumpy guy that always feeds the birds, Keri's grandpa - Joe Taylor.

KERI: *(SL with Sarah)* He's <u>not</u> grumpy!

GRAMMY: *(CS, front of rock)* Yes, dear. I think I've seen Joe around, but not today. Listen Sarah, You may be interested - Keri knows about it... later this afternoon, around 3'ish, we're cleaning up the park and then having a little party for Spikey. *(Keri looks pleadingly at Sarah).*

SPIKEY: Grammy wrote a poem and will sing it! She's been practicing quite a bit!

GRAMMY: Yes. We're going to have special singing and reading. Spikey's singing and reading has improved so much in a year!

SPIKEY: *(points)* Grammy found me over there! In this park, she showed me her care!

SARAH: *(trying to be polite and understanding)* Where did you learn to speak in rhymes?

SPIKEY: I used to sit behind this park bench all day,
   listening to Dr. Seuss and Mother Goose read, in the same <u>old</u> way.

SARAH: So that's the only conversation you know?

SPIKEY: The only conversation I <u>know?</u> Yes, apparently <u>so</u>.

KERI: Isn't it kind of awesome, Mom?

SARAH: Well, uh, it's kind of annoying, but you speak very well Spikey. *(Spikey smiles)*

KERI: Grammy is like his Mom.

SPIKEY: She's the kind lady, who found me by the road.
   I lost my parents, I was sad, cut, bruised - and out cold.

GRAMMY: Why I remember when Spikey first moved in. *(puts arm around Spikey, as they stand)*

SPIKEY: She had so much to teach me. And she did, without getting angry.
   But, we can't celebrate in this mess. Cleaning together makes work time less!

KERI: Mom, can we help clean up? Please?!

SARAH: Yeah, I guess... *(to Grammy)* Sure, we can. *(Grammy claps then high-fives with Spikey)* But let's call your Grandpa first. He'll be wondering where we are.

KERI: Maybe Grandpa will help too? Can we ask him? Just call him on your cell... Please?

SARAH: Oh, all right. He's making lunch now. He does enjoy spending quite a bit of time here.

KERI: *(to Grammy and Spikey)* Mom's calling Grandpa. We'll be right back Grammy. *(Grammy smiles and nods.)* See you right away, Spikey. *(Spikey and Keri wave to each other.)* *(move off side, SL)*

SARAH: We're just going over there. *(Sarah takes out cell phone from purse, as she and Keri move to the left side of the stage).*

KERI: *(from SL)* Thanks Mom. *(Sarah gives Keri a hug. They stand SL at side of stage) Sarah talks in mime, on her cell).*

SCENE 5

SPIKEY: First we say "hi's," then we say "bye's." *(Mark and Ben enter)* Hi to two great guys!!

GRAMMY: Oh, hi boys. Back already? So are you ready to go back to school?

MARK: Don't remind us. *(Ben backs up)* He's okay Ben. Spikey just looks scary.

GRAMMY: He's more afraid of you than you are of him. Trust me.

SPIKEY: *(Puts up hand)* Hey, guys! *(high-fives with Mark)* *(Lisa and Sally get up, and high-five)*
Mark taught me how to high five.

BEN: Hi, Spikey. *(touches Spikey's quills. Spikey touches Ben's blue hair. Ben is NOT impressed.)* *(Sarah and Keri return.)* *(Spikey moves away, sits on rock)* *(Ben tentatively high-fives with Spikey)*. *(Spikey smiles! Ben smiles back)* *(Ben and Mark sit on bench SL, Mark closer to rock)*

LISA: *(to Spikey and Ben)* See, you both have good points!

KERI: Hi, guys! This is my mom.

BEN/MARK: Hi.

SARAH: Hi, boys! I'm Ms. Sarah Bell.

BEN: *(points at Spikey)* You! The porcupine that talks! Dad will never believe this! *(laughs)*

GRAMMY: How is Larry - I mean your Dad?

BEN: He's fine. Sometimes I wish he wasn't a lawyer. His cell is always on!

MARK: He got an important call during catch. But hey, we're here to clean up.

GRAMMY: Great! Well, it's noon. Have you boys had lunch? *(Spikey is thinking and sits on rock. He intently counts on 4 fingers)*

BEN: Yup! Another of Dad's surprises! *(looks questionably at Spikey)*

MARK: We had lunch before we practiced. Ben, let's go get Dad to meet Spikey. *(They start to exit)*

SPIKEY: Hey what word spelled forwards and backwards is the same? Grammy just said it- this is a fun game! *(Boys look confused)* *(gets up from rock)* N-O-O-N. Noon. Ah, you would have gotten it soon! *(All Laugh)*

21

BEN/MARK: Let's get Dad!! *(Mark and Ben exit)* *(Mr. T, enters SR. Spikey rolls into a ball. Mr. T doesn't see Spikey)*

SARAH: Hi Dad, we were just getting ready to leave. I left a message.*(stands in front of Spikey to protect him from Mr. T's wrath!)*

KERI: Hey, Everyone. This is my Grandpa. You can call him Mr. T. *(joins Sarah to cover Spikey)*

GRAMMY: It's a pleasure to meet you. I've heard about you through the kids. I'm Mary.

MR. T: *(enters SR)* I'm Joe. Joe Taylor. But call me Mr. T. Everyone does. *(to Sarah and Keri)* So here you two are, while I'm cookin' away. The burgers are done to perfecto on the barbeque...but they're going to get cold!

KERI: Wow, Burgers for lunch?! Thanks Grandpa!!

MR. T: Yeahhh, Well, you're welcome! *(Smiles at Keri)* *(Sees Spikey and panics/screams)* What in the world is that "thing" doing here!!!? *(pulls Keri SL, protecting her, stands with her)*

KERI: He's a porcupine, Grandpa!

MR. T: Well, stay away from it, Sweetie. It could have rabies or something.

GRAMMY: *(Heavy sigh of exasperation)* Huhhh... I've already taken him to the hospital. He's had his check-up and his needles...

MR. T: Is that what those things are? Needles?

SPIKEY: *(walks away)* This world isn't ready for a porcupine like me.

MR. T: It talks??!! Okay, so **what** is your name?

SPIKEY: <u>What</u> is **not** my name, no <u>siree.</u> My name is <u>Spikey!</u> *(stands far SR)*

MR. T: Spikey, what? *(snickers)*

SARAH: *(CS)* It's just Spikey, Dad. Spikey, you're alright. You're just – <u>different</u> - that's all. Dad, be nice! *(Mr. T makes a face at Sarah, then moves SR towards Spikey)*

MR. T: Be nice?! It would destroy my nerves to be nice. Okaaay... Spikey. I'm sure you have some good points. You are one huge porcupine.

SPIKEY: I'm tall and <u>lean</u>, but I'm definitely, not <u>mean</u>.

MR. T: Good point. I'm sure you're the only porcupine in this world - that talks.

GRAMMY: Possibly. But he's not mean. Lots of people and animals are afraid of each other when they first meet. It's smart to be cautious.

MR. T: Well I'm just trying to be smart and cautious. How would I know he's not going to bite and poison me or someone else?

SPIKEY: I don't <u>kick.</u> But I know I'm <u>not</u> <u>your</u> <u>pick</u>!

GRAMMY: *(Defensively)* That's just it. The best point Spikey has, IS loving unconditionally. *(moves CS towards Spikey, puts hand on his arm)*

SARAH: We can all learn from that.

SALLY: Yeah, he just wants to be happy and helpful! He wants everyone around him to be happy and helpful, too.

LISA: Spikey, you <u>are</u> ready for this world! More ready - than the world is for you!

SALLY: <u>All</u> of us are all like <u>porcupines!</u> *(Mr. T shakes his head, sits on bench SL)*

LISA: You're right! We've got some <u>really</u> good points!

SALLY: And <u>not</u> so good ones...good points – bad points... *(Sally, Lisa and Keri CS)*

KERI: And some <u>BROKEN</u> ones!! *(all laugh)*

SALLY: We get angry and say mean things. Spikey doesn't.

LISA: Why does Spikey even try to be kind and nice – what's the point?

SALLY: Yeah, he just gets bullied anyway. He's helpful even when he gets knocked down. *(Sally goes to get Spikey, and brings him back to CS).* Spikey – YOU are trying to make a <u>difference!</u> YOU are the change, we all want to see!! *(All cheer)*

LISA: World, are you ready for a porcupine like Spikey? Are you ready for all of us...

KERI: With our good and bad points?

SALLY: World – Are you ready, for all of us...

ALL: PORCUPINES?! *(Sarah sits by her dad, Mr. T. She's closest to rock. Grammy on bench SR. All are standing up for Chorus...*

SCENE 6

MUSIC CUE: **<u>WORLD, ARE YOU READY?</u> *(Track 5) (all on stage)*

(Sally sits on bench SL. Lisa sits beside her, closest to rock. Grammy on bench SR)

SARAH: Spikey, we could learn from you. You didn't judge us the way we judged you.

LISA: Do we not like a stuffed animal or toy cuz it's scary looking!? Or the wrong colour!!?

MR. T: *(gets up from bench SL, closest to rock)* Well, my daughter and granddaughter need to eat. The burgers will be cold. Let's go.

KERI: I'm not ready to go. *(beat)* Grandpa, how old do you have to be to do whatever you want?

MR. T: I don't know. No one has ever lived that long. C'mon, let's go.

SPIKEY: You must be happy to have them moving back here?! It's nice to have family near.

MR. T: Yes, it is Spikey. Well, let's hit the road. *(Sarah in front of bench SR)*

SPIKEY: You can hit a ball with a bat to the sky...but hit the road? Why, sir, why?

MR. T: *(cuts him off)* Look Spikey - *(starts to explain, then decides not to)* We're outta here. What a mess this place is. It's been bothering me for a long time. I thought I was going to have to clean it up myself! *(to Keri)* Don't ask again... yeah, I'll come back and help. *(Sarah, Keri and Mr. T exit. Mr. T 'shuffles' off).*

GRAMMY: *(yells in the direction of Mr.T)* We'll be cleaning up <u>soon</u>! *(Mr.T waves, without looking back).*

KERI: *(waves)* Bye Spikey. I'll be back *(loudly to Mr. T)* <u>soon</u>!

SPIKEY: Bye for now, Keri. More of you, I will see.
    (to Grammy) Her Grandpa is kinda grumpy, isn't he?

MR. T: *(from backstage)* No I'm NOT!!! *(Grammy shakes her head).*

SCENE 7

MUSIC CUE: **<u>Look At Me</u>** *(Track #6, OR ACAPELLO) (Spikey's tap dance / rap solo)*

SPIKEY: Thanks for helping here, kids. *(they smile)*
    To help us fill the garbage cans, up to their lids.

GRAMMY: Spikey, kids – let's go home and grab the lunch bags in the fridge. We need food and energy to clean up! C'mon, let's go now. *(to park dancers reading on side)...* You too! *(Spikey, Grammy, kids exit SR) (Ben and Mark enter SL) (Larry is offstage, behind them)*

BEN: *(enters SL, Mark follows)* Dad, where are you, Dad? Dad, Spikey was right here. Mark, where's Dad?

MARK: *(points to Larry)* Oh, he's over there – can't ever be without that blackberry.

BEN: Dad, would you like to meet Spikey? *(boys stand on either side of Larry)*

LARRY: Ummmm. No. *(sits in middle of bench SL)* It's very sweet of Grammy to do this party thing for a porcupine... *(Shakes head, texts on his cell phone)*

MARK: *(Interrupts..sits on right side of Larry)* He talks Dad!

BEN: *(sits on left side of Larry, closest to audience)* And he walks, Dad!

MARK: He was homeless...an orphan. His parents were found, on the side of the road.

BEN: Spikey got hit by the car too, but he survived. It's a miracle. *(Larry puts away phone)*

LARRY: Wonderful! It's a miracle he can talk. Nothing ordinary about that! Now look, I haven't seen Grammy lately. She's very caring, a wonderful woman. I mean – she babysat you kids and many in the area. But I think it's ridiculous having a porcupine party!

BEN: A Porcupine Party in the Park!

MARK: Now that's a good alliteration! *(Ben gives Mark a questioning look)*

LARRY: Boys – he's not human. He's not 'normal.' Let's be realistic.

MARK: Dad!

BEN: You're a lawyer – be fair! *(Larry rolls his eyes and shakes his head)*

25

LARRY: But... when Grammy phoned me, I couldn't say no. *(beat)* Who could have a party in <u>this </u>park? *(boys pretend to pout)* Look, I'll help clean up for Spikey *(boys knuckle cheer)* but paying tribute to his parents?? *(shakes head)* But – for Grammy, I agreed to do it... and I will. *(shakes head)*

BEN: You'd think differently if you met Spikey.

MARK: After all, she <u>has </u>taken care of us, for years!!

LARRY: Yeah, you're right. Grammy's tried to get me to meet him – but I just, haven't had the time... *(takes out phone, texts, doesn't see Spikey. Boys try to get his attention and point to Spikey. He ignores them). (Enter Grammy and kids, SR).*

SPIKEY: Grammy, you make a great sandwich! I have it all – I feel so rich.

GRAMMY: Thanks Spikey. I feel rich too. *(sees Larry)* Spikey, come meet Larry.

SPIKEY: I may scare him – I better not. I've been hiding for about a year, but now I am caught. *(walks away)*

LARRY: *(Jumps up in panic!)* What in the world!!!! I've seen it <u>all </u>now! Hello Spikey. *(Spikey stands...waves sheepishly).*

SPIKEY: *(looks at Larry)* Sorry I scared you. I've done that to quite a few!

LARRY: Ahh – it's not your fault. *(sits back down)* A walking, talking porcupine. I don't believe this. Ahh,- what is this? It talks? It walks? It – oh - this is insane! *(Ben laughs)*

SPIKEY: How many more do I have to meet? Scaring people has me beat!!

BEN: You hurt his feelings.

MARK: Dad, you're the one that says, "It's important to treat everyone fairly!"

LARRY: But...this is...Okay, I am losing my mind. Am I watching a porcupine <u>walking</u> away?! Someone please tell me this is not happening. *(Grammy comforts Spikey on opposite side. They stand looking at Larry).*

BEN: Hate to tell you dad – but it's for real.

MARK: You're the lawyer, Dad. You told me once, you've seen it all.

LARRY: Nothing like this. I won't sleep tonight.

SPIKEY: *(moves in)* Is it because you can't decide, which side? Are your eyes, open very wide?

LARRY: Stop!

BEN: It's happening, Dad! It's the hugest porcupine in the world! Awesome!

MARK: His name is Spikey and he walks and talks...

BEN: Yeah...he speaks in rhymes...

LARRY: Don't go there...!

LISA: It's so COOL! We could all become famous because we know him. We could make a movie!

SALLY: No way!

MARK: Cool! Hey do you think he could play baseball? Dad and I are looking for a back catcher...and we do need a back-up pitcher.

LARRY: A pitcher yeah...but Spikey? Sorry...I'm Larry. I see you have met my boys. *(shakes Spikey's hand)*

SPIKEY: Pleasure to meet you Larry. - but please excuse me...
Do you play with a full pitcher or empty? *(Larry makes face, starts to answer)*
And catching a BAT, can that be done? I know catching my breath – isn't as fun.
Now if a bat were thrown at me, I would definitely RUN!

LARRY: Look, Spikey, *(sits on rock)* it's a BACK catcher, not bat catcher! The back catcher tries to catch the ball, if the batter doesn't hit the ball. Then the back catcher throws it back to the pitcher. The pitcher is the one who throws the ball to the batter. The batter tries to hit the ball...

SPIKEY: Grammy makes cake batter! *(Larry shakes his head, rolls his eyes)*
I think she's trying to make me fatter.

LARRY: I was thinking school is about to start. Many kids hang out here. So I thought maybe we could create a practice field at the back of this park.

BEN: Would we have a ball diamond? *(Larry nods yes)*.

LARRY: It's good to have a diamond, where guys can get together to play catch or hit a ball.

GRAMMY: No Spikey, ball DIAMONDS do NOT sparkle! *(all laugh)*

LISA: Well they could! They could sparkle with excitement!! *(all laugh)*

LARRY: True! Anyway - we'll help fix this park up so kids can play here at noon recess as they come back from lunch.

SPIKEY: I've seen this park at noon recess. It's bigger, I must confess.

LARRY: *(confused)* How?

KIDS: Yeah, how?

SPIKEY: Cuz, there's more feet in it! And hands, with baseballs and mitts. *(all kids laugh)*

MARK: That's good Spikey! I'm one of them. Yeah, I've got years of school left and I'm playin' ball. Thanks, dad – for helping us clean up.

LARRY: You're welcome. This park **is** for everyone. *(to Grammy)* Who knows about the surprise?? *(Spikey gets distracted and picks up garbage around him).*

MARK: Everyone knows but Spikey and Keri. *(Spikey on bench SR, picks up garbage, puts it in can)*

BEN: There's a party at Grammy's after! A fun party!!! Lots of food! I'm always ready for a party! *(Spikey and Grammy return to group) (Keri, Sarah and Mr. T return)*

GRAMMY: Okay – let's get this place cleaned up!!!

MUSIC CUE: **Clean-Up Stomp** *(Track #7) (All sing/dance) (line dance/country,2 step) Mr. T enters with a rake, and is raking. Keri and Sarah enter, pick up garbage and throw it in garbage can. Lisa brings out Blue Recycle Bin and sets it SR. Some pick up garbage/recycling. Others exit / return with lawn chairs and set them up. (Immediately after song, Some get & set up lawn chairs. Mr. T and Sarah on bench SR, Larry, Mark, Ben in lawnchairs SR, Ben closet to audience) Spikey ond Grammy on bench SL. Girls in lawn chairs SL, with smallest girl closest to audience)*

SPIKEY: Wow, everyone – that was so much fun! Helping others has begun! *(INTERMISSION OPTION HERE) (See end of script for Grammy's line option).*

GRAMMY: And now, we can begin! *(Dancers sit) (All sit on lawn chairs, except Grammy and Spikey).*

Scene 8 *(All cast on Stage)*

GRAMMY: It's so-o-o- lovely! What a nice park! Now that everyone's here we'll have our party. I've got all kinds of food at home for later - cake, perogies... and Spikey's favorite - asparagus and pickle sandwiches!!

SPIKEY: Love them to eat! Grammy's can't be beat! *(Sits by Grammy on the bench)*

GRAMMY: Thanks Spikey. But before we eat, we'll sing and Spikey will speak....

SPIKEY: I'm too nervous to speak, even to a few.
　　　Tell the others here, I'm in bed with the flu. *(Gets up to leave)*

GRAMMY: But Spikey, you're fine with speaking, and you're such a good singer.

SPIKEY: Well, I suppose I could sing some. Or I could hum.

GRAMMY: Maybe Joe Taylor could sing a little, too. Excuse me, Joe - do you sing?

MR. T: Do I what? *(Irritated)*

GRAMMY: Sing.... "A Parent's Love." It's a classic.

MR. T: Of course not! Yes, I can sing - but not porcupine stuff. I feed birds. I'm retired. I go to ball games and hockey games but I don't sing **to** or **with** porcupines! Nor do I talk to porcupines! I'm only here because of my grand-daughter Keri.

GRAMMY: *(with sarcasm)* Sorry, Mr. T.

SARAH: Maybe I can help you Grammy. I know the song you said you were practicing.

GRAMMY: That would be lovely, dear. *(Sarah stares coldly at Mr. T)*

MR. T: *(pause, gruffly)* You know, Grammy, my wife and I used to sing that song... That song you were practicing in the park; *(Grammy smiles at him)* to our daughter, Sarah. That's why she knows it. If you're gonna sing - I'm glad you chose that one.

GRAMMY: *(smiles)* I'm glad you like that one, too. Interesting. Larry told me he and his past wife used to sing the same song to Mark and Ben. *(Pause)* You could join me if you like.

MR. T: Nah, I forget the words. *(He walks away)*

SPIKEY: Can I sit here, Grammy? *(Grammy nods, Spikey sits) (Grammy paces nervously)* This party thing kinda scares me.

GRAMMY: Yes dear, I understand. I'm a little nervous too, so bear with me.

SPIKEY: *(comforts Grammy)* Grammy, sorry to say this, but there's no bear with you! Just people, and friends, and a porcupine too. *(All smile/laugh).*

GRAMMY: Right you are, Spikey. He has a way of lightening things up. *(Quickly)* I don't mean lightening in the sky, Spikey. Okay, everyone... Let's get started. Drum roll please. *(All drum on knees /stamp on floor. Grammy takes out notes)* Spikey, you have a way of brightening up any area around you - with your 'presence.' *(all clap)* That he does, folks. All whom have met Spikey, know he has many good points. Thanks everyone for joining us here today. We're here to celebrate Spikey's new life with us. One year today! *(Cheers, as Grammy whispers to Spikey. He nods his head, yes.)* At this time, Spikey has a few words to say. *(Grammy steps back as Spikey gets up. All cheer / clap).*

SPIKEY: Thank you. Thank you very much! And to the dancers, Grammy and my new friends, my life you do touch! *(Spikey takes out his notes)*
Grammy helped me with this. And like her, I feel a little nervous ... *(pause – sighs)*
My stomach is all wiggly goo. Maybe I've got the flu.

GRAMMY: Just relax Spikey. We're your friends here. *(all say yes, Spikey it's okay, YOU CAN DO IT SPIKEY!, etc.)*

SPIKEY: *(big sigh) (reads from notes, nervously)* As I face a world, that at times is not fair,
I feel protected in Grammy's love and care.
I had the best parents a porcupine could have had.
I hold them in my heart, so I don't feel so sad.
They made me feel I could do anything.
They'd be happy to know my new friends here – who've taught me how to sing!
And just because I've tried,
My parents and Grammy are satisfied.
I love my parents now way up there, and all of you here.
And my new 'mom,' *(smiles at Grammy)* is such a dear!
Thanks everyone for letting me be me.
I am, a very lucky and loved Spikey!!
(all clap) (Spikey bows and returns to his seat)

GRAMMY: Thank you, Spikey. I know that was difficult for you. I'd like to thank all of you for coming here today. Thanks to all who sent flowers and gifts, to our home! You shouldn't have made such a fuss, just for us! Oh, I'm starting to rhyme like Spikey! *(Spikey and all laugh)*
But we appreciate your thoughtfulness. I'm very grateful to have Spikey join me in my home and join **us** in our community. *(all cheer)*

One year has gone so quickly. We're here to celebrate Spikey!!! *(all cheer)* We feel saddened by the loss of your parents but we are grateful that you survived. *(cheers)* Thank you. Would you like to add anything, Spikey?

SPIKEY: *(from bench)* Thank you Grammy, you said it perfectly. Thank you all.
You have picked me up from my fall.

GRAMMY: Well said, Spikey. Your hardship taught you bravery, tolerance and patience.

SPIKEY: Later we'll all go back to the house – eat, and open a gift.
My spirits, you really do lift.

GRAMMY: Thank you Spikey. It's your day – your celebration of life and new home! *(pause)* Home is special, wherever it may be!

SPIKEY: Being here is where, I <u>now</u> belong! I think it's soon time, for a song!

LARRY: "A Parent's Love?" I heard Mr. T. singing that one to the birds, in this park last week. *(Grammy, Sarah and Keri look surprised)*. It's a song my wife and I used to sing to our sons. Grammy, I know you know this one. Please come and join us!

GRAMMY: Sure! Mr. T?? *(motions him to join)* *(shrugs shoulders, last to get up)*

MR. T: My wife and I used to sing the same song to Sarah. Sarah, can you join us? *(cheers from the audience)* *(Sarah smiles and waves)* *(She gets up)* Thanks!

MUSIC CUE: **<u>A PARENTS LOVE</u> *(Track #8)* *(If you choose not to have a musical, song could be recited as a poem). Mr. T slowly gets up after music starts. They all sing, while looking at their 'children.' (Guests clap after song.) (Performed by Grammy, Sarah, Mr. T and Larry).*

LISA: Wow, let's give them a hand. *(All applaud)* *(Grammy, Larry, Mr. T. Sarah, Mark, Ben and Keri sit down).*

SPIKEY: Why do we say, "Let's give them a hand?" There are so many sayings like "easy as pie" and "piece of cake" that I don't understand.

GRAMMY: Giving them a hand means clap for them. That song was for you Spikey. It's our tribute to you. You've taught us so much... especially how much we have to learn! You've taught me to reach deeper inside myself and find a special kind of love.

MR. T: You know, that kind of hit me singing that song. It brought back some great memories.

LARRY: *(puts his hand on Mr. T's shoulder)* We can give each other strength during the tough times.

(Mr. T turns up his nose as he looks at Larry's hand on his shoulder. Larry pulls his hand back. Mr. T laughs as he play punches Larry on the shoulder).

MR. T.: *(nods in agreement)* And so we should!

SPIKEY: Our road doesn't end, it just has a bend
We've all become like family, living happily!
Thank you all for being here.
And thanks my Grammy dear.
And now Grammy, I have a tribute for your kindness.
This song will be followed by a kiss.

MUSIC CUE: **<u>TRIBUTE TO GRAMMY</u>** *(Track #9) (Bachata/Macarena/Limbo with rake etc.) (Spikey sings then kisses Grammy). (applause from guests)*

GRAMMY: Oh, thank you Spikey! When something precious is taken away – it's often replaced with something else very precious. We just have to be open to it.

SPIKEY: Yes, like surprises. They come in different sizes.

Scene 9 – Epilogue

KERI: *(Spikey sits on bench beside Keri. Sarah stands behind them, closest to rock) Mark and Grammy on bench SL) (Ben sits on rock)* There's always hellos and goodbyes.

SPIKEY: Keri, Please come back for a visit. On this bench – come again and sit.

LISA: Keri, sometimes things change and we have no control.

SALLY: Or **no** choices.

LISA: Yeah, but things happen for a reason, I think.

GRAMMY: I really believe I was chosen to take care of Spikey... and all of you kids.

SPIKEY: To have love and someone to believe in me, makes me shine.
In this world, I feel like I'm the luckiest porcupine!

SALLY: I would like to say something to you, Spikey and Keri. We'll help you get to know this community better. *(Spikey, Sally and Keri high-five).*

KERI: Sorry, I was kinda mean to you, Spikey, but that will change. *(She gives Spikey a play punch. He gives her one back).*

MARK: Spikey, you can play catch with Ben and I. *(stands behind bench, behind Spikey)*

BEN: Yeah – that would be so cool!

SPIKEY: I'd love to play catch.
Or you throw and I fetch. *(Grammy walks towards Spikey)*
Thank you Grammy for this special day!
I appreciate it more than words can say! *(Grammy smiles as she sits on bench)*

LARRY: You know, Spikey. You've already taught me something. You can't go through life with a catcher's mitt on both hands. Sometimes you need to throw something back. You give a lot more than you take, Spikey. You have great points to share.

SPIKEY: Baseball for me is new. But for your kind words, I do thank you! *(shakes hands with Larry)*

GRAMMY: Thank you Spikey. Oh what would I do without myself?! *(laughs)* You're so easy to please Spikey. *(To Sarah)* Anyway, Sarah, next week would you like to join me in a cup of tea?

SPIKEY: No matter how you sit - You both won't fit!

SARAH: *(laughs)* Sure. Next week it is. *(beat)* *(Sarah sits by Grammy)* This is a lovely event, Grammy. Maybe coming here to teach next year – won't be so bad after all!

SPIKEY: I'd like you to be **my** teacher. That is so – for sure.
You've got class. In my books, you surely pass!
Keri - I wish I could go to school and have your mom as my teacher
I don't know – but I'm sure she would be a feature. *(Keri and Sarah laugh)*

SARAH: *(smiles)* Thank you Spikey! *(Spikey smiles back.)*

LISA: *(to Sarah)* So you're going to teach school here, in a year?

SARAH: Yes, Yes I am. *(smiles)*

SPIKEY: *(to Keri)* Could you imagine a porcupine in school?
That'll be the day – but wouldn't that be cool? *(Keri laughs)*

MARK: Who knows?! Maybe if it was a school where all could work at their own pace.

BEN: A school where everyone passes – well eventually.

SALLY: *(to Spikey)* We mean a school that <u>includes</u> animals!!

SPIKEY: That kind of <u>school,</u> would be so <u>cool</u>!!!!!

LISA: Sounds okay to me!!

GRAMMY: *(takes Sarah's hand)* Everything will be okay, dear. Don't worry.*(They talk on bench SL)*

MR. T: *(slowly moves towards Spikey)* Spikey, you must think I'm the perfect grump.

SPIKEY: Oh no Mr. T...No one is perfect. Not even you and me! *(Mr.T walks away shaking his head.)*

LARRY: Hi Keri. So, you're the new girl my boys Ben and Mark, told me about.

KERI: Yes. Hi. I'll be moving here next summer with my Mom. That's her over there. *(she points to her mom, sitting on bench beside Grammy. They're talking, don't hear Larry).*

LARRY: Riiiight. *(Impressed as he notices Sarah).* You'll like it here, Keri!... Oh, boys. I cooked up a surprise. We'll eat at home, before we go to Grammy's....

BEN: Not another surprise meal, again!

MARK: How about we just eat lots at Grammy's? Ben – Let's fill up at Grammy's, then take leftovers home.

BEN: Sounds like a great plan! I can't take too many more of Dad's surprises.

KERI: Speaking of surprises... What is it anyway? When's this surprise coming?!

GRAMMY: *(CS)* It's a surprise!

SPIKEY: *(to Sarah)* Grammy asked me to ask you to come tomorrow for dinner...*(Sarah nods)* Before Grammy's food, I used to be thinner.

KERI: We'd love to!

SARAH: Yes - of course!

GRAMMY: *(CS)* And now, for something completely different!! *(All stop and look at Grammy) (with excitement)* Sure, we wanted to clean up this park for Spikey's party – ... but there was <u>another</u> reason....

LISA: Spikey, Keri – we know this has been a tough time for you. You're both scared because you're new.

SALLY: Well, Keri and Spikey. We all have something in common with you.

MARK: We're <u>all</u> huge fans of Lady La La too! *(or name of current singing star)*

BEN: And we couldn't get tickets to her *(his)* concert tonight...

LISA: Cuz they're all sold out!

KERI: Duhhhh!!!

LISA: We're not done – just wait, Keri. Well, Spikey... Grammy told us that she tried to get you a ticket but they wouldn't allow a porcupine in the concert hall.

MARK: And Keri – your Mom said she couldn't afford to get you a ticket. Your Grandpa Joe was in line with us to get tickets and <u>none</u> of us got one. So we came up with this idea – with the help of Grammy and Dad, of course.

BEN: And Grammy called his manager to see if he could play a song for us in the park, for a kind of a warm up and something special – for us...

SALLY/LISA: Yeah, and his manager said YES!!!! *(Keri doesn't believe them, shakes her head.)*

SALLY: But we had to promise to keep it a surprise!

MARK: But especially for Keri and Spikey. (*pause*) She (He) should be here soon! Grammy, what does your watch say? (*Grammy shows Mark her watch, Sally shows him time on her cell*).

SPIKEY: All watches say tick tock! Like on a clock! (*Spikey shakes his head in disbelief*) (*Sally and Lisa Look around for the 'Star.'*)

KERI: (*crosses her arms indignantly*) C'mon, she's (he's') a Star! She's (he's) not gonna come here!!!!...to a park! I just wish we all could have gotten tickets!

LISA: (*notices 'Star' from back of theatre **audience,** and gets excited*) Well, all I can say is that it's a good thing we got this park cleaned up and everyone's here for Spikey's party because here's the **grand finale!!!** Cuz everyone...I would like to proudly introduce to you **the one...the only...** (*Bold print – say in unison with Sally & the park dancers.*)

All KIDS: Lady La La!! (*or Justin, etc!*) (*Lady La La sings '**Born This Way!**'*) (*OR play on name of CURRENT star, Justin Timbersood singing 'Mirrors,' Bruno Stars, Katy Berry, etc.*) OR STAR can Sing **'Celebrate Life.'** (*Kids /dancers cheer/scream as they run to Star*) (*Excited Spikey jumps up and runs towards Star*) (*Star enters stage from the back, through the audience!*)

STAR: Whoa!!

SPIKEY: Oops Sorree....I'm just a very happy *Spikey!* (*Star moves towards Spikey*).

STAR: (*FIST pump with Spikey, then Keri and others*) I'm very happy I could be here with you, Spikey, Keri!! And all of you here! (*CS – in front of rock*)

KERI: (*Spikey smiles/dances*) Wow!!! I don't believe it!!!! Mom, you knew about this?!!!

SARAH: (*smugly*) Of course. (*Keri hugs Sarah. Sarah and Grammy smile at each other*).

KERI: I love you!

SARAH: I love you too, honey.

ALL: (*Yell, CHEER!!!*)

STAR: Hey Guys! You all good to go?! (*all cheer!*) (*girls sit by star, face front of stage*)

MUSIC CUE: __CELEBRATE__ or Name of Stars Song, example: ** BORN THIS WAY ** (*Separate Track*) Could be a cover tune or artist's original. (*All kids crowd around Star. Sit on ground, or in lawn chairs SL. Spikey and Larry on bench SR. Mr. T on lawn chair SR. Grammy and Sarah on bench SL*)

ALL: *(cheer and run up to Star)*

MUSIC CUE: ALL: **<u>You Gotta Have a Dream</u>** *(Track #9) (Sing/dance with Star) Immediate exit – (Dancers exit first) (Tap Dancing, Gymnastics, etc.)*

GRAMMY: *(loudly!)* **C'mon Everyone, off to Grammy's!!** *(all cheer as they exit SR, after Grammy.) (Black out)*

BEN: Yeah!! The **<u>PERFECT</u> <u>PARTY</u> <u>PLACE</u>!!** *(Yelling out as he follows)*

If an INTERMISSION is chosen....
On page 23 – after ALL CAST SING "Clean Up Stomp"
you could add / change a line for GRAMMY...

SPIKEY: Wow, everyone – that was so much fun! Helping others has begun!
GRAMMY: *<u>Delete</u>*...Now we can begin!! *<u>Replace</u>* with, **<u>Okay gang, let's all go home and clean up before Spikey's Party!</u>** *(all cheer as they exit).* END OF ACT 1.

*

*Intermission - ACT 2 (BEGINS with Grammy saying, **<u>NOW WE CAN BEGIN!!</u>** Last line of Scene 7, before Scene 8).*

ALL Exit SL For CURTAIN CALL
(LIGHTS UP) <u>*(very fast moving)*</u>

Instrumental MUSIC "Together We Can Make It" During
Curtain call - fade out as all Cast take a bow.

(Cast clap for each other, as actors enter stage for Curtain Call)

EXTRAS: CHORUS / Park Dancers *(if any)....Enter SR (stand at far SR end)*

Chorus *enters SR*

Star *enters Centre, moves SL*

Mr.T *enters SR*

Larry *enters SL*

Sarah *enters SR*

Sally & Lisa *.enter SL*

Ben & Mark *enters SR*

Grammy *enters Centre – Stand SL*

Keri *enters Centre (stands next to Grammy)*

Spikey *enters last, from Centre, stands between KERI & GRAMMY.*

All hold hands, 1 - 2 – 3 <u>*squeeze*</u> *–* **BOW**
*Cast raise hands to Choreographer & Stage Manager(s) as they enter. Cast Applaud
Hands to Lights/Sound Technicians & Director. Cast Applaud*

INSTANT MUSIC CUE: ALL CAST SING: **<u>Together We Can Make It**</u>** *(Track #10)*

As cast finish singing – they exit through the audience to meet guests in the foyer for autographs, etc.

THEME SONG INSTRUMENTAL "Together We Can Make It," plays for the third time, as cast exit the stage. Return to birds chirping, nature sounds etc.

- *Scripts / All Lyrics by: Joy Winter-Schmidt (Pilot Premier 1993)*
  (First Musical Editions - Winnipeg Fringe Fest 2001- 2005.

- *Second edition 2008, for Winnipeg MB, LRSD schools. (Third edition 2013, Fourth Edition: 2015)*

- *Music professionally recorded and arranged by Paul Bergantim (2004)*
  Music for theme song "Together We Can Make It" written by David Schmidt (1993)

CATCH A FRIEND

Spikey's Points: Sequel 2 *Approx. 75-80 min. (Reading time 45 min. Music: 11/12 songs - 30 min.)*

PRE-SHOW Musician could be on bench. (One from Chorus on lawnchair, reading the "Community Quill.")

LIGHTS UP ON SET: *Morning: Projected Park Scene: trees, rock, two park benches SR/SL, small picnic table SR. Sound: Birds chirping... nature music. (Musician exits prior to "Once upon a time" Voiceover.)*

Child Voiceover: *(Spoken Backstage or Recorded. Track #1) (Voiceover Opens ALL Sequels)* "Once Upon A time, not that long ago, lived a walking, talking, singing porcupine, with mostly good points. His name was Spikey. His parents didn't make it across the road. Spikey barely made it. He lay injured on the side of the road. A dear old lady everyone called Grammy, found him and nurtured him back to health. He became a friend to many because he always tried to do the best he could. He lived, he loved, he laughed. He became a great example to follow..."

MUSIC CUE: ***Together We Can Make It**Theme Song Intro Instrumental, track#2)*

During voiceover, Keri *enters SR slowly, texting. Sits on park bench **SL**, puts feet on bench, still texting).*

SCENE 1

Music fades. Spikey, Ben & Mark enter SL with ball and gloves. Mark sets 3 water bottles on bench, SL. (Spikey sets baseball & glove on bench SL.) Mark hands a bottled water to Spikey. They all drink water.

SPIKEY: *(excited as he runs in)* Yay!! To Another Great Day! *(lifts water bottle to cheer, then high-fives with Keri).*

MARK/BEN: Hi Keri! *(She waves and returns to texting. They shrug shoulders, lift hands).*

SPIKEY: Thanks Mark and Ben!! It was fun to play a little catch again! *(high-five)*

BEN: Yes it was Spikey! And Dad's coaching again! Are you happy with Coach Bob, too?!

SPIKEY: Yes, I sure am. *(pretends to hold bat)* He taught me to hold the bat and – wham!

MARK: Spikey, we're glad you joined us to play catch! Speaking of catch, Ben & I went fishing.

KERI: *(not looking up)* Wow, Good for you! What did you catch?

BEN: Uhhh, duhhh – FISH!! *(All laugh, including Keri).*

SPIKEY: My fishing friends Ben and Mark! Good to be with you guys, in the park! *(bang knuckles)* Glad you could play catch <u>early</u>! You'll need quills for pens, <u>surely</u>! *(pretends to pull quill)*

MARK: Thanks Spikey, but we don't need quill pens!!

BEN: Nooo! Please don't give me a quill!! Or I'll be accused, <u>again</u> - of poking a hole in Mr. T's convertible rooftop!! *(Keri looks up. Watches Ben, Spikey and Mark. Spikey and Mark laugh).*

MARK: *(to Ben and Spikey)* Hey! We gotta run. Dad only gave us **15** <u>minutes, to play catch</u>...

BEN: Of course he made sure we had his "surprise" breakfast first. It was **not** good!!

MARK: Thank Goodness for water, *(lifts up water bottle)* and some fresh air ...

BEN: Now we gotta run home - and get ready for school! Not cool!

MARK: School's not so bad, Ben! Glad you could meet us Spikey!

BEN: Knowing we were playing catch with you, Spikey - at PEACE PARK - was the **only** thing that got me out of bed!

SPIKEY: *(smiles at Ben)* Playing Catch is a <u>great</u> **way**, to start a <u>first morning</u> of school, **day**!!

BEN: Right! See you later, Spikey and Keri! *(boys exchange a knuckle greeting with Spikey and Keri)*

MARK: Yeah, see you after school Spikey! We'll practice more catch, later. *(Boys start to exit)*.

BEN: *(to Spikey)* Glad our first day, is just <u>half</u> a day! *(Mark looks at his cell to check time, as Ben peers over to see)*.

MARK: Ben, we <u>gotta run</u>... *(picks up his glove and baseball)*

BEN: But we still have over <u>four</u> minutes!

MARK: It takes five minutes to get home! Bye Spikey! *(Ben makes a face, as he picks up glove. Boys wave, exit SL)*.

SPIKEY: Doodle Doo! I'm happy your Dad's coming to practise too! *(Chorus enters with backpacks, put backpacks on ground, stretch, speak in 'mime.')* Hello park dancers! Do you need an extra prancer? *(prances, chorus smile, stretch) Spikey sits on rock)* Hey, hello there, early morning Keri! You're not looking too merry.

KERI: Hi Spikey. I'm <u>not</u> too merry. Couldn't sleep last night. I miss my old friends, and Lisa too. We just become friends, and <u>she</u> moves!! We're all starting school today, **without** each other! *(big sigh)* And I picked two new hoodies at the mall with Grandpa Saturday.

SPIKEY: That makes you sad? That would make me, double glad! *(sits on bench by Keri)*

KERI: He said he'd pick **one** of them up for me. I got **none**!

SPIKEY: Sometimes adults forget when they have too much to do. They need reminders too.

KERI: But it's the first day of school! Mom got me this one I'm wearing, but it's old and I kinda wanted to wear the new one **I** picked out! Tomorrow's my first <u>full</u> day. Sure hope Grandpa will get it for me, for <u>tomorrow</u>!!!

SPIKEY: Let's not blame your Grandpa Mr. T. He did his best to try and get you, your hoodie! You need to find it in your heart to forgive. *(beat)* Live, and let live!

KERI: *(makes a face)* Oh Spikey, you're strange...but so funny. How can I stay mad, around you?

SALLY: *(Sally enters SR, with little sister **Tia**. If there is no Tia, Sally can say her lines. Girls are wearing backpacks.)* Hi Spikey, Hi Keri! *(Sally, Tia sit at picnic table SR, Stretch with dancers).*

SPIKEY/KERI: Hi Sally. Hi Tia. *(Sally and Tia exchange hello's to all on stage).*

SALLY: *(to Keri)* My sister and I are going to hang out here! We're going over routines, for the auditions. Want to join us?!

KERI: No, Thanks. I'm <u>not</u> going to audition.

SALLY: C'mon Keri, At least try! If we don't make the team, we can still dance in the park!

KERI: Yeah, well, whatever! *(Sally puts hands in air, takes out notes. Sally and Tia stretch, with Chorus)*

SPIKEY: *(to Keri)* Okay, Tell me what your Grandpa <u>said!</u> You've been upset this early morning, since you got out of <u>bed</u>!

KERI: *(speaking quickly)* Well, I couldn't decide which hoodie, so I said '<u>he</u>' could pick one out for me. So, like the next day, after church, Sunday, he calls and says, *(mimics Mr. T)* "I was running late! I was visiting a 'lady' friend. *(Spikey rolls eyes, shakes head.)* When we got to the mall, it was closed! " Whatever! I'm gonna sit and text old friends...

SPIKEY: *(makes face, puts hands up, as if to ask "Now What?)* Today's your first day of school. Try to be positive. That's my rule! *(Chorus, Sally, Tia sit)*

KERI: *(sees chorus)* There's dance auditions at noon! I'm not ready for a new school – not today!

SPIKEY: You'll be just fine. Soon you'll have friends waiting in line! Look around this special park. This is where I caught friends, Sally, Ben and Mark! *(points to audience)* These are friends we haven't met yet. This year will be okay, I bet! *(to audience)* Good to see you everyone! I see you're catching, some Winnipeg *(or name of local city)* sun! *(enter BOB, with baseball and glove)* Hey, Coach Bob is coming by! *(to Keri)* He's a really great guy! He's my **<u>new</u>** friend! We play catch to the day's end! *(Bob nods)*

BOB: Hi there Keri!

KERI: Hi Coach Bob. I met you with Grandpa. You're a construction worker, right?

BOB: Hey, that I am!! I remember meeting you too! Hello there, Spikey! *(high-fives with Spikey)*

SPIKEY: And hello, my friend Bob! I've been practicin' my back catchin' job!

BOB: I can tell! You can even catch the curve balls! Good for you, Spikey! I was hoping to find you here. *(sits on rock, facing Spikey)*. Hey, would you like to help me coach the ball team?

KERI: *(still texting, not looking up)* So, Spikey as a ball Coach??! What next?

SPIKEY: Me!?! *(to Bob)* You make me beam! But what do I know about a ball team?

BOB: Fairness. Besides, all the kids and guys I coach at the back of this park, wanted me to ask. You could be an assistant coach... like Larry. It's volunteer, of course. *(Keri shakes head)*.

KERI: *(sarcastically, without looking up)* Well, we all know Spikey has good points to share!

SPIKEY: Yes I do, so I'd like to play ball and volunteer! I'd like to catch friends far and near. I'll have fun and get fit! A porcupine coach? Who knew it?

BOB: You've already caught lots of friends Spikey! You're friends to all of us here!!

SPIKEY: But some kids and parents may not trust me. I'm pretty scary looking, can't you see?

KERI: *(looks up and faces Spikey)* We can see who and what you are! Spikey, you're MY FRIEND!

BOB: Mine too! We see what matters. I've known Grammy for years. And now I know you.

SPIKEY: You and Grammy are gems. My pin cushions for problems. *(Keri playfully pokes Spikey)*.

KERI: I need some of your good points, Spikey! You're never jealous or mean, never hurt anyone.

SPIKEY: *(Bob nods)* I wouldn't hurt anyone! I just want to have fun!

BOB: Okay, Assistant Coach – here's some <u>fun</u> baseball questions for you. We talked about this in the dugout. Remember? *(Spikey doesn't remember)*. What would you do if it were the bottom of the ninth inning. That means finishing the final inning. There's two players that have struck out and there are three runners on all 3 bases?

SPIKEY: I'd run out of the dugout! So I could see what all the fuss was about!

BOB: You're the back catcher. You <u>wouldn't be in</u> the dugout! *(Keri and Spikey laugh)*.

SPIKEY: Ohhh, I know what this is all about. So, I'd throw the ball at the runners and knock 'em out?! *(Keri and Spikey giggle) (Sally and Tia are at picnic table SR, colouring. They giggle).*

BOB: No Spikey... *(shakes his head)* Let's try another one... Can you stay calm? *(Spikey nods)* Ball players can't get too emotional. Why do you think that is?

SPIKEY: I know that <u>one!</u> You said don't '<u>Choke up</u>,' cuz - we need a home <u>run!</u>" *(Keri rolls eyes)*

BOB: 'Choke up' means, **on the bat**... *(physically shows Spikey)* Anyway ... *(laughs)*

SPIKEY: *(hits mosquito)* Oh, those pesky little Manitoba skeeters!!! *(Coach Bob laughs).* Okay, are baseball umpires good eaters?

BOB: Don't know...

SPIKEY: Yes, cuz they always clean their plate! Now how does that one rate? *(all laugh)*

BOB: Very good. Last question. What do you call someone who 'runs away' from the ball?

SPIKEY: Duhhhh! You think you're a clever fella. Grammy *(Grammy enters SR, waves)* taught me that one...<u>Cinderella!!</u> *(All laugh. Chorus enters to sing/dance). (Grammy, Spikey, Keri, Bob, Sally Tia and Chorus sing **Let's Make A Point!*** *(Option, sing 1 verse, to reduce time).*

BOB: Spikey, don't worry too much about ball practice. It's just for fun!

KERI: I'm sure you're a better ball player than I am!! *(looks at time on her cell and panics)* Oh no!! I've struck out! I told mom I'd be home by 8 am, to get my stuff for school! It's 5 after! She said I needed a few minutes of fresh air. I still have stuff to do! *(runs, exits SR)* Gotta Run!! Mom will be in a panic!

SALLY: We'll meet you back here Keri! We'll practice our audition routine, behind the trees!

KERI: *(running as she exits SR)* Okaaay!

GRAMMY: Hope you have a good morning dear! See you later Keri! *(Keri waves to Grammy and Spikey). (All Dancers exit SL) (To Spikey)* I've got to run too. I'm dropping some knitting off, at the hospital. I'll be back soon. Spikey? Want to go with me? *(Spikey shakes head no).*

BOB: Grammy, I thought we'd practice some catch. There's a few of us ball players back there. Spikey can practice with us. Is that okay with you?

GRAMMY: Of course, Bob. *(Spikey pretends to be a back catcher)* Spikey's ready to play ball! Spikey, you <u>CAN,</u> catch a friend! Bob's your new friend! Bye. I won't be long.

BOB: I have a cooler of food there, for us to eat. *(Spikey smiles, gives a thumbs up, rubs belly)*.

GRAMMY: Great. Thanks. I'll grab something from the hospital. *(she starts to exit SR)*

SPIKEY: To grab is okay – as long as you pay!

GRAMMY: *(turns around)* Yes Spikey, I will pay! See you two later. *(waves and exits SR)*

BOB: C'mon Spikey. I've got some time off! I'll show you some new baseball tricks!

SPIKEY: On the ball diamond, I'm rough. Teaching me, will be tough! *(Bob laughs as they exit SL)*.

SCENE 2

DSC: (SR - Sarah's 'home' set) (SL – Larry's 'home' set)

DSC Scene: In front of Park. Larry enters SL, pushing black office chair, on wheels, with his foot; (or carries chair) while putting a tie around his neck, with one hand. His briefcase is on top of chair, or he is carrying it. Sarah enters SR with small round table, with binder on top. Larry (exhausted) does up tie.

SARAH: *(sets down table)* Okay, Relax. Take a deep breath, Count to 10. I've got that, okay, that's in and *(sighs)* I <u>am</u> ready for the new school. *(She frantically looks through papers in binder, drops some, picks them up, throws them in binder, as Larry looks through briefcase).* My daughter is in <u>my</u> class. *(Larry takes out cell).* She wasn't supposed to be. *(looks at watch)*

LARRY: *(Larry and Sarah <u>look at watch, the same time).</u> (He calls number on cell, as Sarah puts head in hands as she exits SR)* Hello? Mr. Taylor? Yes, this is Larry Law confirming your appointment. *(Sarah quickly returns with briefcase & large purse, drops them on table. Exits SR)* Thank you. Okay, now our morning appointment is fine... *(Sarah returns carrying kitchen chair and keys into 'her' SR room. She drops <u>keys</u> on the floor, by the table).* Sure...I understand. *(Sarah and Larry SIT at exactly the same time).* Yes, my sons and I met Spikey with you, last summer. Yes, I've already met with Spikey. Hmmm, I know, we can discuss it further at our meeting. Correct, he lives with his guardian, Grammy. Yes I'm surprised he'd; okay but we have to prove, no, that's what lawyers are for. *(Continues talking in mime)*

SARAH: *(stands ups, holds back of chair firmly)* I CAN handle this! *(Struts confidently)* I CAN handle anything! I AM in control. I AM invincible. I CAN do anything! *(looks at watch)* Keri? Are you back yet? Keri?! Keri!!!!???!!!! WHERE ARE YOU?! *(exits SR)*

LARRY: Well we can't generalize. There are good and bad lawyers too. Yes, the evidence is there. There are definite holes in the rooftop of your convertible. Uhh Huhh, It seems no one trusts anyone anymore. Well, thank you. Yes, I got my sons to help ... Glad you're happy with the temporary patches... *(mime conversation as Sarah re-enters SR)*

SARAH: *(re-enters with lipstick. She's pacing. She tries to put lipstick on.)* Where is she? Keri – where are you???!!!! Keri! *(She puts lipstick in her purse) (Keri rushes in SR)*

KERI: *(out of breath)* Coming mom. *(Slouches on chair. She's exhausted)* I need a nap.

SARAH: I'd worry about you not getting back up! Glad you're home. You can take a <u>long</u> <u>nap</u> **after** school. I have to be extra <u>early</u> today. Did you get enough fresh air?

KERI: You can never get enough fresh air! *(Almost a whisper, Sarah doesn't hear)* or sleep…

SARAH: Thank goodness for parks! What did you do there, hon? *(puts papers in brief case)*

KERI: Texted my old friends…stuff. Talked to Spikey and Bob **…** and Sally.

SARAH: What did you talk about?

KERI: Nothin'! I'm sooo tired. I never slept, all last night. You woke me up waaay too early! *(with sarcasm)* And I'm just so excited about going to school, with <u>you</u>, today…

SARAH: I'm uncomfortable about this too, hon. Will it make you feel better if I <u>ignore</u> you?

KERI: Oh – so you'll be just like dad?!

SARAH: Keri, C'mon! We're divorced! He's thousands of miles away. He has a new <u>LIFE</u>…

KERI: And a new <u>WIFE</u>!

SARAH: C'mon Keri. This is about you and me! *(pause, gets up)* Honey, *(puts arm around Keri. Keri shrugs her mom's hand away)*. We can't afford a house yet. Our apartment here, by Grandpa's is fine for now. This is our 'new norm.' We'll have to get used to each other in a new place, because this is going to be the *(louder)* best teaching job I've ever had, and the least you could do is be happy for me! *(with hurt, as Keri mouths the following words with Sarah…)* I do everything I can for you. I work so hard and I…

SARAH/KERI: … Have no social life so that you can have a life. *(Sarah's voice trails off)*

SARAH: C'mon honey, we don't have time for this. I need to go… *(continue speaking in 'mime')*

LARRY: *(still on cell)* Listen, Mr. Taylor – I really have to run. Certainly. Hey, and if you run into that porcupine again…uh huh, yes. His rhyming is irritating but that doesn't make him guilty! He doesn't have a motive, yes, you can put me on hold…my son Ben again?....uh huh…

KERI: *(gets up, looks at time on her cell)* It's still too early for me to go to school. Can you drop me off at the park again? I'm too tired to walk back there now. *(Sarah nods)*.

SARAH: *(aside)* Yes dear. What is it about women and guilt anyway? *(to Keri)* Did you finish your breakfast? *(Keri nods)* Brush your teeth? *(Keri nods)* Got all your supplies? Your lunch? *(Keri nods as she picks up backpack and puts it on)*. You still have time to visit with your new friends a bit more. Ill drop you off but don't be late for school…

KERI: Yes Mom. *(moves slowly)* I should've taken my backpack in the first place – then I coulda just walked to school from the park, **with** Sally. *(sighs)* I'm too tired to think...

SARAH: You're nervous about your first day. I understand. *(looks in purse, pockets for keys)*

KERI: Glad I'm walking to school with Sally.

SARAH: We'll need to leave right away. *(Keri nods with eyes closed)* Oh by the way, sweetie, your Grandfather called a lawyer. Larry, remember – Ben and Mark's dad? *(Keri nods)* It's about that porcupine, Spikey. He seems like such a nice porcupine. I can't imagine him deliberately putting holes... *(Keri opens eyes, stops walking)* in the roof of your Grandpa's convertible. Apparently there's a few holes the size of porcupine quills! *(continue in mime)*

LARRY: That's fine. *(Larry looks for keys, in pocket, on floor)* It can wait until our meeting. Listen, I need to get off the phone for a min... I'll call right back. *(checks pockets for keys)*

KERI: Uh huh. Whatever. Spikey didn't do it. *(Larry and Sarah get up/STAND, at the same time).*

SARAH: Your Grandpa is so upset. I sure hope I've got enough gas to get <u>you</u> back to the park and <u>me</u> to school! *(Keri picks up keys on floor, as MARK ENTERS SL, walks to Larry. He holds car keys in front of Larry. Mark hands keys to Larry, at the **<u>same time</u>** Keri hands keys to Sarah. TOGETHER, Larry and Sarah, take a huge sigh of 'relief!')*

SCENE 3

KERI/MARK/BEN: KEYS!

SARAH/LARRY: Thanks. *(Sarah puts keys in purse) (Larry puts keys in his pocket)*

KERI/MARK/BEN: Relax!

KERI/MARK/BEN: You need a "friend."

SARAH/LARRY: No time!

KERI/MARK/BEN: There's gotta be someone!

SARAH: Someone unhappy?!

LARRY: Someone uninteresting?!

SARAH: Unhealthy and unattached?

LARRY: Single and stressed?!

SARAH/LARRY: I'm unimpressed! No thanks!

KERI/MARK/BEN: Don't you **ever,** want to get **married** - again?

SARAH/LARRY: No!!

KERI/MARK/BEN:*(Keri/Mark pick up parent's briefcases, and hand it to them)* BRIEFCASE!

SARAH/LARRY: Thanks! *(Sarah puts briefcase on table,) (Keri picks up kitchen chair to leave, Sarah follows with table, and her 'stuff' on top. They exit SR). (Larry lifts up cell as Ben, Mark exit SL).*

LARRY:*(Speaks on cell)* I'm back. Yes, Mr. T. I care about children, too. Uh huh, better to error on the side of caution, to protect our children. Just because Spikey said he's sorry about your car, doesn't mean he's guilty. He's sorry it happened. We're sure the holes are porcupine quills. But there's no history. We can't judge...he deserves a fair trial... he can't be charged on hearsay. *(pause)* Yes, I'm looking forward to seeing you again as well. Thanks. Bye. *(beat)* Boys! Got your lunch? Got everything?

MARK/BEN: *(offstage)* Yes dad! *(Enter Keri SR with backpack- CS to Park Bench. Keri sits, texts).*

MARK: *(re-enters with backpack)* So dad, are you still coming to this dance tonight in the park? Remember?! I'm helping with lights? Sound? You know, backstage? *(Larry's tying tie)*

LARRY: *(hand to forehead ... he's forgotten)* Right, you told me? Are you getting paid?

MARK: No. I told you that. I'm a volunteer.

LARRY: *(without looking up)* Good for you. Volunteering is good! Very rewarding.

MARK: You're too busy to really listen to me. And you've got that staff golf tournament next weekend...*(beat)* *(almost angry as Dad is ignoring him)* Ben and I miss having a mom...

LARRY: Sorry Mark. So do I. *(Larry puts arm around Mark)* I'll tell you what. I'll skip the tournament. Ben, you and I can go fishing together, or something...whatever you want. Just the three of us. What do you think?

MARK: Awesome!!! There is something good out of the bad.

LARRY: What do you mean, Mark?

MARK: You hug us more since mom died...

BEN: *(Re-enters SL, carrying hoodie and lunch kit)* *(Aside)* ... I feel like I'm forgetting something...*(to Larry and Mark)* Dad? Mark? Are we still playing catch after school?

MARK/LARRY: *(to Ben)* We're in!

BEN: Cool! That works for me! *(Ben high-fives with Larry and Mark).*

MARK: But today, 'Catch' first, then runnin' to the park, for the dance. *(Ben nods).*

LARRY: Boys, you drive me crazy – but it's good to see you becoming friends.

MARK/BEN: What???!!!

LARRY: My day is easier when you two get along.

MARK: No problem dad...

BEN: Now about my allowance...

LARRY: Now about your hair... *(playfully touches Ben's spiked hair)* you still look like a porcupine! Come on guys – Let's get going. You don't want to be late for your first day of school.

BEN: Remember dad, you're meeting us after school to practice catch with the ball team.

MARK: Then the dance thing...

LARRY: Yessss. Enjoy your walk through the park! Remember, I believe in you guys! *(puts arm around sons)* Hope you guys have a great day! *(Boys exit SL. Larry follows, pushing office chair on wheels, or he carries it out. His briefcase is on top of his office chair).*

MARK/BEN: *(offstage)* It's school – dad!

SARAH: *(Enters SR and sits by Keri, on bench. Keri's texting)* Hi hon, I'm settled in my class. Ahhh, just need a minute of fresh air before I go back! *(hugs Keri)* Love you. Are you okay? Remember, hon, I believe in you! It's going to work out... Let's be positive, it'll make our year a whole lot easier. We can make it! Right? It's all okay. *(they fake smile at each other.)* *(Enter Mark and Ben SR. Mark is wearing a backpack. Enter Sally, Tia and Chorus, SL They sit at picnic table).*

SARAH: *(getting up)* Hi boys. How was your summer?

BEN: Way too short!!

MARK: It was fine, thanks. *(Larry RUNS in, from SL! He's exhausted. He hands Ben his backpack).*

BEN: I knew I forgot something!! Thanks Dad! *(Larry smiles as he pats Ben's shoulder).*

SARAH: *(nervously)* Hi! How are you, Larry?

LARRY: Fine thanks, Sarah. Are you and Keri ready for your first day of school?

SARAH: Yes, I think so. *(turns to leave)*

LARRY: I don't know you well, but I believe you'll be a great teacher. Glad you moved here.

SARAH: Well, thank you. Okay. Uhh, bye honey. *(hugs Keri)* I've got to run. Keri, would you like to walk to school with Ben and Mark? *(Keri nods yes).*

KERI: Sure, but it's still early. *(points to picnic table)* Sally's over there. We'll all go together.

SARAH: *(to Larry)* It's our first day. We're nervous! I've got to get to school. Keys?! Yes I've got my purse, *(looks inside)* and my keys. *(exits, yells back).* Don't be late Keri! Bye! Ahh Larry, about that, um I'll call later. *(Larry watches).*

KERI: *(to Larry, Mark and Ben)* So... remember meeting me last summer?

LARRY: Yes, I do. I hope you like your move here.

KERI: Hopefully I will. Thanks.

BEN: Yeah, I remember meeting you last summer... we met in this park. We cleaned it up!

MARK: And had a fun celebration for Spikey, then went to Grammy's after! *(Keri nods).*

KERI: Yeah. Mom and I have been so busy unpacking. We haven't been back to the park much.

LARRY: Well, I have to run. Busy day with lots of meetings. Hope all of you have a great day!

KERI: Thank you!

BEN/MARK: Thanks Dad. *(Larry does a thumb greeting with sons. Exits SL)*

MARK: Keri, you **will** come and watch this dance thing in the park, tonight? Right?

KERI: I was planning on it. Actually I was thinking of auditioning at noon, for the "dance thing." Sally asked me to try out. *(Ben and Sally Cheer)* Grammy made ALL the outfits for it. Sure hope I get to wear one! They're pretty cool! Are you both coming tonight?

BEN: You bet! We've got ball practice after school, but we'll be back here!

MARK: I have to. I'm helping with the lights and sound, so we'll **have to** come back here!

KERI: Maybe I'll come with my mom. Maybe I'll get to dance...

MARK: Hope so. Yeah, well, we'll see you later, umm, at the dance.

BEN: We're playing catch right after school with dad! And Bob, Spikey and some other friends!

KERI: Sure hope I CAN <u>catch some friends!</u> *(All kids on stage sing ****<u>Catch A Friend!</u>**** <u>some/all have solos, Sally, Ben, etc.</u>) (Spikey enters from opposite direction, and joins them).*

MARK: Sally, Keri, are you both auditioning for the dance at noon? *(Sally nods/gives a 'thumbs up').*

KERI: I've been practicing. Can I audition? *(shrugs shoulders)* I don't know... Can I?

SALLY: You **ARE** going to audition, Keri! *(Keri shakes head no)* C'mon - Change **Can I?** to **I CAN!**

BEN: Hey don't be nervous Keri. It's dance, not rocket science! You <u>CAN</u> do it!! *(all cheer)*

53

KERI: Easy for you to say. That's not the point. Jessica doesn't like me. And this dance thing tonight - is HER thing!

SALLY: We just have a few minutes... *(sighs)* Are we ready for our first morning of school?

SPIKEY: Take your good points to school! Learning is a great tool!

KERI: We gotta run! My teacher mom will be looking for us! Better get there before the **first bell**!! *(ALL kids run/exit SR). (Ben makes a loud buzzer sound, as he exits).*

SCENE 4 *(Bob and Spikey re-enter SL)*

SPIKEY: Was my 'playing catch' lesson enough? Hope teaching me wasn't too tough!

BOB: Spikey, you're a diamond, in the rough. *(Spikey's confused)* Hey, did Grammy tell you about the holes in Mr. T's convertible roof? *(Spikey nods)* Someone used YOUR quill to poke a hole.

SPIKEY: Holes, someone did poke! Remember Ben tried once, as a joke? *(pokes Bob)*

BOB: Yeah – some joke. *(Bob sits)* You said you need a break, have a seat. *(Spikey sits)*.

SPIKEY: He was mad at Mr. T – for being grumpy.

BOB: Mr. T said he saw Ben pick up your quills in the park.

SPIKEY: Ben took 'my quill.' It was not 'my' will! *(makes a face)*

BOB: He broke quills trying to poke it into Mr. T's roof top!

SPIKEY: Ben was very sad. He didn't tell his dad cuz he thought he might get mad.

BOB: Why? Larry would understand. Why couldn't he talk to his dad?

SPIKEY: I asked Ben and it caused a stir! He said, "Are you crazy, my dad's a lawyer!

BOB: So then, what did you say to him?

SPIKEY: "Say Sorry for doing something wrong!" I asked if he felt lost and didn't belong?

BOB: Did he answer Yes? *(Spikey nods 'yes')*.

SPIKEY: I said, " You can't carry guilt forever. Keeping it inside, is not very clever."

BOB: *(thinking)* Maybe Ben didn't do it this time. He didn't cause damage, but made a dent. But someone DID succeed this time. Who could it be? *(looks questionably at Spikey)*

SPIKEY: My quills do make quite a point, don't they? They fall out, but 'I' have a price to pay! That's why Mr. T, blames me!! It's always MY bad quill, everyone - does see!

BOB: Ben **tried** to punch a hole in Mr. T's rooftop before. But that doesn't make him guilty **this** time. I just dunno...

SPIKEY: But having quills is NOT my fault! Wish I could bring, quills in others hands, to a halt!

BOB: Ben got caught. His dad made him apologize to Mr. T, for <u>planning</u> to poke a hole.

SPIKEY: Maybe Ben was angry or bored. Maybe he tried doing a bad thing, cuz he felt ignored!

BOB: There's no excuse strong enough to cause damage to property, or to hurt others!

SPIKEY: No excuse – for abuse!

BOB: Right! Larry had Ben rake leaves in Mr. T's big back yard! *(Spikey nods)* Remember, Mr. T thanked Ben and bought us all *(Goldeye) (local ball team)* tickets. That was fun! *(Spikey nods)*.

SPIKEY: At the game I sat between Ben and *(points to Bob)* you! My quills got bent, well a few!

BOB: *(laughs)* Yes, I remember – And now we're all friends, ball players and (Goldeye) fans!

SPIKEY: And Ben's not ignored anymore! He's playin' ball and keepin' score!

BOB: So why'd Ben try again? He's fine with Mr. T now? If at first you fail? Nahhh. So you'll come back and join us after your break? *(Spikey nods)* Okay, So who poked the holes in Mr. T's convertible rooftop, this time!?

SPIKEY: Ohhhh.... it's a mystery! We'll just have to wait and see! *(Spikey remains on bench as Bob shakes his head. They both look puzzled as Bob exits SL).*

SCENE 5

GRAMMY: *(Enters SR)* Hi Spikey. Are you just taking a break? *(Spikey nods)* Good timing! *(sits on bench SL)* Guess, it's just you and me now, with the kids in school. How was your morning practice with Bob?

SPIKEY: It was just fine, thanks. *(sits by Grammy)* But that Bob plays many pranks! *(laughs)*

GRAMMY: He is a great guy to be a volunteer coach with Larry. And you're volunteering too, Spikey, by playing catch with the kids.

SPIKEY: And Mark is volunteering! And you with your knitting! *(they sing **Valuable Volunteer**)* Bob and Larry invited me to play catch today. I hope I'm not awkward or in the way.

GRAMMY: Don't let fear rule. Just do your best, Spikey! That's all anyone can ask.

SPIKEY: Thank You. Bob and Larry say that too. *(sighs)* But Mr. T is so mad at me about those holes in his roof! I feel like giving him one big hoof! *(kicks his foot)*

GRAMMY: Now, now Spikey! Mr. T has put your nose out of joint.

SPIKEY: *(Spikey feels his nose)* My nose is not out of joint. But I do have a breaking point. My nose is fine and in line. But Mr. T is no friend of mine!

GRAMMY: Mr. T's a good man. He does <u>love</u> his convertible! *(beat)* It's a good thing our friend Larry is volunteering with this case. *(Spikey's confused)* No, not a suitcase Spikey. A case, a court case. I'll explain later. No one's saying much. What do you know about the holes?

SPIKEY: Nothing, not me. I wouldn't hurt Mr. T! He's grumpy but he's **<u>not</u>** my enemy!

GRAMMY: Did your meeting with Larry go well, yesterday?

SPIKEY: Yes, he treated me like a king. How about your hospital meeting?

GRAMMY: Very well, thanks. *(She takes out her knitting needles, and starts to knit. Spikey realizes it could be Grammy's needle)*. So who do you think could have done it?

SPIKEY: *(staring at Grammy's knitting needles)*. I know it wasn't me! I am NOT guilty!

GRAMMY: I believe you.

SPIKEY: Thanks, but I feel like I'm striking out! In me, people have doubt! And what are these holes, all about?! *(looks intently at Grammy's needles)*.

GRAMMY: You've got holes in your heart, because you're accused of something you didn't do. That's a crime. Believe in yourself! I know who **you** really are! *(Spikey sings baseball rap,* *****Hit Home With Your Heart*****)* Do the right thing, then it doesn't matter what others think. Do good things and good things will come back to you.

SPIKEY: I need something to give me that power – hopefully within the next hour!!

GRAMMY: You have love and faith. You're strong and at peace. Rise above cruel words. *(Spikey slowly rises, reaches up)* Think good thoughts and stay honest.

SPIKEY: *(sits)* Why do some think everyone's business is theirs? Don't they have their own cares?

GRAMMY: Pity the ones who care more about the business of others.

SPIKEY: Sticks and stones can break a bone. But mean words make me feel all alone!

GRAMMY: Yes, mean words hurt and poke holes in hearts! We should be helping, not hurting. But some are angry, or suffer from something, we don't know about.

SPIKEY: But why do they have to be mean? And accuse me of things they've never seen?

GRAMMY: Human nature. It's not actions but the thoughts inside the heart, that count.

SPIKEY: Well it's too bad some **can't see** inside. They see what **they want,** without any guide! People say porcupines don't see well! I see things they don't, but I don't tell!

GRAMMY: You let them see what you are thinking! That's what good actors do. But you don't act. You're pure, all heart and soul. *(Smiles as she pats Spikey's shoulder)* Maybe someone got inside Mr. T's car. *(shakes her head)* We all have accidents. But some do **plan** to make bad choices.

SPIKEY: I'm not guilty. Soon all will see. Yes at times I do slip up. Then I cry like a baby pup.

GRAMMY: We all slip up sometimes. You're a big innocent kid! We're gonna make it, you and I! *(stops knitting, pats Spikey's hand)* Well, your friends are in school for another year.

SPIKEY: Wish I could go to school. School would be so cool! *(Spikey watches Grammy knitting...)*

GRAMMY: Maybe someday Spikey, but I'm your teacher for now. *(Spikey watches knitting needle).*

SCENE 6

(Enter Keri SL to stand alone. Other kids move towards Grammy, as she looks at her watch).

GRAMMY: Hi Kids *(nudges Spikey)* Where does the time go? School's over?! How was school?

KERI; Yeah, Short day today. *(moves away, to side of stage)*

BEN: I didn't have good points today! I just felt tired and prickly! I'm not ready for school this year – and school's not ready for me!

SALLY: I was excited for school, but I'm so tired now!

KERI: *(sarcastically)* Oh, It's such a beautiful morning! And I sooo feel like singing and dancing!

SPIKEY: So, you <u>think you can dance</u>? *(all nod)* Take a glance while 'I' sing and prance! *(prances)*

SALLY: You CAN join us Spikey! Hi Grammy! We could use some waking up and cheering up! We need to get ready for tonight!! World are you ready for all of us prickly tired, porcupines? *(Bob enters SR with water for Spikey). (Larry, Mr. T enter SL, talking together).*

SPIKEY: Can a porcupine dance tonight, in it? I am pretty fit! Let's all 'practice dance' now! C'mon Keri show us how! *(Spikey pulls her up. She reluctantly gets up, smiles and dances! All cast sing, **World are you ready?***) (All on stage, kids and Grammy join Spikey on chorus).*

KERI: Thanks Grandpa. That was fun! *(high-fives with Mr. T) (Mr. T exits SL)* But I'm still not ready for school ... *(Keri walks away).*

SPIKEY: Please tell me what's wrong Keri? Your sadness, does worry me!

KERI; Well, it was a good morning, good lunch...*(huge sigh, Sally looks sad)* Jessica told me I <u>didn't</u> make the dance team! *(beat) (Keri sits on bench by Spikey, pouting. Grammy stops knitting. Both she and Spikey feel sad for Keri).* I was the first to audition! I think she decided I wouldn't make the team before she even auditioned me! She had a plan. I know she did! She took the new vice-principals daughter Robyn, instead of me! Oh, I hate my life!

GRAMMY: Life isn't fair! That's one of the toughest lessons we learn. It's good to talk about it with friends, Keri. You did catch friends in all of us here!

KERI: Yeah, and I'm sorta friends with Mark and Ben too. *(gets up from bench)* There's nothing left to talk about. Sally feels badly for me, too. What's done is done.

SPIKEY: *(to Grammy)* She's soooo sad. That's toooo bad.

GRAMMY: *(arm around Keri)* You're perfect to me Keri! All of you are. *(Keri hugs Grammy, Sings solo **Nobody's Perfect** All join chorus.)(Larry, Bob and boys exit SR, with bat/gloves).*

KERI: Thanks Grammy. Thanks all of you. Mom's meeting me here soon. Spikey, maybe I'll try out for your ball team! I can probably catch a ball better than catch a chance to dance!

SPIKEY: Sure, we'll play catch...that will be A-okay! Tomorrow will be a better day!

KERI: *(trying to smile)* You're on Spikey! *(high-fives with Spikey)* Maybe we can steal bases!!

SPIKEY: Oh no Keri, stealing is wrong. We'll leave the bases where they belong! *(Keri laughs)*

GRAMMY: Laughter is the best medicine. It helps make us feel better. *(hugs Keri)*

SPIKEY: Yes, friends help fix holes in hearts – when words hit like angry darts.

KERI: *(to all)* You're the best friends, I could ever catch!!

SPIKEY: Meeting in this park is cool. It's been quite a morning at school!

SALLY: Yes it has! But this year - I'm not going to worry so much about what other kids think.

KERI: Same here! This year, I'm dancing for fun! Doesn't matter if I make a team. *(sits)* It was a tough audition! Look, I **know** Jessica doesn't want me.

SALLY: Keri, we're working on Jessica! We can still be park dancers! We'll have a good year! IF we **'choose'** to make it a good year! *(Keri smiles at Sally)*. Yeah, my friend Keri and I help each other with problems and stuff. *(high-fives with Keri)*

GRAMMY: *(Grammy smiles at Sally)* Good to hear dear.

SPIKEY: We've had hole and heart problems to patch. And too many balls to catch. Coach Bob and guys are expecting me. I needed a break, to get back my energy! *(walks away)*

SALLY: Did you have fun playing catch? *(he nods yes.)* Are you going back to play ball? *(Spikey nods yes as he exits SR with glove).*

GRAMMY: Good. Anyway, I need to finish crocheting another baby blanket, for the hospital. *(laughs)* I've loved working with needles and hooks forever. I remember my Mom and Grandma doing Quill embroidery and jewellery artwork. Did I tell you, I was cleaning up and found one of Spikey's quills in our living room? It was an unusually strong hard quill, with a tiny hook at the end. *(laughs)* I instantly thought, "This would be a great crochet hook!" so I put the quill in my knitting bag...*(starts to pull out quill)*

ALL: Grammy! *(All move towards Grammy. Grammy puts the quill back in her knitting bag).*

KERI/TIA: You did it?! *(pause)* Grammy? *(Grammy is day dreaming).*

GRAMMY: Yes? *(pauses as she reads knitting magazine)* I can't hear you when I'm thinking. *(smiles and sighs)* Well, I'd like to stay and chat longer, but I've got some picnic food to prepare for a friend and I. See you tonight at the dance in the park! And Keri, come back with your mom! We'll have fun dancing!

KERI: Okay Grammy, I will. Thanks. *(All watch Grammy as she leaves. They look at each other, thinking Grammy 'could be the guilty one').*

SCENE 7

SALLY: Are you thinkin' what I'm thinkin? And who is this 'friend'? *(Keri and Sally look at each other)* Do you think Grammy would do it?

KERI: No! What would be her point? Okay, so do you guys know anything about the holes?

SALLY: *(Tia shakes her head 'no.' Continues colouring).* Not much. But I'm sure **someone** knows. Would Ben try again? I don't think so. He planned to damage Mr. T's roof last time. Accidents happen but planning something bad, is so - <u>not good</u>!

SALLY/TIA: *(whispering to each other)* Jessica told us, we don't need any more dancers...

SALLY: ...Than we had last year...but she did take Robyn! That doesn't make much sense.

TIA: *(stands boldly)* And right in front of Robyn - Jessica told me not to steal the show again!

SALLY: You did last year! Your first year! ... Oh, Jessica's making too big a deal of this.

TIA: Yeah, What's one more dancer?!

SALLY: Keri, maybe she thinks, you'll be better than she is, or than me. I think I'm her only friend. She picked me because I'm nice to her. So then she picks my little sister, who's better than us! *(Pokes Tia)* Jessica didn't make the volleyball team last year, and probably won't this year. *(Mark, Ben enter exhausted)* Speaking of teams, Hi guys! *(Keri stands to side)*.

MARK: Coach Bob, Spikey and Dad wore us out! *(to Keri)* Keri, trying and failing is better than never trying at all. I'm not the best ball player. I didn't make the team. I play for fun!

SALLY: *(with empathy)* Dance should be fun, not competitive. Jessica lives and breathes dance.

BEN: *(to Keri)* I think she's jealous cuz we're spending more time with you Keri, than with her. Just sayin...

KERI: Well she doesn't <u>want</u> to spend time with <u>me</u>! *(Sally and Tia silently converse)*.

SALLY/TIA: *(jumps up)* We think Jessica punched the holes!!!

BEN: What??!! Why Jessica??!! My dad's working on this case! He knows who did it!!

KERI: *(quickly jumps up)* I bet you're right! *(sits)* NO - Spikey would **not** have let Jessica, pull out one of his quills!!

SALLY: Yeah, but Jessica would have poked holes into your Grandpa's car! With the quill she pulled out from **Grammy's knitting bag**!! *(Keri gasps)*.

KERI: Right, but what's Jessica got to do with my Grandpa? It's **me** she doesn't like! Why would she poke holes in his convertible rooftop?

SALLY: Yeah! No, wait! Your Grandpa helped coach volleyball last year. Right?

KERI: Yeah so?!

MARK: He cut Jessica! Remember!

KERI: He did?!

BEN: Yeah. You weren't here last year – so you wouldn't have known!

KERI: So that's why she cut me! It's all my Grandpa's fault?!! *(Keri shows her anger)*.

BEN/MARK: Sort of!

SALLY: Yeah, so you didn't even have a chance!

TIA: Jessica bullied you!

KERI: *(aside)* Or maybe it's just - I'm really not good enough!

TIA: No, that's not it!

SALLY: *(to Keri)* I told Mr. Law, when I was leaving the mall on Sunday, I saw your Grandpa's convertible, parked really close by... *(enter Sarah)*

KERI: Yeah, he said he got to the mall, too late to pick up my hoodie... Oh, Hi Mom.

SCENE 8

SARAH: *(to Keri)* Hi hon... *(Sally waves to Sarah. Sarah waves back)*

MARK: Hi Ms Bell? How was your first morning?

SARAH: Great thanks! I <u>am</u> going to enjoy it here! *(hugs Keri)* I hope Keri, will too! I ate my salad while working, but still need to go back. *(beat)* How were auditions?

KERI: Don't ask? *(to Sarah)* So - do you know about the holes in my Grandpa's car?

SARAH: Yeah, a little. *(sits, speaks to all)* Grammy and Dad, Keri's Grandpa, Mr. T, told me Spikey helped patch the holes. *(Girls react and look at each other)*. Now, that doesn't make him guilty! That just makes him caring Spikey! He and Mr. Law got together to discuss what happened. It's being responsible. As a teacher, I like knowing what's going on, if it involves students from our school. I'm sure we'll hear more, soon.

SALLY: We had nothing to do with it. *(beat)* So Jessica doesn't want Keri on the dance team! Why do kids like Jessica bully?

BEN: Yeah, some people can have so much going for them, and still be a bully!

SALLY: We've all got faults, but not all can see them!

SARAH: That may be why some bully others, to cover up their own insecurities. Bullies like to cause fear. They feel stronger when they put others down.

MARK: That makes sense, I guess.

SALLY: Jessica's mad. She didn't make the volleyball team last year. They won the provincials.

BEN: She's so competitive. Some people always have to win! "and to be the star."

KERI: And I hear my Grandpa, and another coach - cut her from the team. Probably because of her attitude. So she started this after school dance group, for Grades 2 - 6.

TIA: Cuz she needs to be in charge of something! Control freak!...

SARAH: Be nice Tia ... Kids. You're gossiping. Maybe Jessica's feelings are hurt.

SALLY: You're right. But Keri...I'm still working on Jessica, to get... *(Enter 'dramatic' Jessica. All girls give an 'Ooops' fearful look to each other)*.

JESSICA: *(big voice)* You're working on me!!? For what? What's that supposed to mean!?

SALLY: Uhhh – ummm...It means that it wouldn't hurt us, to add another dancer!

JESSICA: What?! *(points to Keri)* You wanna be on the team <u>after</u> I cut you?! *(Keri's behind Sally)*

SALLY/TIA: *(to Jessica)* Did **<u>you</u>** pull one of Spikey's quills?!

JESSICA: ME?! What?! Who's Spikey? A dog? *(kids laugh)* I don't even know who this <u>Spikey</u> creature is!! So you think <u>I</u> pulled one of Spikey's Quills, when I don't even know who Spikey is?!! And who are you to accuse me! You're the bullies, not me!!

SALLY: Sorry. Okay – maybe you didn't pull it out of Spikey. Spikey's <u>our</u> friend! He would have told us! Maybe you just <u>found</u> his quill.

JESSICA: Excuse me!!?!! <u>Who</u> - **is** - <u>Spikey</u>??!!!

KERI: What?! Everyone knows Spikey! *(Girls giggle, boys shake their heads)*

SARAH: Okay, that's enough! *(extends hand to Jessica)* Hi Jessica, I'm Ms Bell, a new teacher...

JESSICA: *(ignores Sarah's hand)* Yes, I know. I <u>was at</u> the Assembly this morning!

TIA: *(Forcefully moves in towards Jessica)* Hey girl – you got a bad attitude! *(Sarah pulls Tia back). Jessica stomps away as she crosses her arms, and 'pouts' in corner). (Spikey runs in exhausted. Jessica <u>screams, as Spikey</u> plops down on the ground).*

SALLY: Spikey – are you okay? *(Sally, Lisa and Keri go to Spikey. He slowly lifts his head).*

SPIKEY: Another rest and I'll be fine. There's no way I can finish inning number 9. *(drops head)*

JESSICA: Ahhhhh!! What's this sasquatchy, freaky monster thing doing here?!?!

KERI: Actually, he's like a care bear! And he's a great back catcher! *(Jessica pokes her toe at Spikey and steps on him).*

BEN: *(to Jessica)* Hey! Watch what you're doing! You're hurting Spikey!

SPIKEY: *(gets up)* Ouch! You stepped on my good points! And I think you broke some of my joints!

JESSICA: It talks???!!! It walks! Yuck – So you're the big ugly prickly thing I've heard about!

ALL KIDS: '<u>It</u>' is a porcupine!

JESSICA: What are you? What kind of porcupine are you? You're not normal! I'm either in a bad dream, bad play or I'm totally loosing it!

SPIKEY: *(gets up and limps slowly)* Have no fear. There's no problem here.

JESSICA: Look - Porcupines can float. That thing couldn't! And normal porcupines are only about 3 feet long, they're not like that big thing! Porcupines <u>are</u> RODENTS!!

KERI: You be careful what you say!!!

KERI/SALLY: Spikey could throw Quills at you!!!

SPIKEY: My quills are protection not ammunition. I'm not perfect, but my quills are <u>not</u> a defect.

JESSICA: YES they are! A <u>huge</u> defect! You could hurt someone!

SPIKEY: No, not me. I wouldn't hurt a flea. Please Stop, being so mean to me! *(sits, head in hands)*

MARK: Jessica, you hurt people with your words! *(Jessica rolls her eyes and walks away).*

TIA: *(to Jessica)* Don't be a bully!

SARAH: Tia, we can be assertive, without being aggressive. *(Spikey walks away, Sarah pulls him back)* All of you know to say "stop," and walk away from mean situations. Talk to a trusted adult. Talk to me. I care...let's not be bystanders.

JESSICA: *(interrupts)* Whatever!! I didn't **hit** him!! I just <u>stepped</u> on him, accidently!

SALLY: Your words have sharp mean points. *(Jessica Makes face at Sally).*

SARAH: Bullying comes in many forms, making faces, *(Jessica walks away)* lying, stealing, gossiping, name calling, threats, and thinking we're better than others.

SPIKEY: *(to Jessica)* Get to know me. If you gave me a chance, I'd be a friend, you'd see! I try to be trusting and kind. Sometimes we can't see, cuz we can all, be blind.

JESSICA: Porcupines have bad eyesight! I don't!

SALLY: You'll never see what Spikey sees. *(comforts Spikey)*

JESSICA: Yeah, whatever ... *(rudely)* So, where are your parents? How'd you get here?

SPIKEY: I lost my parents on the pavement. It was an accident.

JESSICA: *(coldly)* How?!

SPIKEY: My parents and I were crossing the road. Then all of a sudden, we were out cold.

JESSICA: *(sarcastically)* How sad!

SPIKEY: Grammy saw the car or bus, that hit us. She picked me up without a fuss. She found me by the side of the road. I was quite a load!

JESSICA: All the porcupines I've ever seen, were lying by the side of the road.

TIA: That is **so** rude!

SPIKEY: To my parents we said goodbye. Grammy's love for me, reaches the sky.

SALLY: *(Jessica makes a face)* Grammy is his mom now. All of us have parents that care for us!

JESSICA: Not **my** parents! My dad got transferred, so our whole family has to MOVE after Christmas break! It's **not** fair!! *(Larry enters SL, stands by Ben and Mark. Sarah, by Keri)*

KERI: But Parents DO care! *(Larry and Sarah sing to their children, Jessica AND all kids on stage: ****A Parent's Love****) (NEW Verse, short version/1 verse only - **kids join on Chorus**.) Sarah, by Keri. After song, Larry exits to side SL, still visible to cast and audience. He texts/talks on his cell, in mime).*

JESSICA: Yeah, I know they care. I just really don't want to move again. I'll miss dancing in this park. *(to Spikey)* Is it true that Grammy carried you to this park! How could she?

SPIKEY: No, but she picked me up. She cuddled me like a baby pup.

JESSICA: *(laughs)* How do you cuddle a porcupine?!!

SPIKEY: Very carefully, you do! But she knew I had feelings too.

JESSICA: *(softer)* So where do you sleep? I can't imagine what you'd do to a mattress!

SPIKEY: Grammy has extra padding on it. On the mattress, it does fit.

JESSICA: So you've got a bed? Nothing could soften those quills! Not even hot soapy water!

SPIKEY: So, on the tips, I put marshmallows. But I ate them and got big and fluffy, to my toes.

JESSICA: *(to Spikey)* That's not funny! It's kinda, pathetic!

SARAH: Jessica, choose appropriate words!

67

KERI: Spikey is <u>not pathetic</u>!! *(Sarah pulls Keri back)* **Spikey's my BEST friend!!!** *(all Cheer)*

LARRY: *(re-enters SL)* Hello again everyone. *(All wave, say hello, except Jessica)* Jessica, I'm pleased you could be here.

JESSICA: Yeah, right...

LARRY: *(SL)* Your parents and I agreed, you will need to apologize to Grammy, Mr. T. and Keri.

JESSICA: *(to Larry)* I'm here because ... *(Larry points to Keri)* I have to apologize to <u>Keri</u> ...

SPIKEY: Truth sets you free! Makes you taller than a tree!

JESSICA: Okay, Keri, I'm sorry I was mean and I cut you from the dance. Oh Whatever! I'm startin' to hate this conversation...

SPIKEY: Hate is a disturbing word and can destroy you.
Feeling it shows in things you say and do.
Get rid of the anger deep inside. That way, you don't have to hide.
I feel for you and know you have cried.
But please lighten up, or you'll have a rough ride.

JESSICA: Ahhh... Get me out of here...

SPIKEY: Be as nice as you can be. Life's too short to stay angry. *(Spikey hides behind a tree)*.

SARAH: Anger defeats us. Spikey, shows us that life is an easier ride, when we can all be kind and courteous to each other. *(Sarah and Grammy walk towards Spikey, and comfort him)*.

LARRY: Spikey has taught us, things aren't always as they seem.

JESSICA: Oh pleez!! *(Spikey re-enters with Grammy & Sarah)*.

SPIKEY: I can help Grammy and you guys up those hills. I try not to poke anyone with my quills!

KERI: I don't even notice them that much anymore! They're a part of what makes you - you!

SALLY: We've got our own things wrong with us. We've all got broken points...

BEN: Yeah, we do!

JESSICA: *(sarcastically)* So, am I supposed to say **I do** too?! K, What-ever...

SPIKEY: We all have some things wrong, that's true. But none of you scare people, the way I do.

SARAH: *(to Spikey)* You don't judge things as they seem to be. You dance to your rhythm, beat **your** drum, and teach us to do the same. You accept us. We accept you!

JESSICA: Uhhh … What!? This is all driving me crazy… *(puts her hands to her head)*

LARRY: Jessica … Keri, all of us - Spikey makes us realize that life's not always fair.

SARAH: We all need to rise above things and move on, to try and be our best! But sometimes we need a little help – someone to lean on. *(Keri leans on Sarah.)* You can lean on us Jessica. And your parents. *(Jessica fakes a smile)*.

SALLY: I love to dance but Spikey's taught me not to be so hard on myself. I don't have to be excellent – just good enough **is okay**!

MARK: Spikey's taught us to enjoy life – and HAVE FUN!

SARAH: He's taught me to relax and lighten up!

SALLY: Yeah! He's taught us to "be ourselves!" Thank you, Spikey! *(Spikey is beaming)*

JESSICA: Okay - this is enough! This is really strange! Spikey is one weird porcupine!! But we're all weirder! …because **we're** talking to him! *(Spikey puts head down. He's upset)*

SPIKEY: I have good and bad points like all of you. I'm happy to be on a ball team too!

SALLY: Jessica, so you didn't make the volleyball team last year…

JESSICA: And I won't this year!

SARAH: Well if one thing doesn't work out – it can open doors to other opportunities! Jessica, you started a dance club! And Keri, there's something for you too! *(Keri makes a face)*.

SPIKEY: If we stop the attitude. We can stop the feud!

LARRY: And we'll have more latitude! *(Jessica makes a questioning face)*

KERI/SALLY/TIA: Yay Spikey! *(Larry stands by Jessica, takes her elbow and moves her into group)*.

JESSICA: *(to Keri)* Sorry Keri. Sorry Spikey. *(he smiles)* but you **were** in my way! *(Spikey's deflated!)* Sorry, about the whole quill thing! Sorry Grammy. Sorry world for my future mistakes!! What's the point?! Okay, everyone happy now!

LARRY: Spikey, Are you okay? *(Spikey shakes head no. Larry gestures to all)* We're all here for you.

SPIKEY: *(slowly gets up)* Singin', dancin' and playin' catch wore me out. Now I'm full of doubt.

JESSICA: *(Grammy pats Spikey's shoulder)* Not only do you rhyme, but you sing! *(he nods)* Are you going to sing again?! *(Spikey nods)* Oh no, we're going back to that strange place where people just break into song, like a musical or something! *(she makes a cynical smile)*.

KERI: Yup!! I feel a song coming on... right about - now! *(Enter Mr. T)* Grandpa!! *(Keri hugs him)*

JESSICA: *(hears intro music)* Oh no! Is this my punishment?!! *(Spikey, Larry, Sarah, Mr. T and girls sing **Attitude** (Girls motion for Jessica to join in towards the end) (Jessica and Keri are featured)*.

JESSICA: Thanks. Hey, I'm sorry everyone. I suppose you all know that Mr. Law has been looking after this with my parents. Okay, I know, everyone knows it was me! Especially when Mr. T and Grammy found **my** earring in Mr. T's car. Mr. T gave it to Mr. Law. Mark recognized me wearing that big hoop earring. *(Mark nods)* I was an easy catch...

BEN: So it **WAS** you!! See, I was trying to tell everyone it **wasn't me**! Mark didn't tell me about the earring? *(Mark puts hands in air)*.

SALLY: Yes, I thought Ben or Spikey poked the holes! But the hoop earring threw me off!

KERI: Could have been mine, but it wasn't! Besides I wouldn't do that to my Grandpa! *(hugs him)*

MR.T: I had NO idea who's earring it was, when Larry showed it to me. *(hands up)* Honest!

LARRY: May I approach the bench? *(sits on bench. All but Jessica laugh)* To be professional, we shouldn't discuss confidential information. But you can go ahead and tell them about your community service, Jessica...

JESSICA: *(sighs)* My other punishment...as part of my community service, I'm volunteering with Grammy at the hospital. *(all cheer)* Thanks.

SALLY: So, you really did take the quill out of Grammy's bag? *(Enter Grammy SR, hides by tree with picnic basket)*.

JESSICA: Yes, it WAS me that took the quill out of Grammy's knitting bag!! *(all gasp)* It was sticking out and, yeah, I poked the holes. So here I am. Mr. T said if I apologized ... *(sighs)*

MR: T: I'd take everyone here, yes all of you to a <u>(Goldeyes)</u> *(Local ball team)* game! *(All Cheer!)*

SALLY: Wow, I remember last time! *(to Mr.T)* You drove some to the game in your convertible. Coach Bob took the rest of us in his van. That game was so much fun! *(beat)* So how did this "hole thing" happen, Jessica?

JESSICA: Well, it was while Mr. T and Grammy stopped at the mall on Sunday.

MR. T: My neon yellow convertible is easy to spot! My roof was down, and Grammy had her knitting bag open, on the seat. *(Grammy nods from the side of the stage)*.

JESSICA: This big quill was sticking out...

MR. T: We were only gone for a few minutes because the mall was locking up.

JESSICA: I saw them go in, when I was leaving. Without thinking, I grabbed the quill... and well...

BEN: Took it right out of Grammy's knitting bag!? *(shakes his head as he walks aside)*

KERI: And you quickly poked a few quick holes in <u>my Grandpa's</u> roof?!

JESSICA: Yeah...something like that. I'm sorry. I really am Keri, Grammy, Mr. T.

MR. T: So you threw the quill back in the knitting bag, so everyone would think Grammy did it?

SALLY: How clever – but that would be too obvious!

JESSICA: Probably. *(sits/sighs)* *(looks remorseful)*

SALLY: WHY? Why did you do it?

JESSICA: Funny – isn't it. That's the first question my parents and Mr. Law asked. Okay – so, Mr. T. cut me from the team last year...

MR. T: So you thought you'd get back at me, by ruining my car?? Framing Grammy?... *(Grammy walks towards group. She sets down picnic basket)*.

JESSICA: *(points to Grammy)* Your 'new friend' Grammy. *(all, look at Grammy)* *(Grammy puts hands to her chest, and smiles. She moves to stand beside Mr. T.)*

MR. T: *(He puts his hand on Grammy's shoulder)* You were mean to Grammy, then you cut my Grand-daughter Keri' from the dance team ... *(beat)*

JESSICA: Yeah...

KERI: Wow! You gave it a lot of thought...

SARAH: Premeditated, that's a little...unsettling But do you accept her apology Keri?

KERI: What CAN I say?! – Yeah, I guess so...

SPIKEY: An accident, we could understand. But this was part of a plan. *(shakes his head)*

JESSICA: I'm so bad!!

GRAMMY: No, you just made bad choices.

SPIKEY: We're your friends in the park, when feeling sad. Talk to us, when you are mad.

JESSICA: Thanks Spikey, I will. *(she does a knuckle greeting with Spikey)*

SALLY: Good for you Mr. Law! I'm surprised you found out it was Jessica's earring!

TIA: DUhhh...That's what lawyers **do!** *(Larry smiles and nods)*

SALLY: Grammy will be happy it was just Jessica's earring! *(All Laugh. Grammy stands by Mr. T and elbows him. They laugh).*

SPIKEY: You were smart to tell Larry the truth. Everyone strikes out, even Babe Ruth.

ALL KIDS: Who's that? *(Grammy and Mr. T quietly exit SL)*

LARRY: You're all too young. I told him about the greatest ball player who struck out many times.

MR. T: Spikey is saying, even the greatest, do strike out! *(high-fives with Spikey)*

SPIKEY: Coach Bob told me about Babe Ruth last week. We went on the internet, to seek.

LARRY: He's a legend, alright.

KERI; Who?! Spikey?! *(Larry laughs)* He will be!!

SARAH: Yes he will be. Look girls, forgiveness is something we do for ourselves. Hopefully we can all find it in our heart, to forgive Jessica. *(Grammy & Larry smile).*

KERI: Grammy is teaching Jessica how to knit and crochet. You won't want to see what I've made! She's trying to teach us too! *(Sally and Keri laugh)*.

JESSICA: I'm actually looking forward to it! *(Grammy smiles, as she and Mr. T exit together)*.

KERI, SALLY: Us too! *(all girls high-five)*

SARAH: I'm next for lessons! *(Grammy smiles while she knits)*.

JESSICA: And another part of my community service is to teach Keri how to dance! *(All cheer)*

KERI: Wow - Can I start tonight?! *(Jessica nods YES)* REALLY???!!! *(Jessica nods again, Keri and Jessica fist pump)*. YES!!!

JESSICA: Robyn, the vice principal's daughter, is sick! *(Keri looks deflated, than quickly smiles)*.

KERI: So, I'm dancing in her place?!?! *(Jessica nods 'Yes.' Cheers from all)*

JESSICA: It's Mr. Law's idea, not mine. Well – c'mon girls. We've got a lot of work to do, before tonight's show! *(Girls follow Jessica, then all exit)*.

SALLY/TIA/KERI: Yes!!! *(high-five as they exit following Jessica)*

KERI: Thanks Jessica! Awesome! I get to wear a dancing outfit Grammy made!!

JESSICA: *(almost off stage)* We're all wearing them! Let's get changed!! *(Grammy and girls cheer)*

LARRY: And Coach Bob and I have a treat for all of you before the dance. Pizza! It's on its way to the ball diamond soon. Coach Bob is expecting us!

ALL: Thanks!!!

TIA: Yay, Pizza!!!!

KERI: Let's go! I'm starved! *(All exit)*

SCENE 9

LARRY: *(to Sarah & Spikey)* We ordered pizza for the ball team plus the dancers. It should be there soon. There's juice and veggies too. Spikey? Sarah? Would you like to join us?

SPIKEY: No problem for me to say yes. Food is my weakness, I must confess.

LARRY: Sorry there are no asparagus and pickle sandwiches, today, Spikey.

SARAH: We get them a lot. Grammy always makes them for Spikey, and <u>all</u> of us!

SPIKEY: Pizza is the next best <u>thing.</u> And then maybe a chicken <u>wing</u>... Larry, I do thank <u>you.</u> Food makes me feel brand <u>new</u>!

LARRY: You're welcome Spikey. How about you Sarah? Keri and the boys are there anyway.

SARAH: Considering I don't have to cook tonight – Sure, I'd love to! Thanks Larry. That's a nice break – after our first day of school.

LARRY: You're welcome. I'm glad you can join us.

SARAH: Thanks for helping get the girls and the quill hole in my dad's rooftop, sorted out.

LARRY: No problem.

SPIKEY: Good thing Larry ordered pizza for the ball and dance team... Cuz Grammy's havin' a picnic with her new friend, and is happier than a sunbeam!

SARAH: She's so cute – isn't she? *(Larry smiles and nods)*

SPIKEY: *(centre Stage)* Grammy and Mr. T up in a tree – K I S S I N G...

SARAH: Dad and Grammy are both so happy.

SPIKEY: I have never seen Grammy happier! She needs more in her life than *(points to himself)* this big lump of fur! *(Larry and Sarah laugh)*

SARAH: Dad's so taken with Grammy, he's gotten over his anger about the holes in his roof top. And Spikey, now we all know you didn't do it. Larry told my dad, before their picnic.

SPIKEY: Thanks for believing in me. *(Sarah and Larry smile, nod.)* It makes for a happier Spikey!

SARAH: I believe in you, Spikey. And in you too, Larry. You've had a tough day.

LARRY: You've had a tough day too, Sarah. *(They sit on bench together, looking uncomfortably at each other)*. You'll have a good year. I believe you...*(uncomfortable pause)*

SPIKEY: *(interrupts, stands at back of stage)* Well, I think the pizza's here. I can smell it, so it must be near. I'm hungry too. *(waves goodbye)* Doodle doo! *(exits, then sneaks back)*.

LARRY: *(still looking at Sarah)* It's already paid for Spikey. Enjoy it! *(Sarah, Larry ignore Spikey)*

SPIKEY: Forgot to say, "Thanks Larry." *(aside)* This moment looks a little scary. *(exits on tiptoes)*

SARAH: Thanks Larry for solving this mess. You resolved it before it got out of hand.

LARRY: *(Enter Mr. T and Grammy)*. Ahh, Jessica is a good kid. She's upset with her Dad's transfer.

SARAH: Keri and I 'get' the moving pains. I believe moving here is a good thing. You're a good man, Larry.

LARRY: But I can't cook!! *(They sing **_I Believe In You,_** sitting on bench SR) (Grammy and Mr. T enter and sit on bench SL, at opposite end of stage, with picnic basket. He's carrying a 'mall' bag with Keri's two hoodies in it. Sets it behind bench. All 4 sing. They sing song to each other) (Grammy and Mr. T continue talking/smiling, saying "watermelon." They're visible to the audience, but not to Larry and Sarah)*.

LARRY: You know, joining a whole group for pizza in the park is not a real first date. *(beat)* I was wondering if you had given any more thought to umm, when I asked you, umm about umm – *(Sarah's smiling coyly)* ah, you joining us, no just me, for a real dinner date at that restaurant ummm, with me at that place....of your choice.

SARAH: Imagine, a lawyer lost for words! *(smiles as she raises her right hand)* I Sarah, solemnly swear that I have given your request, <u>very serious </u>thought. I've honestly considered it. *(Larry appears nervous)* And I am totally committed to join you for dinner! *(Larry sighs and relaxes!)* It would be my pleasure and honour. Thank You.

LARRY: *(sigh of relief)* Thank you! What's a good day and time for you?

SARAH: Umm...this Saturday. Anytime after five.

LARRY: 5:30 it is. I think Keri and the boys will have fun at Grammy's, with Spikey. *(Sarah nods)*

SARAH: I'll make arrangements with Grammy. By the way, I love to cook, *(Larry beams!)* so I'll have you and the boys over sometime!

LARRY: Wow! Thanks! My boys will love to hear that!! But for now Sarah, it's just pizza! Ready?

SARAH: I'm ready! *(Larry and Sarah <u>exit SR</u>, smiling together). (Mr T and Grammy <u>continue to sit</u> on Bench, SL. They do not see or notice Larry and Sarah leave).*

MR.T: I am <u>so</u> full. You're a very good cook, Mary. I'm glad we finally got together for a picnic!

GRAMMY: Yes. Me too!

MR. T: While Spikey's been back catchin' - I caught a new friend, in you. *(she smiles)* By the way, I thanked Larry for all he has done.

GRAMMY: He's a good guy. *(pause)* Do you think Jessica has learned her lesson?

MR. T: Yes, I do. At times the hard drives in our brain get overloaded. She's angry because she's moving during the winter break. Hey, Sarah and I went through all that last year with my Grand-daughter Keri! We remember that, all <u>too</u> well!

GRAMMY: *(nods)* That's why **you** understand Jessica. She's a good kid, just misunderstood.

MR. T: She is, but I can be tough. I was tough on her when I cut her from the volleyball team.

GRAMMY: You did what you had to do! Not all decisions are easy.

MR. T: Jessica argued with the other girls. She wouldn't take any direction! What could I do?!

GRAMMY: You did the right thing at the time. She's having a hard time with her move, but she'll turn out alright!

MR.T: That she is! I'll try to forget about it. Actually at my age, it's easy to forget!

GRAMMY: You got that right! *(they both laugh)* Maybe I forgot I did it, but I noticed my hooked quill was in a new place in my knitting bag. I was suspicious when I found the earring! *(she pokes Mr. T and she laughs. He smiles).*

MR. T: So was I, but there's no one else but you! *(Grammy smiles)* You know, just knowing my grand-daughter Keri, is on the dance team, is worth me paying my own repair bill! But Jessica and her parents have agreed to pay for it.

GRAMMY: Good for them!

MR. T: Her dad told me her allowance is cut, until my new roof is paid for. Larry got it all sorted out. *(pause)* Hey, I'm sorry I accused Spikey. He's an easy target – poor guy!

GRAMMY: Ahh, it's all over now.

MR.T: But I still need to apologize to him. I was being a bully.

GRAMMY: Yes you were. So, don't let it happen again! *(She playfully pokes him with knitting needle)*

MR. T: Ouch. Is that bullying?! Your point I do feel! *(laughs)* Coach Bob would say, "Give bullying a curve ball!"

GRAMMY: Yes, he would! *(beat)* It was a good idea to have a picnic, then go for a long walk.

MR.T: Yes it was. I needed a good long walk, after all that food!

GRAMMY: You're never too old for a 'picnic in the park'!

MR. T: How true. And what a picnic! I am soooo full. That's supper too. I'm glad you decided to have dessert <u>after</u> the dance show? I couldn't eat another bite!

GRAMMY: Me neither.

MR. T: I'm glad it wasn't Spikey that poked holes in my car. I mean, it'd be awkward for us to keep seeing each other, wouldn't it? *(both nod, then laugh)*

SPIKEY: *(Enter Spikey, kids, SR)* Hey Grammy and Mr. T. Want some left over pizza, from Coach Bob and Larry?

GRAMMY/MR. T: No...ooo ...*(they groan)*

MR. T: We already ate, but thank you, Spikey. So, girls, how was school today?

KERI: Okay.

SALLY/TIA: Fine, thanks!

MR. T: What did you learn?

ALL: <u>**Nothin'!!**</u> *(Mr. T and Grammy look at each other).*

MR. T: We can learn something every day! Appreciate each day! Because we never know what tomorrow will bring. Don't take life for granted!

GRAMMY: Right, live every day with gratitude! Each day is a gift! *(she looks endearingly at Mr. T) (Jessica moves towards Grammy. Grammy takes her hand).*

SCENE 10 Epilogue

JESSICA: *(walks to Grammy.)* Sorry Grammy. Sorry Spikey. *(Grammy pats Jessica's hand, Spikey and Jessica do a knuckle greeting).*

GRAMMY: Thank you Jessica. Apology accepted. It's over now dear. *(enter Sarah)*

MR. T: *(to Spikey)* Spikey, I know I said it before - but I really am sorry. I didn't show much class and you're a class act! Sorry for accusing you, when I didn't know the facts!

SARAH: Thanks Dad!

SPIKEY: Thanks Mr. T. Apology accepted graciously. Maybe we could be friends, you and me?

MR. T: Yeah, Spikey, you caught another friend in me! *(they high-five) (Sarah high-fives with Mr. T.)*

JESSICA: *(beat)* Well, I didn't show much class, either.

SPIKEY: I just want to be **in** a class! *(all laugh, even Jessica)* I wonder if I could pass? Grammy says 'Good Manners is Class!' Both Rich and Poor, can Pass! *(Grammy smiles, pats his arm).*

JESSICA: I don't know if I can pass everything. I'd like to be an actor, dancer or a star!

MR. T: It's okay to reach for the stars - just keep your feet on the ground!!

SPIKEY: If you don't become famous or perfect, that's okay. We all have to find our own way.

SARAH: And learn not to be so hard on ourselves, or others. It's about acceptance.

SPIKEY: Yeah, forgive others and yourself. It's good for your health!

SARAH: Because forgiveness is something we do for ourselves.

SPIKEY: Forgiveness is a key. Get rid of anger, to be the best you can be!

SARAH: Anger is baggage. Get rid of it!! Be nice. Even if you don't like someone, or feeling resentful – be polite! Your day will be easier.

KERI: Be sweet like my Grandpa and me!! *(they smile at each other)*

MR. T: Yes, *(gruffly)* Don't be grumpy!!

KERI: Yeah, we all make mistakes. I just keep trying to be the best I can be!!

LARRY: I tell my sons, be patient, understanding and have a goal.

SARAH: And reach as high as you possibly can...

SPIKEY: But don't be too hard on yourself or others, to get way up there! *(points up)* Always remember to, play FAIR!!

GRAMMY: When life's changes get in our way...we keep trying! We don't always get where we want <u>because</u> of things...

SALLY: Yeah, Look at Spikey! He's kind **in 'spite'** of things!

SARAH: We can get where we want with some hard work and at times – in <u>spite</u> of things.

BEN: We just have to, **Take a Chance!!**

MARK: Hey, I'm taking a chance on doing sound for the dance! All I can do is **TRY!!** Hey Ben, want to come back with me, to get the sound system?

BEN: Sure! You're taking a chance on me!! But I can "try" to help! *(they exit)*

KERI: I have huge goals. I'd like to take a chance - but I make mistakes...

JESSICA: Me too, and well, that's why you, 'Keri' get a chance to make our team! *(cheers)*

KERI: So, if I do well tonight – I could make the team?! That's my dream! *(covers head with hands)* Oh No!! I'm rhyming!!

JESSICA: Yes, you're in, Keri!

SALLY: *(to Keri)* Yes!!! We all know you CAN dance!!

SARAH: *(to Keri)* But you have to work <u>hard</u> to be on a team. There's no 'I' in team. Being committed, a good attitude and being on time is good manners. It shows respect.

KERI: Mom, we ALL know that! Thanks Jessica! *(Keri starts to hug her, but Jessica is uncomfortable, and backs away).*

KERI: I just want to <u>dance!</u> I don't care about being "The Star!" *(Enter Bob. All exchange hello's)*

SPIKEY: Exactly! Like and accept who you are! You don't have to be a Star!

GRAMMY: <u>To catch A friend, you just need to be one!!</u>

SARAH: Right Grammy!! What's important is doing our best! As a teacher and mom, it's all I expect. We've all made good and bad choices. *(Bob talks to Larry).*

KERI: But sometimes we don't get a choice. Like me not making auditions!!

SARAH: Yes, but often we <u>do</u> get <u>second chances!!</u> *(looks and smiles at Larry)* You may discover a new talent. So keep trying.

KERI: You're right. I'm just so glad I get to dance tonight!! No more finger pointing at me! I'm in! What do you think of people who point fingers? What's your opinion Grammy?

GRAMMY: If anyone points fingers, they have three pointing back at themselves. *(Spikey, girls place fingers as Grammy said)* My opinion is, keep our opinions to ourselves.

MR. T: I second that! Unless, someone **asks** for our opinion.

SARAH: Exactly. My opinion is - at times we don't have control what happens. But it's our choice <u>how</u> we <u>react</u>, if something unexpected or cruel happens to us.

JESSICA: *(nods from rock)* Yeah, *(huge sigh)* Well ... I'm trying ... *(Sarah smiles)*

KERI: Me too! *(Sarah smiles).* Grammy did you ever dance, or do fun things, when you were young?

GRAMMY: Yes, been there, done that, seen, heard it all. Only trouble is, I don't remember...

KERI: We never know what the next few minutes will bring, do we?

JESSICA: And you don't know what I'm going to say now. First of all, Mr. T – I am so sorry for poking holes in your roof top. I don't know what I was thinking. I was just so mad about – everything! *(Mark enters carrying his sound system. Ben follows).*

MR.T: Apology accepted, Jessica. Forgiving you, also helps me. There's no sense in staying angry. I believe you're sorry.

JESSICA: Thank You Mr. T. *(They exchange a knuckle greeting as Mark sets down sound system. He and Ben 'fake' set up).*

MR. T: Ben, Spikey, I'm sorry I thought it was either of you. Can I make it up with Goldeye **Season Tickets** for you two, Mark and your Dad!! I put him through a lot of hassle. *(Larry smiles, as Mr. T. and Larry shake hands)*

LARRY: Thanks! You do believe, in paying it forward!!

BEN/MARK/SPIKEY: You got it, Mr. T! *(High-five/knuckle greetings. All sing)* **_Pay It Forward._**

JESSICA; That's awesome! Now it's my turn to pay it forward! We've got some fun choreography I've been working on in this park! Ready girls?! Keri, Tia, Sally?! *(Option: I invited the park dancers to join us!)* Okay team ready to dance?! Keri, it's the same routine I taught at the auditions! *(Keri smiles and nods. She and Jessica give a thumbs up to Mark! He returns a thumbs up) (Girls dance, featuring Keri/Jessica!) (Spikey, all on stage, sing/dance to* **_Celebrate Life!_** *FEATURE dance number) (girls in 'new' outfits by Grammy) (Near end of song ALL chant 'Celebrate Life' moving downstage).*

KERI: *(Jessica moves to Keri. They high-five).* Yes! Celebrate life! We're not victims, we're victors!

MR.T: Now that's a victory! *(thumbs up)* Oh by the way, Keri, I've got a double treat surprise for you.

KERI: Can I have a hint? Double dipped, double scooped ice cream?

MR T: Yeah, we can do that soon. But that's not it. *(hands her 2 hoodies!)*

KERI: Wow!! **Two** Hoodies!! *(very excited!)* Grandpa! Thank you. *(hugs him)* Sorry I was mad at you. Sorry I'm not the perfect grand-daughter.

MR. T: I'm not the perfect Grandpa. Life can be tough. No family is perfect. That's normal!

KERI: So we're normal?!

MR. T: Yep! If anyone thinks their family is perfect – they haven't looked back far enough!

GRAMMY: *(to Jessica)* How is your family, dear?

JESSICA: They're okay. I'm not. I'm moving in the new year. So I'm still upset with my parents!

SARAH: Deja vu! Life changes and we need to learn new coping skills. It'll all work out, Jessica.

KERI: Hey, I've Been There! Done that! Jessica, we can get together and talk about it! *(knuckle greeting with Jessica).* I'm happy here now. My Mom and Grandpa, are awesome! I love them both. But Grandpa, I love you twice as much *(holds up her two hoodies)* as I did before!

MR. T: Glad you like your two new hoodies. Love you too, honey. *(notices Jessica walking away.)* Jessica, I'm too old to be coaching volleyball anymore but I can give you volleyball tips.

JESSICA: Thanks Mr. T, but I'll be **too busy** dancing. I'll think of packing and moving later!

SALLY: We can help you pack.

KERI: Yes! Yeah...yes we can!

SALLY: Life's about choices but sometimes we don't get choices.

KERI: Sometimes there are "no choices," and we just have to "ride along."

TIA: My choice is just to 'dance.' It's all I want to do!!

KERI: Me too! I'm so happy I got a chance to dance tonight!!! It's not about making the team! That's for Robyn to decide after Jessica leaves. Thanks Jessica, for this chance now!! Maybe dreams can come true! *(Keri notices Jessica standing alone, looking sad).* Jessica, we got off to a bad start, but I know how you feel. I moved and am the new girl here now. I was sad, and angry too. *(Spikey, Grammy, Sarah, Mr. T, Sally and Tia nod 'yes!')* Lisa moved, now you! I miss my old friends, but we text each other! *(pause)* When you move, we could keep in touch. I could text you too...if you want?

JESSICA: Really, you'd do that?! *(Keri nods)* You're on the dance team as long as I'm here! *(cheers)* We could be friends!? *(Keri nods)* Look Keri, I'm kinda jealous of you, you're popular and...

SALLY: Everyone wants to be friends with Keri now! We stopped hanging out with you, Jessica.

JESSICA: Yeah. But I don't blame you. I was mean! But not anymore!

SALLY: *(to Jessica)* We can be 'mean girls,' or choose to be nice. I'll text too! No cyber bullying!

KERI: We can be friends on Twitter and Facebook! We'll send selfies! *(Girls pose for selfie).*

JESSICA: I've <u>caught friends</u>!!

SPIKEY: And we've caught a new friend, who's a <u>hit</u>! Jessica, please come back again, and <u>visit</u>!

SALLY: Yes, please do! I'm so glad we all got a chance to dance together! *(high-fives with Keri, Tia & Jessica) (All on stage sing **You Gotta Have A Dream!**)* Keri, can we be new best Friends? *(Keri nods yes. They hug).* And I'm not moving! *(Mr. T 'high fives or does a hand greeting' with Spikey, Mark and Ben. Grammy with Sarah and Keri with Sally and Jessica).*

SARAH: *(moves to Keri, hugs her)* So glad you got to dance! *(pulls in Jessica and hugs her too)*

TIA: And Catch FRIENDS!! *(Sally, Tia and other dancers, join Sarah for a group hug).*

SARAH: *(to Keri)* Yes especially that!

JESSICA: I'm so sorry...

GRAMMY: Never underestimate the power of an apology and a hug! *(joins in on group hug).*

SARAH: Exactly!! *(releases 'huggers')* *(to Keri)* Now you my dear – need a good night's **sleep**!

GRAMMY: Yes, right after we all **Celebrate**!

BEN: ...with Dessert at Grammy's! Let's Go!! *(All cheer, Yes!!, etc. Exit SR, following Grammy. Spikey turns to exit SR as Misty, female porcupine, enters SL).*

MISTY: Yoo hooo. Hi Spikey! *(he turns around)* I've been watching you back **catchin.'** You're awesome! Can we meet tomorrow after your practice? *(He nods, mouth open.)* *(Misty blows Spikey a kiss. He pretends to "catch" it. Misty waves Good-Bye, as she slowly exits SL)*

KERI: *(re-enters SR, but doesn't see Misty exit)* Spikey...Spikey?! Are you day dreaming?! *(Spikey smiles and nods 'yes.')* Well, everyone needs to have a dream...*(she takes Spikey's hand)* C'mon, let's go to Grammy's! She got dessert, but she's also got... *(mimicking Grammy)*

ALL: Asparagus and pickle sandwiches!! *(Keri and Spikey walk SR, holding hands)*

SPIKEY: Sometimes we are misunderstood. But Life is still so **very, very** good!

KERI: And Life is full of surprises! We can **catch** them without even looking!

SPIKEY: Ohhh that's so true!! It's happened to me and you! I just want to dance and **sing**! I wonder what tomorrow will **bring**? *(Spikey happily skips, as he exits SR with Keri!)* *(Lights instantly out as Keri and Spikey exit - **BLACKOUT**)*

(The END!)

*(Lights up as Instrumental THEME MUSIC **Together
We Can Make It**starts, for curtain call.)
Cast move quickly to Enter/Form Curtain Call line. Wait
while previous actor receives their applause.*

Chorus *enters SL*
Misty *enters SR*
Coach Bob *enters SL*
Mr. T *enters SR*
Larry *enters SL*
Sarah *enters SR*
Ben & Mark *enter SL,*
Sally, Tia *enter SR,*
Jessica *enters SL*
Grammy *enters SR*
Keri *enters SL*

*SPIKEY Enters LAST, from Centre. Stands between Keri
and Grammy. All join hands, Smile/Bow!*

*Theme Music fades. Cast acknowledge Stage Manager, Director/
Crew. All stage sing *Together We Can Make It.**

*Cast immediately Exit down aisles to greet audience in foyer,
as THEME MUSIC plays for the third time...*

*CATCH A FRIEND Revised Editions: 2009/2013/2015 – *by Joy Winter-Schmidt (From
Five original scripts/lyrics written for musicals performed at: The Winnipeg Fringe Festival,
Manitoba Canada, 2001–2005)*

SPIKEY'S COOL SCHOOL!

Spikey's Points: Sequel 3 *(75-80 min.) (Reading time approx. 45 min. Music: 11 songs - 30 min.)*

Child VOICE CUE: *(Spoken Backstage or Recorded. Track #1) (Voiceover opens ALL sequels)* "Once Upon A time, not that long ago, lived a walking, talking, singing porcupine, with mostly good points. His name was Spikey. His parents didn't make it across the road. Spikey barely made it. He lay injured on the side of the road. A dear old lady everyone called Grammy, found him and nurtured him back to health. He became a friend to many because he always tried to do the best he could. He lived, he loved, he laughed. He became a great example to follow..."

MUSIC CUE: ***Together We Can Make It**Theme Song Intro Instrumental, track#2)*

<u>Lights up:</u> *Enter Chorus from back of aisle, dance – sit in park, read the "Community Quill,"*

LIGHTS UP ON SET: *Morning Park Scene. - trees, rock, park bench. Sound: Birds chirping.*

(The role of TIA, a 7–8 year old girl, could be eliminated. Her Sc. 2 lines could go to Robyn. Her other lines to Misty, or deleted.)

SCENE 1 *(music fades). Spikey is backstage with baseball glove.*

SPIKEY: *(yells out as he enters SL, running from backstage)* Where are you? I'm gonna get you! You got away again, you little fly. I can't catch you – I wonder why. *(Runs SR, off stage, to catch fly. Spikey re-enters SL as Misty walks in SR).* I'm gonna get you! Yes, I am. I'm gonna get you! *(He runs into Misty. They both stumble).* Ooops. Fancy meeting you like this. Sorry I bumped you, Miss... *(puts his glove on bench and offers hand to help her up).*

MISTY: *(rubs head)* Thank you. I'm Misty. Remember me? We met in this park last year.

SPIKEY: Yes I do!! Happy to see you! I'm sorry as can be, for bumping into you, Misty!!

MISTY: Apology accepted. Thanks for saying sorry. Your name is Spikey, right?

SPIKEY: Spikey. That's me. I was just playin' with a fly. He was my little friend, until he flew, 'goodbye.'

MISTY: I can be your friend! *(Spikey nods 'yes' excitedly)* I watched you playing catch a few times, last year. I heard the kids call your name. I'm glad you're here today.

SPIKEY: Me too. Yahoo! How do you do? *(extends hand, shakes Misty's hand)*

MISTY: I'm fine thanks. It would be nice to plan to meet here again.

SPIKEY: Hey, maybe my Grammy could send you an email?! My typing would fail! My pencils are dull. I'm pointless, can't write a note! *(beat)* But I can rhyme and quote!

MISTY: *(she laughs)* Is Grammy your guardian? *(he nods)* I don't think I could write or type very well either. *(both laugh as they look at their hands)* It would be awesome to meet in this park sometimes! Funny how life happens. We don't always know when, where or how we'll meet again...

SPIKEY: I feel so silly and dumb. Umm, so where did you come from?

MISTY: Just like you. A porcupine family. Oh Spikey, you're not dumb, but you're silly!

SPIKEY: *(laughs)* Where do you live, is what I mean? It's been a year, since each other, we've seen. Where have you been?

MISTY: Lockport *(name of suburb or local town)* is where I live. Winnipeg *(or name of local city)* is the furthest I've been.

SPIKEY: Are you locked in a port? Is it like a fort?

MISTY: *(laughs)* A fort? Lockport is the name of my town. It's near here, but too far to walk. I was hoping to find you, right here in this park! I've looked for you here, a few times before today.

SPIKEY: Before today? It's too bad I was away!

MISTY: We come into Winnipeg sometimes, to do some shopping.

SPIKEY: Porcupines can do a lot of things. Do they drive, or does your family have wings? *(giggles)*

MISTY: *(giggles)* No, I live with a really nice family. The parents drive. I'm like a pet for their children. But they're all teaching me things, like how to read and speak.

SPIKEY: Wowee - just like Grammy teaches -me!

MISTY: Yes! *(Spikey nods)* This couple found me. Well – actually I found them. I watched them eat hotdogs with their kids. One of the kids wanted one of my quills. So, of course I had to give both kids a quill. And well, the parents saw me and thanked me. Then they bought me a delicious hotdog. It was love at first bite. The first and best hotdog I've ever had! Hotdogs are now my favourite! They kind of adopted me after that.

SPIKEY: Yes, we're both adopted. Someone cared and kept us fed!

MISTY: There's some <u>really</u> good people in this world. Our world is mostly good, don't you think?

SPIKEY: Yes, I agree. We're so lucky, aren't we? You know what I think? *(Misty shrugs her shoulders)* I think we're the luckiest porcupines to link! *(links arms with Misty)*.

MISTY: I think so too. I'll be right back. I need to tell my family I found you!

SPIKEY: I'll run and tell Grammy too. She'll want to meet you! *(Misty exits SL. Spikey skips then exits SR) (Bob enters SL. Misty and Bob don't see each other until they bump into each other)*.

BOB: *(Enters SL, wearing Construction hat. Looks around)* Spikey?? Where are you? Hmmm, thought I'd find you here. *(picks up Spikey's ball glove and puts it down again)*. Spikey, wanna play catch? I'm working around the corner from here. I'm on a break. Are you hiding from me? I've got some plans I'd like to talk to you about! Maybe another time? Spikey? Spikey? *(Bob turns to exit SR) (Spikey slowly enters SL, whistling). (An excited Misty enters SR and bumps into Bob)*. Ahhhhhhh!! Who and what are you? *(Spikey laughs)*

MISTY: I'm Misty and I'm a bit clumsy. *(pause)* Sorry! Ahhhh. Oh no, I'm rhyming like Spikey! Hmmm...To rhyme is kinda cool!

BOB: Oh great! Another walking, talking porcupine!

MISTY: I don't rhyme like Spikey, but I sing too!

BOB: *(Bob shakes his head)* Oh, umm, that is wonderful. It's nice to meet you Misty.

MISTY: Spikey and I are just getting to know each other. We're brand new friends!

BOB: I'm happy for you both.

SPIKEY: *(Moves from SR to CS)* Coach Bob, hello! Done making dough?

BOB: Sort of. Hey there, Spikey - I'm working in the area. I'm just on a break – but I'll be back, off and on during the day.

MISTY: *(to Spikey)* He makes dough? *(Bob laughs)*

BOB: Misty, dough is just an expression for making money. Dough is money. *(she makes a confused face)* Spikey, I'm thrilled you found a new friend. Spikey, you look so happy! *(Spikey sings verse 1 of, **__Let's Make A Point!__** Misty & Bob join in on chorus and verse 2.)* Hey Spikey, I've got some ideas for you. I'll share them with you later. I'll let you two get acquainted. We'll play catch another time. *(begins to exit)*

SPIKEY: Thanks for understanding, Coach Bob. Glad you got a good building job.

MISTY: Bye Coach Bob. Nice to meet you!

BOB: You too, Misty. See you two later. I'll come back on my next break. *(Bob exits)*

MISTY: Okay. Spikey, why do you always rhyme? It's not contagious is it?

SPIKEY: Oh my goodness, no! One rhyming porcupine is enough to know!
It's all those rhyming books I heard, and was read to, a long time ago.

MISTY: Ohhh, thaaat's why!

SPIKEY: *(rubs tummy)* It must be almost lunch time. My friends will be finishing their morning of school, anytime.

MISTY: It's Friday. One week finished today! *(Spikey nods)* So, you're waiting here to meet them? *(he nods again)* And then I came along!

SPIKEY: Good for you and me! School is one place I'd like to be. My school friends you'll soon see!

MISTY: Yes good for me! It's so good you're here! We may be the luckiest and the smartest porcupines, but I also think, we're the weirdest!! *(they laugh)*

SPIKEY: Then this is the start of a weird and wonderful friendship. Hey, wanna come to Grammy's later for veggies and dip?

MISTY: Sure, I've had an early lunch, so I'd love too, later. I'd love to meet Grammy.

SPIKEY: I just asked her now to come here and meet you! She said *(mimicks Grammy)* "I'm meeting Joe, but we'd love to meet Misty too!"

MISTY: Wonderful! Who's Joe?

SPIKEY: Mr. Joe Taylor, Mr. T, is her 'special' friend. Many love emails, they do send!

MISTY: Ohhh. Sure, I'd like to meet them both - Just as long as I meet back at the grocery store by 3. Can you tell me when it's 3 o'clock?

SPIKEY: *(uses fingers/hand to demonstrate)* Big hand at 12, little hand at 3. I'll ask Grammy or Keri to remind me. *(sees Bob carrying tool box)* Hey my friend Bob, Passin' through again with your job? *(Bob nods)*

BOB: Yes, my friend Spikey. The park is a great shortcut to the school AND where we're working today. I'm just going to deliver this tool box...

LARRY: *(enters carrying lunch bag)* Hey my friends Bob and Spikey. *(to Misty)* Ahhh, and who have we here? I'm Larry.

MISTY: Hi Larry. I'm Misty.

SPIKEY: She's my new friend and will be to the end. *(music starts)* *(Misty smiles coyly)* *(Spikey, Misty, Larry and Bob sing first verse and chorus of **FRIENDS.*** *(Bob exits after verse 1 and chorus. As they finish singing - Keri, Sally, Robyn, & Mark enter from opposite side. They're all shocked). (Larry hands a lunch bag to Mark and Ben, then exits).*

SCENE 2

(Robyn screams, then other girls scream. Misty moves away. Spikey takes her arm to comfort her).

TIA: Did you see that? <u>Two</u> walking, talking, singing porcupines?!!

SALLY: Yes, I saw them too! I only know about one. And that one is you, Spikey!

ROBYN: Isn't one enough? *(Spikey/Misty hide by tree)* Mom and I moved here to see that?

KERI: Well, my mom and I did! I'm new too. I've learned to "expect the unexpected!"

ROBYN: Yuck!!! I won't be able to eat my lunch now!

MISTY: *(to Spikey)* As if it's our fault! *(Spikey makes face in agreement)*

SPIKEY: We must be the only two on earth. Now we feel, we have no worth. *(Misty and Spikey smile sympathetically at each other).*

ROBYN: I'm sorry. I didn't mean to hurt your feelings. Hi – I'm Robyn.

MISTY: Hi Robyn.

ROBYN: My mom's the vice principal at the school.

SALLY: *(to Robyn)* I met Spikey last year, he's a good guy! We gave Spikey a chance. We should give his new friend a chance too!

KERI: Right! We're all sorry. *(all agree, nod, say sorry)* Of course you have worth.

MARK: Both of you have special qualities. You're wonderful, unique...

SALLY: Loving, kind...

TIA: And cute too! *(Spikey and Misty put their faces/cheeks together/smile).*

SALLY: Your friend is a...a surprise.

BEN: First there's just Spikey! Is the world ready for <u>two</u> walking, talking porcupines? Spikey, who's your friend?

SPIKEY: Misty is her name. I'm so glad she came. But your screams almost scared her away. *(Misty nods)* And I really want her to stay.

ROBYN: Sorry...

TIA: Please stay, Misty.

MISTY: *(shyly)* Okay. I'll stay. Hi everyone...

ALL: Hi Misty.

MARK: We're all Spikey's school friends. I'm Mark. *(Misty waves to Mark)*

BEN: I'm Ben, Mark's brother. *(Misty waves to Ben)*

SALLY: Nice to meet you. I'm Sally.

TIA: I'm Tia. Sally's my sister. *(Misty waves to Sally and Tia)*

ROBYN: Where are you from, Misty?

MISTY: Lockport. *(This town can be changed. Add your own pertinent history!)*

KERI: I know about Lockport! It has an over 100 year old lock and dam, we learned about in school.

BEN: Yeah, and the bridge connects two rivers!!

SALLY: I just know about the hot dogs!

MISTY: Yes, they ARE good. My parents met as kids years ago, near the waterslides.

BEN: Waterslides! Dad said they've been closed forever!

MARK: There's still more to Lockport than a dam and hotdogs.

MISTY: No, that's pretty much it. *(Pause)* Spikey. you're lucky to have all these friends.

TIA: Yes, we're all friends of Spikey's!

ALL: *(GREETINGS: Hello Misty ... Hi Misty, Nice to meet you, etc.)*

ROBYN: Now this is probably none of my business, but Spikey, why is going to school so important to you?

SPIKEY: I have so much to learn! I have energy to burn. But with me, I think the teachers will have to be stern.

TIA: Do you think some kids would be scared of you?

SPIKEY: Yes, some fear me, grown-ups too. Many think I belong in a zoo!! *(Tia laughs)*

KERI: Yeah, some do. Some people are prejudiced against porcupines. *(Misty looks confused)* Prejudice means some people think they're **better** than porcupines!

TIA: Really? Some people are prejudiced against porcupines?!

BEN: Unfortunately, yes!!

SPIKEY: Yes, unfortunately so. Why? I don't really know.

MARK: We want to INCLUDE Porcupines! So, Spikey and I discussed having an animal "cool school" meeting here tonight at 7:30. Everyone coming? *(all nod. Misty is confused)* It's our version of a "court."

BEN: Dad's taking Spikey's case!!

TIA: We're all going! Isn't that right everyone?! *(all cheer, yes, sure am, etc.)*

MISTY: I'm going to see if I can get permission to come back here for 7:30. I want to go to court with you!

MARK: It's not a real court, Misty. It's us kids running it.

BEN: But that's our way of getting our point across!

SPIKEY: *(to Misty)* I'd be so happy if you came back for me! I'm lucky to have friends standing up for me!

SALLY: Because **you** have good points, Spikey.

MISTY: *(sits)* I'd like to come back! Now, I'll just sit here with Spikey, while you tell us good points of your first morning of school. I wish I could go to school!

SPIKEY: You too?! I wish I could go with you!

MISTY: See how lucky you all are. We want to go, but we can't. That's too bad. So how was your morning?

KERI: We got through it. It wasn't so bad. I can't believe our summer is over!

BEN: I know. It went so fast! Yeah, school isn't so bad. *(they nod)* In a way, I'm kinda excited about school. Field trips and stuff.

KERI: I'm even getting used to my mom being in the same school.

BEN: Well at least she's not teaching you!

KERI: Right! Other than Leadership class.

ROBYN: It's worse being the Vice Principal's daughter!

SALLY: Yeah, that would be tough!

TIA: I can hardly wait until I'm old enough, to be in Leadership class! But I wouldn't want to be the vice principal's daughter! *(all laugh)*

BEN: Hey, guys, do you wanna eat your lunch at my place? We still have some chocolate chip cookies left!

MARK: Grammy made them for us!

BEN: They're really good!

KERI: I'm in!

SALLY: I'd love to join you for lunch too!

TIA: Me too! Sally's taking me back to school. I'm with Sally, until our parents pick us up.

BEN: Good. Then you'll be able to come to the court case AND to Grammy's after. We always go to Grammy's after, <u>everything</u>! Okay, let's go eat lunch!

KERI: Sure! And we'll keep having dance rehearsals in <u>this</u> park. Does that work?

ALL: Yes, yup, etc. *(all agree!!)*

KERI: We're going to be outside, in fact, right here – at period 2 anyway, so...

BEN: Wassup in period 2?

MARK: Huhh, Ben?! The vice principal announced it.

BEN: She did?! Oh yeah, now I remember!

ROBYN: Yeah, my mom, usually makes the announcements!

SALLY: It's Leadership class!!

BEN: *(mimics announcer, with microphone)* "Anyone in Grade 7 or 8 interested in participating in Leadership Classes; please meet in Ms Bell's room, number 108, period 2, after lunch today." *(hands pretend mic to Keri)*

KERI: Good Ben! *(takes pretend mic, and mimics announcer, with microphone)* "She will be taking you outside, to the park across from the school. Come prepared with pen and notebook."

MARK: Yay, I'm joining. You guys too? *(all agree, nod)*

SALLY: Our dance class is now part of Leadership thanks to Keri and Robyn! *(Keri and Sally and Robyn high-five).* That's so cool!

TIA: Leadership class sounds so cool! Someday I will be in it!!

KERI: It's been good for me. When I first came here, I didn't get along with anyone. Remember all my arguments with everyone Sally? *(Sally nods)* I argued with everyone except you, cuz you're always so nice!

SALLY: Yeah, but when you're the nice, good student – you may as well be invisible.

KERI: Well you weren't invisible to me! I don't know what I would have done without you. You were always there for me. You didn't move away! I was mad because we had to move here. Now it's HOME! Especially this park!!

ROBYN: And it's great we're all friends now! *(Sally nods)*

BEN: We're older, more mature and grown-up! I'm in Grade 7.

KERI: And the rest of us are in Grade 8. Besides, if I'm going to be in a Leadership role, I have to be a good role model. It's hard to believe this is our last year here. I think I'll run for student council this year. All in favour?

BEN: You got my vote! *(All raise hands, cheer, etc.)*

SALLY: We're your friends. Of course we'll vote for you.

KERI: Thanks guys. I'm so lucky to have moved here and to have made such good friends! Now we all have a new friend in Misty, as well as Spikey. *(All sing 2ⁿᵈ verse and chorus of **_FRIENDS_**)*

BEN: Come on everyone, Spikey, Misty – my place for a quick lunch! I'm only a minute away.

MISTY: Thanks, but I've had lunch. Spikey – did you have lunch? *(he nods)* Spikey and I need to stay here. I'm meeting Grammy and Mr.T!. *(All say goodbye, exit SR)*

SPIKEY: I'm excited to meet **your** family! But my tummy feels a little queazy!

MISTY: Then it's good we're not eating! Let's take a minute and walk your queazies out! *(Spikey nods yes. They exit SL)*

SCENE 3

(Enter Grammy SR, looks around, sits on bench. She picks up Spikey's glove, shakes her head as she puts it in her knitting bag; looks at watch.. Enter Mr. T, SL)

MR. T: Hi Mary.

GRAMMY: Hello there Joe!

MR. T: Good timing.

GRAMMY: Yes, it is. Just think, it's our Anniversary today. We met here for a picnic on this bench, one year ago today.

MR. T: Yes. Trust you to remember the exact day! So, that's why you called me here?

GRAMMY: No, but isn't it romantic to come back to the same place?

MR. T: Yes, it is. But why right NOW? The time was to be 5 o'clock. It was after school. We agreed on that yesterday. Let's come back at that time, to have our picnic. Okay? *(He gets up to leave).*

GRAMMY: Okay. But you know women like to change their mind. I want to tell you something....

MR. T: *(panics)* Oh No! You're not going to change your mind, are you?!

GRAMMY: What? Oh we'll still meet here at 5. *(Mr. T breathes a sigh of relief)* I just wanted you to meet someone 'new,' *(Mr. T looks shocked)* because 'she's' leaving at 3.

MR. T: *(sighs)* Glad you said, "She." Oh. *(pause)* I made your favorite muffins. I made banana chocolate chip muffins, just for you. I'll bring them later, at 5!

GRAMMY: Oh, Joe – you shouldn't have! But I'm glad you did! I have a little surprise for you, too.

MR. T: *(smiles, as he elbows her)* And I have another little surprise for you, too.

GRAMMY: Oh, the muffins are enough. I can hardly wait to try one! I don't need any more surprises. But, you are going to meet someone, very special.

MR. T: *(looks endearingly at Grammy)* I already have.

GRAMMY: Thank you. *(Grammy smiles, as she looks around)* I told them to meet us here.

MR. T: Who? Meet who? *(enter Spikey and Misty SR)*

GRAMMY: Hello!!! *(stands up and waves to Spikey and Misty)*

MR. T: *(Sits. He's in disbelief)* What – now there are **two** of them! Am I seeing double?

MISTY: Oh I'm sure there are more of us. They're just too shy to come out.

SPIKEY: There you two are, under a tree. Hello, Grammy and Mr. T, I'd like you to meet my new friend, Misty!

GRAMMY: Hi Misty! What a lovely surprise!

MISTY: How do you do, Grammy and Mr. T?

MR. T: Fine. I think...

GRAMMY: It's a pleasure to meet you, Misty.

MISTY: Spikey told me about you, two. All good points of course.

MR.T: *(With sarcasm. Grammy gives him a cold look).* Yes, you two would know all about good points. *(Spikey and Misty laugh)* (BEAT) *(Mr T gets up)* Look, why don't we all go for a drive in my convertible. We can get to know each other a little better. You two just make sure you don't poke any holes in my rooftop!! *(Grammy elbows Mr. T)* Okay, I'll put the rooftop down! I don't want to take any chances! Besides it's a great day! I don't always get a chance to drive with the top down! Today's the day!

GRAMMY: That would be a great idea, Joe! It's a beautiful day, to drive with the rooftop down! *(Spikey looks for his glove)* *(Grammy smiles and waits)* Oh, I've got your glove here, Spikey. *(lifts glove from her bag, to show him)*

SPIKEY: Thanks Grammy! You look after me!

MR. T: *(trying to be polite)* Misty, I know you need to meet your family by 3 o'clock. I'll make sure we'll be back by 2:30. *(Misty smiles and nods)* How about we go for burgers – then ice cream!

GRAMMY: Another great idea, Joe. Spikey needs a change from asparagus and pickle sandwiches!

SPIKEY: They'll always be my favorite treat. Grammy's asparagus and pickle sandwiches can't be beat! *(Grammy smiles and puts her arm around Spikey).*

MISTY: I'd like to try them sometime, too!

SPIKEY: You would!? *(looks questionably at Grammy. She nods)* Yes!! Grammy said you could!

MISTY: Yes!! *(smiles)* It's a wonderful, most fabulous day ever!

GRAMMY: Because we all had an early lunch - I brought some veggies and dip, another of Spikey's favorite. We can eat them during our drive.

SPIKEY: Yes! Today is the best! Friendship, veggies and dip, hamburger nip and then ice cream with chocolate dip!

GRAMMY: Life is good. How can it get better? *(Mr. T smiles smugly at Grammy and takes her hand as they exit SL)*

SPIKEY: Misty, you're smart, you're funny, you're cute, you're hip. I think this is the start of a super friendship! *(Misty smiles. They hold hands and skip. All four, Exit SL)*

SCENE 4

(Sarah and Leadership kids from school, enter SR)

SARAH: Okay, valuable Leadership students. Hope you enjoyed your lunch hour. Thank you for joining this class. Just find a comfortable spot in the park. We'll get started soon. *(aside)* I love this park. *(To Mark)* This is where I met you Mark, your brother Ben and your dad. Yes, good memories seem to start here...

MARK: Dad said we're having a late dinner with you and Keri. He said he's meeting you here at 5 or so, to drop something off first.

SARAH: Yes, my scarf. I forgot it in his car. He wants to meet here for a few minutes first. Not sure why. *(Keri and the boys exchange "we know something you don't" looks).* Okay everyone, now that you found a place to sit. Let's get started. What does being in a leadership class mean to you? *(pause)* Anyone?

KERI: It means we can be trusted to take responsibility. *(Sarah nods, points to Mark)*

MARK: And that we are responsible for our actions. We're polite, not rude.

SARAH; Yes, of course. Anyone else? *(Ben raises his hand).* Yes Ben?

BEN: We can be safe and responsible leaders. Truthful, fair ...

SARAH: Very Good. That says we have value and values. *(Sally raises hand)* Sally?

SALLY: We raise our hands, speak when asked. We're caring, kind, helpful and respectful.

SARAH: Excellent. *(Ben raises hand)* Ben, you have more thoughts?

BEN: We control our tempers and our actions. We listen more than talk. We're loyal.

SARAH: Very good. *(Robyn raises hand)* Robyn, do you have some ideas?

ROBYN: I do. It can also mean standing up for your rights. Being an UPstander, not a bystander! Standing up for what you believe in! *(Sally has hand up, Sarah points to her).*

SALLY: *(puts hand down)* Helping others when they get knocked down. Even if you know you could be ridiculed... *(Sarah nods. Points to Mark, who has his hand up)*

MARK: *(puts hand down)* It means that changes can start with us. We can all make a big difference, by doing small things together!

SALLY: And together we can build something big!

SARAH: Very Good, all of you! Yes, of course. Sometimes it's difficult to stand up for something you believe in, especially when you feel there's too much opposition, to take a stand. It takes more than talent, determination and brains. Thoughtfulness and good points can be your best weapon, or best way to get your point across. *(Bob & Larry enter, with draft plan. They show Sarah. ALL sing ****It Starts With Me!***** (Bob & Larry exit with draft plan).* Okay, any other thoughts before we head back to class? *(Mark raises his hand)* Yes Mark?

MARK: So you're saying your best defense should be a kind approach, not a vicious attack?

SARAH: Exactly! Okay, let's open this topic up for discussion.

BEN: Attitude and fairness is everything. That's the way to find **justice!!** *(all cheer)*

KERI: Wow – you'd think your dad was a lawyer or something!

SALLY: Don't you all get it? Talent and brains ALONE, don't win battles.

SARAH: Yes, win them with kindness! It's more empowering to be the **peaceful hero**!

BEN: Spikey's our hero*! (all cheer)* Ms Bell, guess what Spikey told us? He told us he wants to go to school.

SARAH: Really?!

MARK: Yes. He wants the chance...

SALLY: And choice!

MARK: Yeah - to learn things like everyone else. He said we are so lucky to have such a wonderful opportunity, to go to school!

SARAH: And you are. It's truly a privilege to be able to go to school and learn about so many things. Sometimes we take things for granted. You are all fortunate to be able to go to school. Education **is** important!

SALLY: Even just learning how to get along, is important!.

SARAH: YES it is!! *(sees Ben's hand up)* Yes Ben?

BEN*: (puts hand down)* And how to be a good leader and helpful team player. *(Sarah nods)*

ROBYN: *(raises hand, Sarah points to her)* So, shouldn't Spikey have that right? Shouldn't all breathing things – including animals be able to voice their opinions? Shouldn't they get the respect we do? Come on, we're all animal lovers. We're all the same here! We're all made up of <u>cells</u>! Hey, do I have support here?

SARAH: This is a good discussion.. Brainstorm, ask questions. Look at both sides.

KERI: *(raises hand, Sarah points to her)* Okay. What are you getting at Robyn? What do you want from us? And even if we agree – what are we supposed to do about it?

ROBYN: *(raises hand, Sarah nods)* In order to make a change, we all have to do a little bit!

KERI: *(lifts hand)* Yes! We're the nucleous! This is a leadership class!

BEN: And we're LEADERS!

SARAH: Correct. And Leaders have good Attitudes. They don't bully or attack. If everyone does a little, progress can be made. But remember, we all need to pull together. Tug o' wars keep us at a standstill. You can't move forward. *(beat)* ****ATTITUDE **** *(ALL CAST)* Right. The secret to making things work is pulling together! We need to stay open to others' thoughts and ideas. Yes, sometimes there IS a better way than ours! Be OPEN to it! Always play as a team. One person can't do it all.

SALLY: Yeah! We have to **pull together** to be strong...to build or start anything at all!

BEN: So, what if we start a **petition** to get Spikey in school?! *(Sarah shakes her head, side to side)*

SARAH: That's not exactly what I had in mind. *(Mark raises his hand)* Mark, do you have something specific in mind?

MARK: I'm putting together a court? ... for Spikey. *(Sarah shakes her head)* He's going to be here tonight at 7:30 pm. Who wants to join me?

SALLY: Why are you telling the teacher! *(kids raise uproar, yeah why, it's our thing, etc.)*

SARAH: Ohh oh....I'm losing control here. *(looks at Mark)* Mark, a court? What are you talking about?

MARK: It will be a mock court. We'll discuss the pros and cons of an animal school. We'll probably need some specially trained teachers.

BEN: Ms Bell, why did you become a teacher?

SARAH: *(smiling)* To teach children how to make the world a better place. *(looks at watch)* Okay class, it's time to go. Remember, it's early dismissal. We'll continue our leadership discussion tomorrow. *(starts to exit, but stands aside listening, smiling)*

SALLY: Mark, I can be here early, by 7, in case some come early. I can start setting things up.

MARK: Thanks Sally! All interested, meet me <u>right here</u> at 7:30 pm. I'll be early too.

TIA: I'll be early too! I'm coming with Sally. There might be others here early too!

KERI: Don't worry Mark. We'll all be here by 7:30! *(Sarah shakes her head side to side, in disbelief, as she continues to smile. All exit SR)*

SCENE 5

(Enter SL: Grammy, Mr.T, Spikey and Misty).

GRAMMY: That was so much fun! I feel like a young girl again!

MR. T: We are young! Just like school kids!

GRAMMY: Yes, with the wind blowing in our hair!

MISTY: Thank you Grammy and Mr. T, for everything.

MR. T: It was our pleasure.

GRAMMY: Spikey, please walk Misty back at a quarter to 3.

SPIKEY: A quarter is 25 cents. A quarter to 3, doesn't make any sense?!!

GRAMMY: *(laughs)* Spikey, you know 3 o'clock. *(Spikey nods)* A quarter to 3 is the same thing as 15 minutes to 3, or before 3. A clock is divided into quarters. There are 4 sets of 15 in ONE hour. Just like 4 quarters equals ONE loonie, or one pie can be divided into four quarters. *(Spikey is confused)* I'll explain it to you again later. Ask Keri, to remind you two.

SPIKEY: Yes, no problem. Keri's my friend and a gem.

GRAMMY: She is. I trust she'll remind you. Yes, Spikey, you do need to be in a school!

SPIKEY: I DO really need school. I don't wanna be anyone's fool!

GRAMMY: You're not, Spikey! You've got more common sense than all of us! Well, we're going to run along now. Hopefully we will see you all in court!

MISTY: I'm really going to try and get back! It was nice meeting you two. Thanks for the wonderful day! It must be almost time for me to go. *(Grammy nods)*

GRAMMY/MR.T: You're welcome. Bye now. *(Grammy and Mr. T exit SL as kids enter SR).*

SPIKEY: *(to kids)* You're all outta school! Yahoo!!

KERI: *(to Spikey and Misty)* So glad it was early dismissal!! How was the car ride with Grammy and my Grandpa?!

SPIKEY: Wonderful, but I'm so full!

MISTY: Me too!

ROBYN: What's your favorite food, Misty? *(Misty shrugs her shoulders)*

TIA: Mine is sausages and perogies with bacon bits and sour cream. *(or can name ethnic, cultural food)*

SALLY: Really?! Perogies are my favorite, too.

MISTY: I like hot dogs! Spikey, what's a perogie? I'd like to try one sometime!

SPIKEY: You will! They're yummy. But when I eat too many, I hurt my tummy.

SALLY: Where's Mark?

BEN: Mark went to ball practice. But he'll be back here at 7:30.

KERI: Are you all in favor of Mark being the judge?

TIA: He told Sally and I that he would <u>really like</u> to be the judge!

ALL: Sure, fine, sounds good, etc.

ROBYN: Spikey, how is going to school going to make a difference in your life?

SPIKEY: I need an education to get a job ... in building, construction, like Coach Bob!

BEN: That sounds good, Spikey. *(Misty nods)*

SPIKEY: Do you guys think I could get into school? Do you think Misty could too?

BEN: Maybe. That's why we're having a court. Maybe all the people that come to the park could be our jury? Maybe they can help us sign a petition? See, I've already started one! Okay guys, sign up!! *(All on stage sign petition)* I even got Ms Bell and a few other teachers. I'm working on this! We start with small steps, a few signatures; then ...

SALLY: Small steps? We need to make a big point! We have to get our point across, strong and clear!! *(Spikey and Sally high-five)*

KERI: I agree. We need strong power on our team!! Hope you can make it back, Misty!

SPIKEY: Yes, Thanks Misty for supporting us. I hope getting back here is no fuss!

MISTY: I'll find a way! I need to get back here for court!! Keri, Can you please tell me when it's 15 minutes before 3?

KERI: Certainly! *(looks at cell)* Almost. Okay, for court, we'll need a judge, baliff, and a ~~defending and a prosecuting lawyer...~~

BEN: We need a fair judge and jury. A judge who doesn't judge! No prejudice!

SALLY: Right! Some people see what they want. They pre-judge before they know the truth. We can't be like that. We'll win fair and square!

BEN: Right! We don't dislike certain people or animals, for no reason at all!

ROBYN: Well, I'm not sure how crazy my mom will be about having porcupines in school! She was great about helping me organize the park clean-up, remember?

ALL: *(Yeah, she was. I remember, etc.)*

ROBYN: But agreeing to porcupines in school?! She wouldn't see the point!!

SALLY: But no one is better than anyone else! *(beat)* If porcupines went to school, then maybe they'd learn more things!

KERI: Yeah - so they could be better and smarter than they ever were before!

ROBYN: Good point! They could contribute to society.

SPIKEY: We could learn to read and write better. Then I could write Misty a letter!

TIA: If you had a bigger computer - you could text! And type your own emails!

SPIKEY: I tried Grammy's, but couldn't read what I wrote. Couldn't even type a quote.

BEN: They need to make HUGE spaces between the keys. I see the problem. How could a porcupine ever text! *(Spikey and Misty laugh)* Maybe we could get someone to make a special computer and a cell for porcupines!!

KERI: I wish they could go to a school, that has computers for them.

SALLY: Yeah...A school that understands them and meets their needs.

KERI: *(looks at cell)* Oh. Time to go Misty. We'll walk with you. It's on our way home.

MISTY: Thank you Keri.

SPIKEY: We're gonna build a school fort! *(beat)* But first – let's take it to court!!! *(All laugh as they exit SL).*

SCENE 6

(Enter Larry SR, stands, looks around, then at watch). (Enter Mr. T SL, stands, looks around, then at watch). (Enter Keri, Mark, Ben and Spikey SR. They quietly hide behind a tree).

KERI: It's almost 5 o'clock. I'm so tired after early morning dance practice! Where's mom?

SPIKEY: Where's Grammy? It's a mystery...

BEN: Where is Mark? Ball practice <u>is</u> over!

MARK: *(runs in)* Hi! I was at home looking for a judge robe and a gavel. Hope Dad's Grad gown and a hammer will do. Did I miss anything? *(Keri and Ben shake head no).*

KERI: No, Shhh, they can't know we're here. This shouldn't take long. Then dinner at my place!

(Intro music for Keri's solo - **When you've got Love**** *Harmony: Ben and / or Mark, Chorus.*

(Grammy enters SL, Sarah enters SR)
(Larry and Mr. T turn to watch 'their ladies' walk towards them. - as **Keri starts to sing.)**
Sarah greets Larry as Grammy greets Mr. T.
Grammy and Sarah sit on bench.
Larry sits on bench by Sarah, as Mr. T sits on bench by Grammy. (possible brief ballet solo dance, 10-12 seconds)

Mr. T hands Grammy a muffin. (boxed ring inside)
Larry hands Sarah her scarf made into a bow. (boxed ring inside)

Grammy takes a bite of muffin, smiles and gives Mr. T a thumbs up!
Sarah continues to untie the bow in her scarf. (Ballet dancer exits)

Grammy's next bite is on box. She looks disgusted. Mr. T laughs silently.
Grammy laughs and pokes Mr. T.
Sarah sees box and is very excited!
Mr. T and Larry take the white boxes, then get down on bended knee.
Larry takes Sarah's ring out of the box, the same time Mr. T takes out Grammy's ring.
Both women are beaming/smiling.
Both men mouth "will you marry me?" and hand the rings to their future brides.
Both women <u>lift up hands</u> (cue) and mouth "Yes!" at the same time.
The men put the rings on the fingers of their new brides to be.
Larry and Sarah / Mr. T and Grammy hug and kiss. Kids and Spikey are very happy.

Keri's solo song "When You've Got Love" <u>ends.</u> Sarah, Larry, Grammy and Mr. T join in on last chorus.

LARRY/SARAH/GRAMMY/MR. T: <u>We're engaged</u>!!

(Each Couple looks at the other couple, in shock!!!) All see each other for the first time. Spikey, Keri, Mark and Ben Cheer! Yeah! Congratulations, etc. All form group hug!

GRAMMY / SARAH / LARRY /MR.T: <u>YES!!!</u>
(Both couples and kids high-five with each other then ALL exit SR).

SCENE 7

(Sally enters SL, singing/humming "Together We Can Make It." She's carrying in 2 lawn chairs. Sally removes garbage from garbage bin. She turns garbage can upside down, on top of garbage. It is used as the Judge's podium). Ben and Spikey follow, joining Sally singing. They are each carrying 2 lawn chairs.

SPIKEY: Where's the judge? Where's the judge? *(sets down lawn chairs with Ben)*

SALLY: We're 20 minutes early. Some are still home eating dinner. The judge isn't here yet! I'll be the Bailiff. I help swear in the witness. They put their hand on the bible. *(Keri and Robyn enter. They set down lawn chairs)*

BEN: I could be the defense lawyer, if Dad doesn't make it!

ROBYN: I could be the prosecuting lawyer. Actually, no, because my mom may take the witness stand. Maybe Keri should do it! Can you Keri? *(Keri nods yes)* You know I'm 100% in favor of supporting Spikey going to school, right ...? *(all agree, we know)*

MARK: *(Enter Mark in black robe, carrying a hammer for a gavel)* Here comes the judge! Here comes the judge!

BEN: Okay, we have our team! Let's practice.

ROBYN: I'll play my mom, the vice principal. *(clears throat)* I believe porcupines do not belong in our school! I refuse to sign your petition. *(crosses arms indignantly)*

BEN: But you have to!!

ROBYN: See, that's just it! I don't have to! Everyone is entitled to their own opinion!

BEN: You're right.

ROBYN: Everyone has the right to refuse. After all, that's what life and this trial is all about...rights! Everyone in this great country of ours has the right to make their own decision. It's called freedom! If anyone decides not to help Spikey, we HAVE to accept that.

BEN: But it's also our right to continue fighting for the cause we believe in!! We all have to have a dream! This is Spikey's dream, and we're here to support him!!
*(Cheers. ALL SING **'**You Gotta Have A Dream****CS with Spikey, Sarah, Larry enter, stay in SR wing/sing to each other. Grammy & Mr. T enter /stay in SL wing/sing to each other. (Spikey and Grammy do not see/acknowledge each other.) (Spikey, Bob, Larry, Sarah) (Grammy and Mr.T exit)*

BEN: Okay Sally, let's start again!

SALLY: All rise! *(All are talking)* Quiet! Now I know how teachers must feel!

MARK: <u>Order in the court!</u> *(bangs hammer gavel)*

SPIKEY: Your Honour, who buys? I'll have a cheeseburger and fries! *(Mark rolls his eyes)*

KERI: So, Mark, how did you learn to be a judge?

MARK: Mostly through trial and error...But I won't make any sudden or rash decisions.

TIA: What's a rash decision?

BEN: I know! It's when you cross a judge with poison ivy! *(all laugh)*

KERI: Okay, that's enough! We're off track! We need perfect peace and quiet!

SPIKEY: None of us said, 'we're perfect'. Even a mirror, sees a defect!

MARK: Okay guys! Keri's right. This is a court. Silence in the court! We are here to determine if Spikey is guilty, for wanting to learn.

TIA: That's just stupid!

KERI: Life is sometimes! Okay, Let's start practicing a - gain! Okay Sally, you're the bailiff, **again.**

SALLY: All rise!

KERI: Oh no, we can't start without Misty, Grammy my mom or Mr. Law! And Coach Bob too! Do you think they'll come back? *(Mark shakes his head, side to side, impatiently. Big sigh)*

ROBYN: And my mom! This IS school related! I think they all just went for a walk.

SPIKEY: They know I want to learn school stuff. Knowing nothing, makes life rough!

ROBYN: But your Grammy has taught you things. It's not a crime to learn!

KERI: Right Robyn! Spikey, you are not guilty of anything. My mom is a teacher, She said her goal was "To teach children how to make the world a better place."

MARK: And I asked my Dad why he wanted to become a lawyer, and he said... "To help people when no one else will."

BEN: Spikey, on behalf of my Dad, **<u>if</u>** he doesn't get here, I'll take your **<u>case</u>**!

SPIKEY: Will you bring it back, after you unpack?

BEN: Not that kind of case, Spikey. I'll defend you in our court!

SPIKEY: Cool! Do I need special court shoes. Will you give me some cues?

KERI: Spikey, if you win this court case, you might be able to do what no porcupine has ever done before. You will be able to go to school. And school is so cool!!!

BEN: You are taking a big step, to change the world! We each have to do our part. We'll help and encourage you!

GRAMMY: *(ENTER Grammy with Spikey's lunch kit in her big knitting bag) (Mr. T. follows) (All cheer)* There you are Spikey. Are you hungry? *(he shakes head no)* I've been looking everywhere for you.

SPIKEY: Well no wonder you couldn't find me yet. I haven't been everywhere yet.

GRAMMY: You didn't eat much for supper. *(Grammy hands him lunch kit. Spikey shakes his head 'no')*. I'm glad you came here early. I know you're anxious about this court case, and... you can eat later. *(Spikey nods yes, as Grammy puts lunch kit back in her knitting bag). (pause)* No Misty yet? *(Spikey shakes head "no." Grammy hugs him.)* Hope she makes it.

SPIKEY: Me too. I'm feelin' blue.

MR. T: *(to Spikey)* It's not 7:30 yet. *(sees Keri)* How's my only Grand daughter?

KERI: *(anxious)* Good, thanks Grandpa. Glad you're here. I hope mom's coming soon.

MARK: So, everyone here... as a practice judge, Spikey, if I find you guilty, I can give you a choice, *(Misty tiptoes in and listens. No one sees her)*. $500 or a month in jail.

SPIKEY: Oh, I'll take the money, your Honour, yes siree. *(all see Misty and cheer)*

MISTY: *(runs in playfully) (to all)* Hi!! *(to Spikey)* Spikey, you <u>want</u> dough? You're sooo funny.

SPIKEY: *(proud and happy)* You came to support me! You could help lead me to victory!

MISTY: I sure am going to try, Spikey! I'm here to listen and support you! *(Misty sings **<u>I Believe In You!</u>*** to Spikey.)*

ROBYN: Okay, let's get this show on the road!! So what if someone's missing, we've got to get rolling... Maybe mom's not coming....the vice principal <u>should</u> be here - Whatever! ...

TIA: Cameras, lights, action!

SCENE 8

KERI: *(Ben follows Keri, pretending to be a camera man. Keri holds pretend mic)* Good Afternoon. This is Keri Newscaster with the evening news, broadcasting live from the Personal Rights Advocacy Court building, right here in this lovely park in downtown Winnipeg. What began a few weeks ago as a young porcupine's curiosity has now grown into a full scale search for justice! Spikey the talking porcupine, will finally have his day in court. Today I will be speaking with Spikey's guardian, Mary...

GRAMMY: Just call me Grammy. Only Joe calls me Mary. Everyone else calls me Grammy. *(Ben does a camera CLOSE-UP on Grammy).*

KERI: Okay, Grammy. My first question for you is... How did you meet Spikey?

GRAMMY: Five years ago, I was driving home from the hospital where I worked - and I saw a cute little, well, big porcupine on the side of the road. I could tell he was badly injured. I could see he was trying to cross the road. He made it alive, but was in pain. *(head down, sadly)* His parents didn't make it across the road. They became separated. It was very sad. I nursed him back to health and *(proudly)* raised him, like my own son!

KERI: I understand that you and Mr. Joe Taylor are neighbors. Apparently there have been reports that Spikey likes to cause trouble.

GRAMMY: Oh, he's your typical mischievous teenager. He's growing up.

KERI: Grammy, I'm afraid that's all the time we have here today. Are there any final comments you'd like to share for the evening news? *(Ben comes close-up with pretend camera. Grammy boldly speaks to audience).*

GRAMMY: Yes. We're gathered here today, to find a way to open a school for Spikey! We need as much support as possible! We need to all help a little, to make a difference! Together we can make a big change! *(all cheer)*

KERI: Thank you Grammy. I mean Mary. *(Enter VP Radcliffe, SR, with lawnchair. Keri runs after her).*

ROBYN: Thanks Mom!!! Glad you could make it!!

MS RADCLIFFE: I'm here for you, Robyn.

KERI: Wonderful news! Ms Radcliffe is here! Ladies and gentlemen, with me at this time is Vice Principal Ms Radcliffe. We are so pleased you could join us today. Ms Radcliffe, what are your thoughts on today's trial, in this park?

MS RADCLIFFE: *(stops CS)* Oh good grief. I don't understand any of this. All I do is continue to enforce one of the oldest rules of a school. All animals, dogs, cats, birds and <u>porcupines</u> are not permitted in school! *(sees Misty)* Oh my goodness, there's two of them!

KERI: Yes, Spikey and Misty, his new friend from Lockport. So, this is NOT a personal issue with Spikey or the students?

MS RADCLIFFE: Oh don't be silly. Of course not.

KERI: I understand that your daughter Robyn has joined several other students in objection to your decision.

MS RADCLIFFE: No comment. But I must say, it's nice to see the students take an interest in something that doesn't involve <u>I pods and cell phones.</u> *(add current fad)*

KERI: What would you do if one of your teachers testified on Spikey's behalf?

MS RADCLIFFE: No comment. Actually everyone is entitled to their own opinion. *(sets her lawn chair dawn and sits)* But – It doesn't make them right.

KERI: There you have it ladies and gentlemen. An exclusive interview with Vice Principal, Ms Radcliffe. Any final comments? *(mic back to Ms Radcliffe)*

MS RADCLIFFE: I am curious to what you kids are up to. But it's a public park and I can't stop you. *(looks around)* Is everyone invited or did all these people just <u>show up</u> on their own?

BEN: *(puts camera down)* Most of them came because they <u>wanted </u>to. Some may be here because they felt pressured. Many of them signed our petition. Would you care to sign, Ms Radcliffe?

MS RADCLIFFE: Oh don't be silly! You know how I feel. Look - I'm <u>here</u> aren't I?

BEN: Sorry. You're right. We do respect your feelings Ms Radcliffe. But the students are here to support Spikey. Students, do you have faith in Spikey?

KIDS: Yes!! Spikey rules! *(Ben pretends to hold camera, spans audience)*

MS RADCLIFFE: How is Spikey going to pay for this trial? *(snickers)* Do porcupines even use money, or do they trade for things with sticks and stones?

MISTY: Maybe Spikey can use **<u>dough</u>** like Coach Bob!

ALL: Huh??!!

MS RADCLIFF: What kind of desk do porcupines need? They'll leave quills all over the place. Or do you plan on using their quills for pens? I can't believe I'm even discussing this!

ROBYN: Mom!!!

MARK: I think we need a recess...

SPIKEY: *(jumps up)* Recess like school? *(Mark shakes his head no).* That would be cool! *(Spikey sits).*

ROBYN: How many signatures do we have, Ben?

BEN: Ninety seven, including mine. *(Ben picks up Petition, hands it to Sally).*

SALLY: I have one hundred and fifty one. Here, see this!

BEN: Wow, thanks Sally! So that makes...okay 97 is almost 100, plus 150, so I'll estimate, and that makes 250!!

SALLY: Not enough. We still need more! *(Disappointed Ben puts Petition in his pocket).*

KERI: How are we going to get more signatures?

BEN: We can ask people right here in this park. *(Points to kids on stage, then audience)* They could also be our jury! We have to have a jury!

KERI: Can we do that? Okay, people in the park – let's vote. How many would like to be on the jury?

SALLY: All of us do – but we need 12! *(looks into the audience)*

MS RADCLIFFE: Good grief. This is unethical!

SALLY: I think it's a great idea! Do you?! *(Sally looks on stage and into audience. Kids on stage and some placed in the audience, raise hands and cheer).*

BEN: We have to send a message that everyone should be allowed an education. Being different IS okay!! Everyone has a right to learn!

MS RADCLIFFE: This isn't about Spikey or prejudice. It's about common sense. Good Grief. *(Enter Larry with briefcase, and Sarah with pen & paper on clipboard). (All cheer!)* Hello Sarah, Larry.

SARAH: Hi. So glad you could be here! *(shakes MS RADCLIFFE's hand)*

LARRY: Hello. Nice to see you again. *(shakes MS RADCLIFFE's hand)* We're here for the court case! I will be the defence lawyer. Keri said she could play the prosecuting lawyer. *(Keri shakes her head NO, then puts her head in her hands).*

SARAH: And me ... her mother, will play the silent court reporter.

SALLY: So when does it start?

MARK: *(looks at watch)* Right now! *(Mark leaves)*

BEN: Great! Okay, let's try this again, guys. Everyone take a seat. Sally is our bailiff... One more time! *(Keri removes her hands from her head and sits upright).*

SALLY: *(Mark enters)* ALL RISE!! This court is now in session. The Honourable Judge Mark Law, is presiding.

MARK: You may be seated. *(kids talking)* Order in the court! *(bangs gavel. as Sarah opens her notes and takes out pen)* Call the first witness please.

SALLY: Ben Law. *(Ben takes the stand and puts his hand on the bible to be sworn in).* Put your left hand on the bible and raise your right hand. *(Ben gets hands mixed up)* Let's try this again. LEFT hand on the bible.

BEN: Right! And Raise my RIGHT hand! At school it doesn't matter, we just raise...

SALLY *(cuts Ben off)* **Do you** swear to tell the truth, the whole truth and nothing but the truth?

SPIKEY: Swearing on a bible? Is that acceptable?! *(Grammy motions Shhh)*

BEN: I Do!

TIA: This is just like at a wedding! *(She giggles. Grammy motions Shhh)*

MARK: I will now call on Defense Lawyer, Mr. Larry Law.

LARRY: Thank you, your Honour. May I approach the bench? *(Ben nods)* Now Ben, for the benefit of the court, please tell me everything that happened September 6th of this year...your first day of school?

BEN: Well, our class went out to clean the school ground at our Elementary School at 10:30 am. Spikey saw us. I think he thought it was recess.

LARRY: Ben, please, tell us what happened just before Ms Radcliff arrived?

BEN: Sure. I saw Spikey and invited him to help clean up. He was so happy, he started singing! *(Spikey reacts, smiling)* Soon, all the kids joined him. Ms Bell took us outside to clean up the school grounds. She hadn't seen Spikey. But unfortunately Ms Radcliffe did. Spikey made picking up garbage so much fun!

LARRY: Were you enjoying being outside, <u>after</u> Ms Radcliffe sent Spikey away?

BEN: No, not at all! It wasn't fun anymore. We understand rules are rules, but no one ever told us porcupines weren't allowed at school! He was just trying to help! He wanted to be with us. We gave him a purpose! *(Spikey nods)* Everyone needs a purpose!

LARRY: Were any children afraid of Spikey?

KERI: *(stands)* Does this have any relevance to the case? *(Mark bangs gavel, she sits)* Ooops, sorry.

MARK: *(boldly)* Could we move this along, Counselor? Will the witness please answer the question.

BEN: Yes. I mean, no. They were not afraid of Spikey.

LARRY: No further questions, your Honour. *(Enter Keri)*

MARK: Call the next witness please.

SALLY: Ms Radcliffe. *(She takes the stand and puts her hand on the bible. She's sworn in.) She puts her left hand on the bible and raises her right hand.)* Do you swear to tell the truth, the whole truth and nothing but the truth?

MS RADCLIFFE: I do.

KERI: Ms Radcliffe, we've heard versions of events that transpired. Could you please tell the court what really happened, that day?

LARRY: I object, your Honour. *(smiles at Mark, then Sarah)*

MARK: Sustained. Miss Keri Bell, I suggest you re-word your question.

KERI: Ms Radcliffe, what happened from your point of view?

MS RADCLIFFE: I was in my office when I heard laughter and singing. When I went outside I saw this huge porcupine!

KERI: Was he disrupting the class?

MS RADCLIFFE: No, not really, but I reminded the students that pets do not belong on school grounds.

KERI: Did you feel they were using the porcupine to undermine your authority?

LARRY: Objection, your Honour.

MARK: Overruled. The witness will answer the question.

MS RADCLIFFE: Yes, I did!

KERI: I understand you have strict policies with your students.

MS RADCLIFFE: Our school has an excellent reputation! I'm new here – and I'm not going to be the one to make changes!

KERI: No further questions, Your Honour.

LARRY: Do you have a daughter, Ms Radcliffe?

MS RADCLIFFE: Is that relevant to the...? Yes, a wonderful daughter, Robyn. She's here.

LARRY: Would you let her choose her own behavior, her own schooling?

MS RADCLIFFE: No, she's still a child.

LARRY: Does she need <u>you</u> to be responsible for her? Does she need your guidance?

MS RADCLIFFE: Well, of course!

LARRY: No further questions, your Honour.

MARK: Please be seated. Bailiff, call the next witness.

SALLY: Spikey Porcupine. Do you swear to tell the truth, the whole truth and nothing but the truth?

SPIKEY: Cross my heart, hope to die, stick a needle in my eye.

MARK: That won't be necessary, Mr. Spikey. Please have a seat.

KERI: Spikey, when you were in the playground, what was going through your mind?

SPIKEY: I was as happy as could be! I thought going to school would be great for me!"

KERI: You were guilty of being on school property. *(kids fake a gasp)* Did you leave immediately after you were asked?

SPIKEY: I was scared of course! I ran faster than a racehorse!

KERI: Do you think you were asked to leave for the children's protection?

SPIKEY: Yes. I must confess.

KERI: No further questions, Your Honour. *(Keri sits. Larry gets up)*

LARRY: How do you feel through all of this, Spikey?

SPIKEY: I feel like I don't belong. I just want to be loved, is that so wrong?

LARRY: What valuable lesson have you learned?

SPIKEY: One lesson I have learned – respect can't be demanded, it must be earned.

LARRY: I couldn't have said it better myself. No further questions.

MARK: I'd like to call on Larry Law to defend his case.

LARRY: *(quickly, forcefully)* Thank you, your Honour. The only crime here today, is preventing a kind gentle porcupine from getting an education!! *(all cheer)* We need to put ourselves in Spikey's shoes before we judge this case. *(beat)* I agree we need rules. If we didn't have rules, people would do whatever they wanted. Rules protect people's rights and remind us of our responsibilities. But school is more than about learning. The students <u>would benefit</u> from interacting with Spikey and Misty. School is learning about other cultures, animals, developing social skills during group projects, and playing fairly at recess! *(beat)*
Spikey and Misty don't want to cause trouble. They want a chance to learn! Spikey wanted to help his friends pick up garbage, just to be with them! He had no harmful motive. He just wanted to be <u>included!!</u> We all need to be included! *(Pause) (beat, softer tone)* Have you ever been teased? Felt different? Last chosen for gym games? Now consider being left out <u>forever,</u> as Spikey and Misty are! We all need a sense of belonging. Spikey and Misty are now <u>excluded.</u> *(Pause, beat) (STRONG Voice!)* Let's give these porcupines a chance! Let's respect them! They deserve a VOICE too! Your Honour, we are not asking that the rules be eliminated, just adjusted in this case – for everyone's benefit! I'm sure we can find a compromise to work this problem out. Spikey does not want to create hard feelings. Spikey just wants an education! Thank you, your Honour. *(Loud Cheers from all kids)*

MARK: *(bangs gavel)* ORDER! Order in the court! I'd like to call on Ms Keri Bell to defend her clients case.

KERI: Your Honour, *(All look confused)* I can't even pretend to say anything against Spikey! I agree with the Defense lawyer! So, I'd like to call on Ms Radcliffe. Spikey's my friend. I'm sorry. I don't know what else to say … I can't do this.

MARK: Permission granted. Ms Radcliffe, please take the stand.

MS RADCLIFFE: Thank you, your Honour. *(firmly and quickly!)* I have 300 students I'm responsible for. Their parents would be in an uproar, <u>if</u> Spikey were allowed in <u>our</u> school.

And then there's Misty. How do we know there aren't more like these two, trying to prove a point? We don't have room. Our classrooms are too large already. I'm very busy. It's stressful. I work long hours. Running a school takes a great deal of time and dedication. I've had too many years of responsibilities that don't allow for much free time. In fact, I'm also here on behalf of our principal, who is working overtime tonight! *(Beat)* Now in Spikey's defense, kids can be cruel. Can porcupines handle the name calling and the teasing they will ultimately be subjected to!? I think not. *(beat)* Students and parents get very upset with teachers and administration, if they feel they're being unfairly treated. No one wins if the school can't stop mean students or bullies. How do we know Spikey and Misty won't be bullied, or - bully others? *(all protest)* Fairness is on trial, here! Each student has their own style of learning. We can't keep changing the level of the bar! We are <u>accountable</u> for what happens to our students. We measure and assess <u>each</u> student. We try to provide every student with learning tools to give them the skills they need. *(pause)* Maybe I'm being too protective of our school; but I prefer to error on the side of caution. There's no room for porcupines at our Elementary School. I'm sorry. *(silence)*

BEN: Now what?!! *(Throws his hands in the air. All look beaten and depressed....shrug shoulders, etc.) (Kids circle around Spikey)*

KERI: There's been a huge mistake! Spikey, I wish you could see yourself through our eyes. We all think you're perfect! Sorry Spikey. We don't know what to do now!

SPIKEY: I'd like fighting to cease – so we can all live in peace. *(beat)* Well, we could... just sing a song! Everyone - sing along! *(ALL sing, **<u>Give – Don't Give Up!</u>**) (Ms Radcliffe and Sarah look at each other, then sing, as they both sit, write notes).*

SARAH: Spikey, you're our moral compass! You don't put any labels on yourself or others. You give us direction.

SPIKEY: *(trying to be optimistic)* North, South, East and West. I'm just tryin' to do my best!

KIDS & SPIKEY: North, South, East and West. We're just trying' to do our best!

SARAH: Yes! You're thinking of others before yourselves...trying to support a cause. You're sincere. When you're honest and real, you're beautiful. But pleasing everyone is impossible!

KERI: But upsetting everyone, is a piece of cake!

MARK: We can either find a way, or an excuse. We have to believe there's another way! *(All kids cheer).*

SARAH: *(smiles, as she speaks to all kids)* Exactly! Don't Give up. Know in your heart, you're doing what's right. The adults here aren't judging you. We know the motive behind your actions is positive! You're not wrong or hurtful. No one here has any malicious intentions... *(Spikey and Kids try to smile but are feeling defeated)*

117

SCENE 9

(Bob. Enters) (He's wearing a construction hat. He carries in drafting papers). (All cheer)

SPIKEY: Hey there, Coach Bob! Can you <u>please</u> help with this court job?!

BEN: Yeah, We've lost our case! *(all speak out)*

MARK: *(bangs gavel/hammer)* Order in the Court!

BOB: Well! Have I got a plan for you?!! Your Honour, may I address the court?

MARK: Go ahead.

BOB: I've changed hats to help you! I have a very special surprise for you!

BEN: We need a surprise! We've been here an hour and nothing's happened yet!

SPIKEY: We sure need a miracle now! Our plan kinda went **ka-pow!!**

KERI: Are you getting frustrated, Spikey?

SPIKEY: Nope, Coach Bob has a new hat. Just wait until <u>he</u> gets up to <u>bat</u>!!!

BOB: Well, I've designed a special plan! My team and I have plans for the COOLEST SCHOOL! *(all cheer)* It will be separate, but could be <u>attached to</u> the school you're in now. *(all look confused.)* The present school is FULL, but there IS extra land space, to build beside it! *(all kids are happy!)* Sometimes we have to make compromises to make things work effectively. If we're not willing to be flexible, and go to a Plan B, there may be no progress at all! Of course I will need school board and city council approval. But if all of you agree, I will get going on the NEW School! *(cheers, except from Ms Radcliffe)* I was thinking of a name, how about, <u>Porcupine Community School?</u> *(cheers, except from Ms Radcliffe)* Okay, Please pass these plans around and tell me what you think? *(Ms Radcliffe looks at Drafting plans with Bob. He also shows his Drafting plan to others).*

SPIKEY: Grammy taught me to hold a knife and fork, so I could hold and cut up my pork.
But I want to learn more school stuff! Then maybe life won't be so rough.
I'd like to find what I'm really good at. I know I'm good with a ball and bat.
Grammy's teaching me how to tell time. And how to add a nickel and a dime.
But there is so much more to learn and do! So many things that are brand new.
Like making friends and work in a group. I don't want to be called a nincompoop.

MS RADCLIFFE: *(gets up)* Okay enough! I've got the point! Listen. I didn't realize how much this meant to Spikey and all of you! When I asked Spikey to leave our school, it never occurred to me that I was segregating someone based on his or her appearance. After listening to all the discussion and testimonies here, I realize now that it would be wrong to deny him of something he wants and needs so much... an education. *(cheers)* An education, is your security blanket. It's your shelter in the storm. Your job, family, pets, self esteem, money, material things - can all be taken from you. But your education remains! What you learn through life in school, travel and growing up - are educational treasures! No one can take them away from you! *(all cheer)* However, *(smiles at Bob)* it's because of Bob's brilliant new community school idea...that I have decided to support Larry, Sarah, Bob and all of you! I will do what I can to help Bob pursue his building plans! *(cheers from all on stage)*

SPIKEY: Wowee! I'm very happy! You all did this for Misty and Spikey!
(Ms Radcliffe smiles and high fives with Spikey).
I could learn more than to subtract, multiply and divide,
I could learn about this wonderful world, far and wide.
I want to be as smart as I can be.
I'm glad that doesn't make me guilty.
Thanks to Coach Bob and Larry,
A new animal school could make history!! *(all cheer)*

LARRY: See, Misty ... Bob is just like the Lockport dam. Both created a bridge so we could get across. *(to all)* Sometimes, we shouldn't try to see which side is better – or right or wrong. Sometimes we need to concentrate on finding the best solution. It's teamwork! Whether in a classroom, a ball team, or a dance team – we need to pull together ... build together! A bridge must be created to close the gap.

KERI: And as long as the bridge is in place – we **are** connected! Thank you Coach Bob, for saving our day! *(all cheer)*

BOB: Thank you, but Larry is our peaceful hero! He opened the door to make it possible to build that bridge. You supported Spikey! Thank You! *(cheers)*

SPIKEY: *(To Larry)* Yes, just in case – **You took my case!** *(Larry smiles. They 'knuckle greet')*

TIA: ALL of us wanted to help! *(all cheer)*

BOB: Just remember, everyone – the most precious things in life can NOT be built. *(All look confused.)* It's about finding happiness, it's about things you see and hear.

GRAMMY: Bob's trying to say, it's the special feelings in our hearts. It's about feeling appreciated, respected and loved.

SARAH: Yes, Love is the greatest gift of all. And a sense of belonging, being included! *(smiles at Larry, Grammy and Mr. T.)*

LARRY: How true. Thank you Bob and Sarah.

SALLY: *(proudly)* I always believed in Spikey!

KERI: Spikey, we all believe in you and love you!

LARRY: I've always believed everyone should have the education they want and deserve. I will <u>stand</u> behind the new school, and support it! I will start by helping Bob check out gov't funding! *(cheers)*

MS RADCLIFFE: *(gets up from writing notes)* Count me in too! *(All gasp)*

BOB/LARRY/ALL: Thank you Ms Radcliffe!

SARAH: I would also like to help be a part of this strong bridge and wonderful team! I've already talked about this with Larry, last week. This school will require specially trained teachers. I've decided I'd like to work part time at Porcupine Community School! *(all cheer)* following it's completion of course. I'd teach at both schools, if possible! I'd like to help strengthen the bridge for this very cool new school! *(more cheers)* I will be taking many courses to provide me with the skills required to teach porcupines and other animals interested in learning. Teaching touches lives forever. *(Ms Radcliffe cheers!)* To help someone learn and believe in themselves, is the best gift I could give anyone! *(cheers)* *(Sarah shakes hands with Ms Radcliffe. They sit and share notes).*

LARRY: Thank you, Ms Bell. *(Sarah smiles back at Larry)*

MARK: What do you think jury? Do you need a recess?

BEN: *(looks at audience, stage)* No, I don't think so. Who's in favour of Spikey's new cool community school? Raise your hands and yell out, 'yes!'

ALL: YES!!! *(including Ms Radcliffe, as she gets up and looks at Drafting Plans with Bob).*

MARK: *(bangs gavel / hammer)* This court is officially dismissed. COURT IS ADJOURNED! *(bangs gavel again).*

ALL: Hooray! Yippee! *(Ms Radcliffe moves to talk to Sarah. Sarah is writing notes. Kids join them. Sarah, kids and Ms Radcliffe stand near Spikey and Misty).*

SARAH: Misty and Spikey, we all have a few questions for you to see if you're ready for school. Now everyone will work at their own pace. First one. What is a synonym?

SPIKEY: Grammy pours it on apple pies, and in coffee cakes that rise! *(Sarah smiles as she shakes her head, from side to side).*

MISTY: I can help! A synonym is the word you <u>use</u> - when you can't spell the other one!

MS RADCLIFFE: Okay. These are just sample questions, to see what level we will start you at. Next question. Contractor Bob could answer this one. What about a Music Room?

BEN: Music Room?! Great Idea! Contractors like heavy metal! *(he laughs as all look confused).*

MS RADCLIFFE: Well what about making a <u>bandstand</u>?

SPIKEY: That's easy, take away their chairs! They could stand on the stairs! *(Ms Radcliffe shakes her head)*

SALLY: Do you like <u>music</u> Spikey?

SPIKEY: Sort of, but I have no time! I'd much rather rhyme!

KERI: This is a science question. How many bones are in your body?

SPIKEY: Hundred's or a whole bunch! I had <u>sardines</u> for lunch!

BEN: Okay, this is a trick Math question. If I had 20 marbles in one pocket, 17 dollars in coins in another, and 11 rocks in my back pocket, what would I have?

MISTY: Very heavy pockets! *(she high-fives with Spikey, as all laugh)*

KERI: This one is about fractions. Do you know what a fraction is?

MISTY: It's when you break something!

MARK: I have one about division. If a pie was divided into 6 pieces and only one was gone, what would that mean?

MISTY: The pie wasn't very good. *(all laugh)*

MARK: What is matter?

SPIKEY: Everything is made of matter! It means that we all matter!

TIA: What does colourblind mean?

MISTY: When all people and animals look the same, inside and out.

BEN: What is further away? Australia or the moon? And why?

MISTY: Australia is further away, because you can **see the moon**! What a silly question!

SARAH: Last one. What is Global Warming?

MISTY: When the whole world finally starts, warming up to everyone! *(Sarah and Ms Radcliffe smile and nod 'yes' at each other. They give Misty and Spikey a 'thumbs up').*

KERI: *(to Bob and Larry)* It looks like Spikey and Misty are on their way to school! *(Spikey and Misty hold hands and jump up and down together).*

SPIKEY: Thanks Larry and Bob. You started this job! *(puts arm around them)* *(Bob sees Ms Radcliffe)*

BOB: And thank you Ms Radcliffe for helping us build a bridge. *(they smile at each other)*

MS RADCLIFFE: No problem, Bob.

GRAMMY: Let's celebrate Spikey's first big step at my place! *(cheers)* We've got asparagus and pickle sandwiches, perogies, veggies, fruit, hot dogs and cake!

MR. T: There's always great food at Grammy's. That's one of the reasons why I'm marrying her. *(all cheer)*

GRAMMY: Well we'll celebrate two porcupines going to school <u>and</u> two engagements?

ALL: What? Who else?

SARAH: *(proudly)* Larry and I.

SALLY/TIA: Get out?! *(all cheer)*

LARRY: *(takes Sarah's hand)* I have the "honour" of sharing my life with this wonderful woman and teacher! We've decided, we're going to get married next summer!

MR. T: So did we!! *(all cheer as they start to exit SR)* *(PUNKY, a baby porcupine, male or female, enters SL. He or she crawls towards Sarah. Only the audience sees Punky. He puts his arm/paw around Sarah's leg. Sarah jumps up and screams. Her scream scares him and he backs away and huddles into a little ball).* And then there were THREE!

SARAH: Oh my goodness – what happened.?! Oh no little guy I didn't mean to scare you away. *(Keri is the first one to run back in).* Come back. Do you have a mommy? *(Punky shakes his head no).*

KERI: Mom, he's so cute! Where did he come from? *(Sarah shrugs her shoulders, not knowing)* Can we adopt him?! *(Sarah looks terrified!)* Please?!

BEN: Look at his head! He has coloured Spikes like I used to have! How cute!

MARK: Do you talk? *(Punky shakes head no)*

MISTY: Well, not yet!!! Spikey and I can help teach him. We speak the same language.

BEN: Do you understand us? *(He nods head yes).*

KERI: Did you find coloured markers on the picnic table, and paint your spikes? *(he nods)*

SALLY: Did other kids help you do this? *(he nods)*

KERI: Do you want us to wash the colours off? *(he nods no)*

BEN: Can we name you PUNKY?! You look like a little Punk rocker! *(Punky nods "yes " exuberantly!)*

KERI: So you like your coloured points!? *(Punky nods yes)* That's so cool! Can we keep him, Mom? *(Mark turns over garbage can)* *(Punky hides behind garbage can).*

SARAH: Well, maybe, maybe not ... we'll talk ...

GRAMMY: It takes a village! No worries! Punky can stay with Spikey and I! *(Mr. T nods)*

SPIKEY: That's awesome!!! Another porcupine has a mom! *(all cheer)* I'm feeling so terrific! And Ms Radcliffe's change of heart was fantastic! But I knew Larry and Bob, would not fail! In the end – we will prevail!

BEN: *(rips up petition)* I guess we don't need this any more! *(throws torn sheets in garbage can)* *(Sarah and Keri go to Punky. Each take his hand and bring him to centre stage as cast sing. All greet Punky during song.)* *(ALL CAST ON STAGE SING **WORLD ARE YOU READY?*** FEATURE Dance number!)* Spikey, we ARE ready!

ALL: We're all ready!

BEN / MARK: For porcupines in our world!! *(All Cheer!)*

GRAMMY: Yes we are!

MR: T: And we're ready to go to Grammys and Celebrate!

GRAMMY: C'mon, everyone – you too PUNKY! *(Ms Radcliffe starts to walk away SL).* You too, Ms Radcliffe! Let's go to Grammy's and celebrate! *(Grammy exits SR. Cast follow).*

BEN: Great, Cuz Punky and I are <u>very hungry</u>!!! *(Bob exits with Ms Radcliffe. Ben and Keri take Punky's hands, lift him up – then exit, SR with the rest of the cast).*

B L A C K – O U T !

T H E   E N D

LIGHTS UP FOR CURTAIN CALL

Cast return for curtain Call, with instrumental theme music.

PUNKY *is first to crawl / walk out SL. Stands centre then moves aside*

Tia *enters SR,*

Alternate Cast *enter SL/SR*

Grammy *third last, to enter*

Keri *second last to enter*

SPIKEY *is always last to enter.*

ALL BOW, Music Fades when all cast are on stage.

All Cast sing: *"Together We can Make it!"*

Instrumental theme song music for the third time, as cast exit stage, walk through the audience to meet/greet with young guests.

Lyrics /Script: Joy Winter-Schmidt
Aug. 2007, re-write Jan. 2011 /'13/'15

Theme Song "Together We Can Make It"
Music: David Schmidt 1993

All other Music/Arrangement by Paulo Bergantim

*"Spikey in School" was in Joy's vision since she started a school Drama
program in 2000! The 'kids court scene' - Sc. 8, in Sequel 3, was partially
based on a 'shorter adult court scene' from 'We Want Spikey' by Derek Grech,
2003,' edited, produced and performed by the Cast, Crew and Joy.*

Happily Ever After!

Spikey's Points: Sequel 4 – Final Sequel *75 min. (Script. Approx. 45 min. Music: 30 min. 11 songs)*

Guest on bench, reading the "Community Quill." Someone else could be on other bench, or rock, playing flute or guitar. (Exits with...)

Child VOICE CUE: *(Spoken Backstage or Recorded. Track #1) (Voiceover opens ALL sequels)* "Once Upon A time, not that long ago, lived a walking, talking, singing porcupine, with mostly good points. His name was Spikey. His parents didn't make it across the road. Spikey barely made it. He lay injured on the side of the road. A dear old lady everyone called Grammy, found him and nurtured him back to health. He became a friend to many because he always tried to do the best he could. He lived, he loved, he laughed. He became a great example to follow..."

MUSIC CUE: **Together We Can Make It**Theme song intro Instrumental, track#2)

Morning Park Scene, trees, rock, benches. (Sound: Birds chirping.)

Gradual Lights Up on Set: *Spikey enters SR carrying baseball and glove. (He sets ball and glove on bench). Grammy, Misty and Punky follow, laughing. Grammy carries half of red ribbon. Misty and Punky carry opposite end. They wrap themselves and Spikey, in ribbon.) (Music Fades.) This same red fabric could be used as 'red carpet' for the brides and grooms to walk down 'the aisle' for the wedding scene.*

SCENE 1:

Spikey, Misty, Punky and Grammy move DSC, with long red ribbon, wrapped around them. Keri, Sally, Tia, Mark, Ben, Robyn and Chorus follow.

SPIKEY: *(All Cheer)* That was the best school Grand Opening that ever could be! I got to cut the ribbon, eat cake and drink ice tea!!

GRAMMY: Yes, it was fun, wasn't it! Oh, it's such a beautiful summer morning! Spikey, Misty, Punky? Are you excited about starting your new school in September!

MISTY: *(all cheer)* Now, is everyone ready for <u>educated porcupines</u> and other animals?! *(Spikey, Grammy and Punky nod) Misty sings verses of **You Gotta Have A Dream.** Grammy, Spikey and all on stage, join in on chorus.)* So are we ready for our NEW alternative school?

ALL: YES!!!

SPIKEY: Miss Sarah Bell will be teaching quite a few. Part time at our attached school and her other school, too!

MISTY: A school where porcupines and other animals will feel safe and successful!! *(all cheer)* A school where we can all learn at our own pace!

PUNKY: Cuz life is not a race!!!

MISTY: You are so right, Punky! I'm ready for our new school! I'm so happy my 'adopted parents' and I are moving near the new school.

SPIKEY: Me too! We're both adopted and I'm ready for school with you! I'll be in school with my new best friend Misty and Punky too!!! We're ready to make a <u>point</u> at <u>Porcupine Community School?!</u> That's sooo Cool?! *(cheers)*
*(Music Cue for **Let's Make A Point!** Misty moves DSC with Punky. Cast enters. Misty leads song. All sing. Girls dance with red ribbons on stick batons.) (All exit after song, except Grammy and Spikey. Misty leaves with Punky, Larry, Ben and Mark leave together. Dancers exit together. Sarah, Keri and Mr. T, leave together. Robyn exits with her mom, Ms Radcliffe.)*

SCENE 2:

GRAMMY: What a wonderful day! The morning opening for Porcupine Community School, is tied in with our wedding today! That way, everyone could be here! It's a day of celebrations! *(beat)* Our home is ready for a wedding reception! Just don't get too close to all the balloons!! *(they laugh)* Thanks for helping put our favourite, prickly cactus centre pieces, on the tables!

SPIKEY: You're welcome Grammy dear. Look, guests are already here! I bet they came from far and near.

GRAMMY: *(laughs)* Oh Spikey, they're not all here for the wedding! The wedding's not until 5 o'clock! It's a public park we share. But they're welcome to watch!

SPIKEY: I can hardly wait to eat your good food. It always puts me in a wonderful mood!

GRAMMY: Good! I made lots for the reception!

SPIKEY: Yeah, you've got all kinds of food for the wedding!
Your porcupine meat balls, are fit for a king.
Salads, cabbage rolls and perogies, to name a few.
And my favorite, asparagus and pickle sandwiches, too!

GRAMMY: *(smiles)* So Spikey, What did you want to talk to me about?

SPIKEY: Someday I'd like to be with Misty and adopt Punky. But now my education, and a good job is the key!

GRAMMY: Yes, education first, then the job. Now, you're Punky's hero, and you are setting a good example. Having a dream is important to keep our spirit alive! We all have a purpose in life!

SPIKEY: Construction, would be my dream job! ... with my friend Coach Bob!

GRAMMY: It's important to set goals. Coach Bob has been very encouraging to you! Construction sounds wonderful! You need to do what makes YOU happy! *(Spikey nods)*

SPIKEY: Building together, would be so much fun! He let me help build, to get the school done!

GRAMMY: Yes he did. We build with one brick at a time. That's like taking one small step at a time. Good for you to have goals, Spikey! *(beat)* Yes, Bob did a wonderful job of building Porcupine School! Bob trained to be in construction, like me being a nurse.

Bob can teach you! *(pause)* But we don't just walk in and pick a job, or whatever we want. Nothing comes overnight. We need to work at it. Life's not, a candy store.

SPIKEY: I'd be happy working in a candy store! I'd be happy working in a food store, even more!

GRAMMY: *(laughs)* A career, friend, and partner can make us feel complete. True friends stay with us. That makes us happy! *(hand to heart)* True love never dies. And that's why I'm getting married today! *(smiles)* In this lovely park! But a "Happily Ever After" feeling must be found within us...a peace, inside. Then we appreciate all things more. *(beat)* Was there anything else you wanted to talk about, Spikey?

SPIKEY: Ummm...So, you are ready for your big day! *(Grammy nods happily, as Spikey looks down).* Grammy, I really don't want to <u>give</u> you away.

GRAMMY: *(laughs)* Oh Spikey, don't be silly! You're not giving me away! I'm not leaving you! You and Punky will still be living with us. We're family! We all <u>need happy relationships;</u> to feel loved, appreciated... respected. If you don't have feelings, emotion and love – what's the point? *(beat)* Spikey, you're just<u> walking me down the aisle!</u> That's all! I adopted and chose you! You're like my son! I <u>chose</u> you, as Mr. T and I chose each other.

SPIKEY: *(huge sigh of relief!)* Ahhh, Lucky me! Thank you Grammy! So, you will be walking down the aisle with me? Just until I drop you off to Mr. T?

GRAMMY: Yeah, kinda like that. Come on, we're here, so let's practice. *(She links arm to Spikey's).* Let's try this out. *(She let's go of Spikey)*
First Larry will walk down the aisle. *(She walks)* His sons will follow him. Larry will stand here. *(She points to Stage R and stands in Larry's spot).* His sons Mark and Ben, will stand beside him. Then Keri and Punky will walk in. Punky, will be the best little ringbearer!
Mr. Joe T will walk in with his daughter Sarah. Sarah will stand beside Larry, as Joe stands to the side to meet me. Well I hope he does! *(She laughs and stands SL).* Then I will walk down the aisle with you, my dear Spikey. That means Joe will stand between you and I, Spikey. Then you can *('points' then guides Spikey into position)*... stand on the opposite side of Joe.. *(Spikey is confused., puts hands to his head. Grammy doesn't notice).* His Grand-daughter Keri, will sing during the signing of the register. Sarah, will be so proud of her daughter! Oh, and, Keri will stand near her mom, Sarah. Punky will stand near Keri. *(She finally looks back at Spikey).* It's just like the rehearsal last night. Does all that make sense?

GRAMMY: *(Spikey shakes his head no). (Beat)* Anyway, on this bench *(points SR)* will be Larry and Sarah. Keri and Punky will be in chairs between the two benches, beside Sarah. Mark and Ben will be in chairs, beside Larry. On this bench *(points SL)* will be

Mr. T and me. You will be in the chair beside us. Keri will stand between the benches to sing. Well, that's the plan. Life doesn't always go according to plan!

SPIKEY: *(sighs)* I'm just so nervous. What's my purpose? What if I trip us? I'll cause a fuss!

GRAMMY: Don't worry Spikey – you'll be just fine! I'm nervous too! I've never married before!

SPIKEY: You're so perfect, just like your wedding cake, you did make! I'm so scared, I'll make a mistake!

GRAMMY: I'm not perfect. No one is! Look, just go out there and don't think about being perfect. Just think about being <u>average</u>! Relax! Be yourself! Just say, "I can do this!" Grammy believes in you! *(Spikey smiles, looks confident). (Enter Mr. T, SL)*

MR. T: Hello, Hi there Mary and Spikey.

GRAMMY: Hi Joe!

SPIKEY: Well, hello there, Mr. T. Our very soon, groom to be! *(shakes hands with Mr. T.)* Are you nervous about the wedding – like Grammy and me?

MR. T: Ahhh, there's nothing to be nervous about. And, how's my bride to be? *(she smiles)* *(he hugs Grammy)* So, Mary? Are you still ready to marry me?

GRAMMY: I don't know. You know how women like to change their mind. *(Elbows Mr. T)*

MR. T: What do you think of marrying a grumpy old guy like me?

GRAMMY: Umm, I don't know. I guess it depends on how much like <u>you</u> he is! *(all laugh)*

MR. T: *(to Spikey)* She'll never change! *(to Grammy)* Just letting you know that Sarah and I got all the ceremony flowers. I dropped them off at Sarah's place.

GRAMMY: Thanks so much, Joe! I've used all my garden flowers for the reception!

MR. T: Garden flowers are nicer than the florist ones. It's been a great morning! Great breakfast at the school ceremony and soon a wedding, and a getaway! Well, time to get my convertible washed, waxed and polished!

GRAMMY: To get away in your convertible, will be so lovely, Joe!

SPIKEY: A clean yellow wedding car! Do you have to go very far?

MR. T: Nahh, there's a car wash just around the corner.

GRAMMY: I'm glad you came back to see us at the park.

MR. T: Me too.

SPIKEY: First a fun school opening! And soon, a double wedding!

GRAMMY: Such a nice day for both! It's a beautiful day to be walking home through the park.

MR. T: Yes it is. I can see why you didn't want a ride home. I was driving to drop off the flowers at Sarah's. I saw you were still here. I just wanted to let you know where I was going.

GRAMMY: How thoughtful! Yeah, we both have to get used to that, don't we?!

MR. T: I guess we do. I will try to do my best!

GRAMMY: *(to Mr. T.)* You always do! You restore my faith in humanity.

MR. T: Marriage is togetherness. That may be hard for us to get used to. We've been on our own for a <u>long</u> time! We're like two porcupines. Sometimes we'll need our own space. Right? *(Grammy nods)* Speaking of porcupines, where's Punky?

GRAMMY: Misty said I needed a break. She volunteered to take Punky to the library to get a book to read to him. I've told Punky, it'll be a shorter reading time today! He's very excited, so I don't think he will nap much today!. Misty's bringing Punky back to the park, to meet me. Then we'll go to my place....I mean '<u>our</u>' place.

MR. T: It will be 'ours' soon. It's everyone's place. That's what I love about it!

GRAMMY: Ahhh, you're such a sweet man! I should marry you! *(Spikey looks confused)* Would you like to join me for a special wedding today?! *(she smiles endearingly at Mr. T)*
Hey? Aren't we supposed to wait for the wedding, before we see each other?

MR. T: Too late now! We've already been at the Grand Opening together, had breakfast, and then cake! Well, better run. *(starts to exit)* I've got my cell on me, if you need anything.

GRAMMY: Thanks. I need to run soon, too. I'm pretty much ready, but there's always last minute things to do. We're starting and ending the day with CAKE!

SPIKEY: Sounds good to Mr. T, and to me!!

MR. T: *(Gives Grammy a hug, pats Spikey's shoulder.)* Sure does!! See you two later! *(Mr. T exits SL, Spikey and Grammy yell goodbyes to Mr. T.) (Grammy watches him leave. She puts hand to her heart).*

SCENE 3:

GRAMMY: *(to Spikey, looking dreamy as she holds Spikey's hand)* Everyone needs a hand to hold and a heart that understands them. I love being in this park. *(Spikey nods in agreement)*. It relaxes me. We need a special comfort place ... a great place for a wedding ...

SPIKEY: A double wedding place for two grooms and two brides. Grammy, Mr. T, Larry and Sarah will be standing by each others sides!! *(beat)* Together forever, like geese and penquins. *(Grammy makes a questioning face)* Soon you'll be signing with QUILL PENS! *(holds one of his quills, as Grammy laughs)*.

GRAMMY: I can tell you're remembering things you read and learn. Well, after the ceremony - we'll eat and dance. Then you and Punky will be staying for a few days with Sally and Tia's family. Remember? *(Spikey nods)*. I'm so glad Ms Radcliffe was able to get CONCERT Tickets for you and all of your park friends!! *(Spikey happily reacts)*. She's taking all of you, plus Coach Bob - to the LIVE, one and only ------ *(Lady La La, Justin Timberwood, etc. whatever name was used in Sequel #1,)* **Concert!** *(Star's name taken from a CURRENT Singer!)*

SPIKEY: *(nods happily)* I can hardly wait! I'll be first in line at the ticket gate! I remember watching the rehearsal in this park! We were sung to, before it got dark!

GRAMMY: Yes! And while you're at 'this' concert, Sarah and Larry are flying away, for their honeymoon. Mr. T and I will be driving on our honeymoon.

SPIKEY: Is there honey on the moon? Will that be soon? *(Grammy nods)* What's a honeymoon?

GRAMMY: Ohhh Spikey. A honeymoon is a place where newly weds take their honey pies! *(Spikey rubs his tummy)*. They go away with stars in their eyes! *(pause)* That rhymes. *(Spikey nods)*

SPIKEY: Honey pies! They sound good to eat! Honey pies sound like a real treat! *(beat)* Grammy I don't have a wedding gift for you and Mr. T. What present would you like from me?

GRAMMY: Your presence is our gift. This moment today is a gift! That's why it's called the present. *(Spikey shakes his head. He doesn't understand)*. YOU being with us today, is our gift!

SPIKEY: Thank You very much, Grammy! How about I volunteer to clean up, after the party!?

GRAMMY: Thank you! That's a <u>very</u> special gift! Seems like just yesterday, we volunteered to clean up this park. Remember our one year anniversary with you staying with me? *(Spikey nods)* Now, we're decorating for a wedding! *(beat)* Mr. T and I will only be gone for a week to the States. *(pause)* I always feel a little sick the night before a trip.

SPIKEY: *(ponders)* Maybe leave earlier by a day! That will get the travel sickness out of the way!

GRAMMY: *(shakes head, smiles)* You always have such good points, don't you?! Anyway, Keri, Ben and Mark will stay with friends for two weeks. Then they'll join "their new set of parents," for a family camping trip. I bet you can hardly wait until they get back?!

SPIKEY: Yes, I'm excited to join Larry, Ben and Mark for a day of fishing!! Maybe I'll catch the big one this time – I sure am wishing! We're going to a big lake near the hills. Punky and I will catch fish on our quills!

GRAMMY: *(laughs)* I can't stay too long, my quilly friend. *(pause)* This park calms me down. *(Spikey nods)* We've got a wedding to get ready for, soon. Spikey, can you carry some chairs from our place, to the park later?

SPIKEY: Of course, I'm on it right away! There's a "Double Wedding, on it's way!"

GRAMMY: Don't stay too long playing ball at the school. Glad you're meeting friends there! *(Spikey nods)* No more writing on signs! Like the "BUMP IN THE ROAD," sign? *(Spikey nods)*

SPIKEY: Yeah, I added, "FIX IT PLEASE!" But a bully broke the sign and threw it at my knees!

GRAMMY: Oh no. Was it the same bully that stole your black permanent marker?

SPIKEY: Yeah, when I fixed the stop signs. Over my words, he drew black lines!

GRAMMY: Spikey, you did **not** <u>fix all those</u> stop signs!! To stop hate, stop racism, stop prejudice, stop speeding and stop bullying are good points. But writing those words on a stop sign, is defacing public property! That's why you got grounded!

SPIKEY: I learned my point, yes I did. I'm just really, a big bad kid!

GRAMMY: Oh no. You're not bad. You just made a bad choice. You're young and learning. I'm trying to teach you right from wrong. I don't want you to be a bully, but I don't want anyone to hurt or bully you either. It's wise to be with friends, to make you feel safer. *(Spikey nods)*.

SPIKEY: I've been bullied by quite a few! Has anyone ever, bullied you?

GRAMMY: Yes, bullies are everywhere! Schools, work, streets, home, all over. *(sighs)* A bossy woman I used to work with; always <u>finds</u> fault in me, my driving, friends, my weight, my cooking and I'm too nice?! What's with that? She's not a happy lady! Remember, she's the one who called you "A needled nemesis!" and said your "quillies give her the whillies." *(Spikey nods)* She's upset about some things in her life, but it's no excuse to hurt us...

SPIKEY: Yeah, before she judges, she should get to know us first! She seems to think, we're the worst!

GRAMMY: You're right. I thought she was my friend! I'm still polite to her, but we're not friends. She said she was just 'teasing' me. But I didn't like the teasing, so it's bullying. *(Spikey nods)* Adults can be bullies too. They can cut in front of you in line, or in traffic. At times it's hard to ignore the rude things they do! Spitting out mean words, is like vomit to the heart. *(She pats Spikey's hand)*. Seeing and hearing violence can destroy us. Let's focus on those who love and care about us. We all make mistakes, but we can chose to take the high road. *(Spikey looks confused)* Not road, you know what I mean. But we can be the ones who 'let it go.' Try to forgive and forget. *(Spikey nods in agreement)*.

SPIKEY: YOU always, do forgive me. Even that day, I got stuck up a tree!

GRAMMY: *(laughs)* I forgive, because it helps me! We've all been wrong, but we can chose to be patient and say kind words. *(Spikey nods)* Always tell someone you trust, when you feel bullied.

SPIKEY: I will, cuz mean words and bullying is wrong. When we walk away, we are <u>strong</u>! *(pause)* Grammy, do you get paid to look after me? *(She shakes her head no.)* So you volunteer, with no dough or money?!

GRAMMY: No payment, but many rewards! We're family, we <u>protect</u> each other. I found you by the side of the road and we found Punky last year in this park! Everyone needs and deserves respect and a safe happy home! You babysit Punky and volunteer on Coach Bob's ball team. *They sing* **_Valuable Volunteers._** You're peaceful and kind to all... rich, poor, disabled and bullies too. Life's about relationships, good or bad. *(pause,)* Life isn't fair, but we're grateful for what we have! Being grateful and helping others, makes us happy! Well, I should be moving along!

SPIKEY: Thanks Grammy for being you! You make a difference, too! We should be known for how we treat others. You treat me and others, like your children, sisters and brothers. *(Grammy smiles as she walks away.)* But before you move along – I have for you, a little song. *(Kids return as Grammy stops.)* *(Spikey sings,* **_Tribute to Grammy_***) *(Kids join in on chorus. All dance)*.

GRAMMY: *(Grammy claps)* Thank you Spikey, for being you! Here, *(to Spikey)* I have a little something for you for later. *(Spikey's surprised)* *(She takes bow tie from her purse, and puts it against his neck)* It's a bow tie. You look so handsome! *(he smiles)* Do you like it? *(Spikey nods)* I'll leave it in your room. Hope this makes you feel better.

SPIKEY: Wow, Grammy, already I do! Thank you! I'll be wearing this tie before you say, "I do!"

GRAMMY: I sure hope so!

KERI: Spikey, your mom and my mom are getting married today. I'm so nervous. And then some kids in the shoe store laughed at me yesterday. They made fun of me while I was trying to walk in high heels. Mom said they looked good with my dress but they sure don't make me feel good! And I can still hear those kids laughing. So how am I supposed to feel pretty?! Just sayin...

GRAMMY: Let it go Keri! Some bullies have been bullied. Sometimes they need someone who cares about them, and someone to talk to. Sometimes it's wise to avoid them! Always tell an adult you know and trust, when bad things happen...it's good just to talk! *(looks at watch.)* Misty will be here soon! Then Punky and I will be on our way home, so he can get a little nap. Keri, you'll be beautiful, with or without heels! *(Keri smiles)*

SPIKEY: *(Spikey plays with ball)* To be with friends by the school, I will soon go. But not until after singing a song we all know! *(Music **CATCH A FRIEND!** **(All on stage sing, Misty and Punky enter. Punky could sing/dance or read a book) (Girls enter SR for dance routine, then exit SR).*

Scene 4:

MISTY: Spikey - Punky has a question for you.

PUNKY: *(to Misty)* No, you ask him! Ask him what I asked you.

MISTY: Punky asked me why you have a "ey" in your name and he and I just have a "y"? I have tried to explain to him that a name is a choice. There's no right or wrong. Grammy named you. The kids in the park named Punky. And my parents from Lockport named me Misty. It's like, Anne of Green Gables has an 'e' at the end. And some Ann's don't. It's like Sarah, Keri's mom. She has an "h" at the end and some Sara's don't. *(Punky looks bored). (Misty holds Punky's hand).*

SPIKEY: Yes, and some names end in "i" and some names end in "y."

MISTY: Right! Different is just, different! Different isn't wrong!! It's like being left handed or right handed.

PUNKY: *(to Misty)* Okay. Let's go read my book now, pleaseeeese?!

MISTY: Yes, reading helps us learn better! We'll go now. Spikey, maybe I can meet you back here when Punky has his nap.

SPIKEY: Oh Yes, that sounds great! Can you bring back, some wedding cake?

MISTY: *(laughs)* Sorry Spikey. I think you'll have to wait until after the wedding!.

PUNKY: Bye Spikey! *(pulls Misty SL to Grammy's) (Misty waves affectionately to Spikey. Spikey waves back affectionately).* I'm going to Grammy's for my nap!

SPIKEY: We'll see a rested Punky at the wedding. *(to Misty)* Again, I will soon hear Misty sing.
(Misty smiles endearingly at Spikey as Punky pulls her away. Misty & Punky exit SR with Grammy). (Spikey picks up his baseball from bench, starts to exit SR, whistling/ skipping. Sees Larry entering).

SCENE 5:

(Larry enters SR, carrying coffee and a small bag with Sarah's scarf).

SPIKEY: Hi my dear friend Larry. Today is the day, Sarah you will marry!

LARRY: Yes it is my friend. *(they high five)* We have lots to do today, but I'm going to meet her here for a few minutes. Where are you off to? *(Larry sits on bench SL He looks at Cell)*

SPIKEY: *(shows him baseball)* I'm off to play catch with Coach Bob by the school. Gotta run – Doddle doo! *(they wave. Spikey exits SR)* *(Larry drinks coffee nervously, fidgets with hands/feet).*

SARAH: *(Enters SL)* Hi Larry. Sorry I'm a bit late.

LARRY: No worries, Sarah. I just got here. Mark and Ben are at home washing and cleaning my car. What a great gift! I needed the walk down here, anyway.

SARAH: Me too! How nice of your sons! *(Larry hands Sarah, her scarf.)* Thank you Larry, for bringing back my scarf. I always forget it at your place, don't I. *(beat)* You look terrified. Are you nervous?

LARRY: Yeah. Why? I don't know. I mean I love you. Wow – a lawyer used to court scenes, afraid of his own wedding!

SARAH: Hey, hope you don't have cold feet! Look, we're not even supposed to see each other on the day of the wedding!

LARRY: That probably doesn't include us. We've both been married before and have kids.

SARAH: Yeah – you're right. Speaking of kids, are your boys ready for today?

LARRY: Yes, they're excited for us. They really like you, you know.

SARAH: I like them too. So does Keri. She says you'll be a great stepdad. My daughter's a nervous wreck practicing her solo. Little Tia will be singing as well. She's only 9 and a half, and not as nervous as the rest of us!

LARRY: The park kids are all growing up. It's hard to believe our kids Keri and Mark are finished Grade 9.

SARAH: Same with Robyn and Sally. And Ben going into Grade 8.

LARRY: Yes, they're good kids. Time flies...*(pause)* And how about you, Sarah? Are you okay?

SARAH: Yes, *(pause)* I am. I know I'm marrying the right man! Our relationship is based on friendship. A friend is someone who understands and 'gets you. Right? *(nervous sigh)*

LARRY: Right, friends and soul mates. We'll make a happy home...

SARAH: Together! Two families, second marriages, it's scary, but everyone deserves a second chance, right? Marriage, kids... It's relationships. It's trust. A little give and take.

LARRY: Yes, we need it as parents and in our careers. You're a kind teacher and mom.

SARAH: Thanks. *(pause)* We all dream of a "Happily Ever After, don't we?" *(beat)* but no one takes time to appreciate this magical park. Cars drop people off and quickly turn around. Everyone's too busy to savour the moment. *(directly to Larry)*... Let's keep coming here. *(Larry nods)*. I want our marriage to include many walks to this park.

LARRY: I think we can make that work.

SARAH: I hope I can be a strong role model for your kids. I've told Keri, there'll always be someone wanting us to fail....waiting for us to fall. I want to be there for you, for our kids.

LARRY: Me as well. We can make our marriage, and family, work! Like you said, life's about relationships, good or bad, in business, work, friends, teams, and us.

SARAH: Yes, it is. I try to choose friends and words carefully. I think in this day and age, we all need to be, a little kinder than necessary.

LARRY: So true! Everyone you meet is fighting some kind of battle. *(pause)* Well, I know we both have things to do, before our "I do's." *(beat)* Don't worry. This is the best decision of my life. You encourage me rather than find fault. I will stand by you and defend you.

SARAH: Perfect lawyer words! *(pause)* Being in this park always makes me feel better. It's not just a place – it's an experience...gives me an inner peace...*(deep breath)*...so I can relax. *(big sigh)* Yeah, I'm very nervous. *(laughs nervously)* Thanks again for my scarf.

LARRY: No problem. I think we needed to see each other, anyway. *(Sarah nods.)* We better run.

SARAH: We need a hug...

LARRY: You're right, again. *(they hug)* *(Both get up from bench and hold hands as they exit, SR)*.

SCENE 6: *(Robyn, Sally, Tia and Keri enter SL)*

ROBYN: Hmmm. I thought Spikey would still be here.

SALLY: Did you talk to Spikey at the Grand Opening? He's so out of it today!

ROBYN: Be nice. He's just nervous. And excited Misty is here, for the wedding.

SALLY: So glad we're finished that crazy netting stuff! That's exhausting!

TIA: Yeah, It was hard to loop all that netting through that white lattice arch.

SALLY:. Glad you could help Keri,

KERI: Yeah, I needed a break from practising my song!

SALLY: We all made the arch look nice with those little lights!

TIA: Yeah, the arch with the lights looks pretty over Grammy's Cake table.

SALLY: The amazing wedding cake Grammy made!

ROBYN: Well, now's our moment to have our break! Keri? How is your song?

KERI: I'm too nervous to sing. I need to relax here for a bit. *(slumps on bench SR)* So - this is it guys...where the magical double wedding is going to be – just a few hours away.

SALLY: And what a gorgeous summer day! *(sits on rock)*

TIA: So Keri, your mom is marrying Ben and Mark's dad? *(sits by Robyn)*

KERI: You got it!

SALLY: *(stands behind bench)* Yup, and Keri's Grandpa, Sarah's dad, Mr. T., is marrying Grammy.

ROBYN: Today's weddings are getting too complicated and wacky for me. But what's wackier is my mom's marrying all of them!!

TIA: What?!

ROBYN: Really! The real minister has a last minute funeral and can't marry them! My mom just became a JP, so she's doing it!

SALLY: Your mom's our Vice Principal! What's a JP?

ROBYN: You know – Justice Of The Peace. She can marry people! It's her new part time summer job. This is her first wedding, so she's very nervous! Especially because she knows both brides and grooms!! *(Ben and Mark enter)*

TIA: From a VP to a JP. At least she can marry them in this park. It's a nice place to have a wedding.!

ROBYN: Hi guys! *(they wave)* This park is a meeting place, and our dance rehearsal site.

MARK: Last year it was a court room to build a school for Spikey - and today it's a wedding place!

BEN: It's just a park! A plain ordinary simple park!

SALLY: But a very special park. It's not ordinary. Together people make things work out here. There's something special about this park.

TIA: You're right. It makes me feel safe, at peace, happy...

SALLY: It's like there's some kind of special feeling that connects people here.

TIA/SALLY: It's like...magic!

KERI: Exactly! There is something...a presence that protects everyone that comes here. A spirit that gets inside of you... Yeah, Magic! The experience of being here gives me roots and wings...makes me a different person.

TIA: *(sarcastically)* An expression on your heart... *(Ben and Mark roll their eyes)*

SALLY: Exactly, And you'll never be the same, once you've been here!

ROBYN: You're right. It fills your soul with a peace, a love...

BEN: Oh, c'mon guys - it's just a park. It's just a wedding. It's just...

TIA: It's just a peaceful, happy place!

ROBYN: Yes it is. This park is like a haven. It protects you. And four people who met here, are getting married today. They're happily in 'love.' It's a Happily Ever After, kind of day!

BEN: It's just in your mind... There is no "Happily Ever After!"

SALLY: Sure there is, if you believe in love and staying together. Like penquins and geese. *(all girls look confused)* Yeah?!! You know, they meet and they're together forever. Didn't you know that?!

BEN: Oh yeah, We studied that last year. The commitment part, not the love.

ROBYN: You can't see love, it's in your heart.

MARK: I guess you just have to believe in it.

KERI: We need love...or at least acceptance. We need this park!

BEN: We need air and water! And clothes – Yeah, this park is nice – but we don't 'need' it.

ROBYN: I do. I think it's a perfect place for my mom to marry two couples.

SALLY: And it was perfect for a STAR to have their rehearsal, RIGHT HERE, four years ago.

TIA: That was so awesome! And now, it's a perfect place for a wedding!
Grammy says meeting Mr. T, here...is the best thing that's ever happened to her!

BEN: Keri's grumpy old Grandpa!!

KERI: He's not grumpy! No one in our family is! I need to go back to practice my song. See you later.

TIA: *(to Keri)* Sally said your Grandpa was a good volleyball coach!

SALLY: Yeah, he was!

KERI: Thanks, I heard he was! *(all say goodbye. Keri exits)*

SALLY: Did you know Grammy and Mr. T's engagement was a secret?

ALL: No!

SALLY: Well, so everyone says!

TIA: So Grammy, or 'Mary' is a retired nurse. Does she still volunteer at the hospital?

BEN: Yup. She's a worker bee. She's got like 5 eyes, and knows everything that's going on!

ROBYN: She'll always volunteer at something!

MARK: She does a lot for the homeless too, like adopting Spikey and Punky! She's all good and kind!

BEN: I don't know how Grammy does it! She made the wedding cake, prepared all the food, made <u>her</u> wedding dress <u>and</u> Ms Bell's! She did Keri's alterations. She's like a dolphin!

TIA: What?! A dolphin?!

MARK: Yeah, cuz dolphins never really sleep. I remember talking about them in school last year, too. The things we can learn in school!

TIA: Oh yeah! Did you guys notice Keri? She's sooo nervous. She's still practicing her solo and trying to walk in her new pointed spikey toes and 4" spikey heels!

SALLY: Yeah, she told me at rehearsal last night, that she's <u>really</u> nervous about singing and tripping in her heels.

TIA: Her "designer' dress cost more than her mom's wedding dress to make!

ROBYN: Hey, Be nice. That's gossiping. Keri's our friend! Her dress is a gift from her mom.

TIA: Well, I know Keri is worried about singing her solo. Misty is singing too – but she's not worried! She's just excited! I think she really likes Spikey.

SALLY: Oh she does. I'm so glad they met! And they met in this park too! He likes her a lot! Spikey is the most nervous of all! He's been so silly.

BEN: Yeah, you know what he said to me the other day? *(laughs)* Remember our friend Lisa used to say, "My 'different' colour of skin, doesn't give you the right to call me names!" *(all nod and say yes)* I asked Spikey if he knew what a racist was. He threw his hands in the air and said *(mimicks Spikey)* "Of course, it's someone who races and runs <u>really</u> fast! They're the ones that never come in last!" *(all laugh.)*

MARK: Why people are racist beats me! But friends don't talk about someone behind their back. Let's talk about winners. She is a winner. Spikey is a winner. And so are we!

SALLY: Yeah! Winners are above name calling! We can ignore the mean stuff, because we know who we really are!

BEN: You're right, Sally! But it still hurt her, hurts us. It's like someone sticking quills in me and I can't pull them out. And even when I feel good about myself, there's always someone who tries to push me down. But, I won't ever stay down!! No one is going to bully me and get away with it!! I like myself!

TIA: Yeahhhh!! You Go Ben!!

ROBYN: It's not our fault if someone is a racist! They're the ones with the problem.

MARK: They're the ones that can't see!!! They're the losers in this race. Why can't people see past the skin colour?! Kindness IS colourless! *(cheers)* Well, I promised Spikey I'd play catch with him on the ball diamond, so gotta run! *(he exits, as all say goodbye)*

SALLY: What if the world was colour blind?! *(beat)* Did you know Porcupines are almost blind? They have poor vision.

ROBYN: If we could all see through Spikey's eyes, this world would be a better place.

TIA: What are you talking about?! And what's that got to do with...*(Music cuts her off. All girls sing **__ATTITUDE__**)* *(Spikey runs in and collapses on bench by Robyn).* AHHHHH!!!!! Spikey, what happened to you???!!! *(Mark runs after Spikey. Keri follows).*

SCENE 7:

SPIKEY: I'm a racist! I was chased by mean fists! *(He makes two fists)*

ROBYN: *(runs to Spikey)* You were racing, but you're not a racist, Spikey. Are you okay? *(he shakes his head no)* Did you get hit in the eye? *(he nods)*

SALLY: What happened?

BEN: What bully punched you?!!

TIA: Yeah... What bully did this to you?!

MARK: Okay guys. Spikey can't calm down when we're all throwing stuff at him. He'll talk when he's ready. Keri and I saw him get hit. She texted 'HELP' to Coach Bob, then ran to him out in the field. Coach Bob is talking to the kids now. He and Keri will be here soon!

ROBYN: I'll run home and get an ice pack for his eye. We've got to get the swelling down before the wedding! *(starts to leave SR)*

SALLY: We've got to do something! What iS wrong - is if we do nothing!

BEN: Right! Let's find the bullies and beat them up! *(all give Ben a cold look)* Don't say it, I can control my attitude. *(Girls give him a cold look)* Hey, I was just kidding!!

ROBYN: *(SR)* We know fighting never solves problems! It just creates violence. I'll be right back. *(exits to go get an ice pack)*

TIA: *(leaning over Spikey)* Can you talk Spikey? No, not yet?! I hope someone stopped the fight.

SALLY: I hope so, too. Ignoring is the SO wrong thing to do. Mark and Keri stood up to the fighters. They're heros! *(Misty enters SL, runs towards Spikey)*.

MISTY: Oh no – what happened?! *(Robyn whispers to Sally and Tia)*.

SPIKEY: A bully stole my glove and ball, then started a fight.
A girl nearby, was part of the terrible sight.
She could have called for help, but called me names. She was part of his mean game.
Keri and Mark, my friends came by. Wow, life can change in the blink of an eye!
Keri texted Coach Bob, as Mark tried to stop the fight.
Coach Bob came at the speed of light!
Their anger and hatred was very dangerous.
Their foolish words and punches were senseless.

Bob got the kids off of me. It wasn't easy, I could see.
I can't really think <u>now,</u> cuz I still feel the KER POW!! *(sighs)*

TIA: *(enter Coach Bob and Keri)* Hi Coach Bob and Keri! *(all exchange greetings)* Robyn's gone to get ice.

COACH BOB: Good for her. We'll need it! Bullying has become a whole new <u>ball game</u>!! Never trample on someone's hope. Sometimes it's all they have left. Often people don't know what the problem is or how it got started. For example, is the problem the pencil or the sharpener?! *(all look confused)* Anyway, each are trying to make a point!

MARK: So who's fault is it if the point keeps breaking? Anyway, these kids think they're fixing the problem by keeping Spikey <u>off</u> the field. They keep breaking him!! It's not fair!

COACH BOB: Good Point. I don't know. Who knows why this kid started bullying Spikey. He tried to create fear. That fear alters thinking, so much that Spikey doesn't feel normal. He made Spikey feel that somehow, Spikey is the cause of the problem – not him.

KERI: Spikey is too trusting! Maybe if we never trust anyone, we won't be disappointed, and just brush off the bullying?!

MARK: There'll always be some we don't like, or some who don't like us!

KERI: That's normal!

MARK: That kid was mean to Spikey, He told Spikey ... actually Keri, do you remember?

KERI: I Sure Do!! The bully said "What happens in the park, stays in the park!" We said, <u>"No it Does NOT! NOT in this park!"</u>

MARK: He yelled back at Spikey, <u>"I wish you could just unzip yourself!"</u> *(Keri nods).*

KERI: <u>"Get out of that ugly dark skin!!</u>

MARK/KERI: <u>"You with your useless points!"</u>

TIA: That's so terrible!!

SALLY: It is!! It's almost worse than cyber bullying! Thanks for getting rid of the bullies! *(Bob smiles/nods)* How did you make them go away?

COACH BOB: Mark and Keri did it all.

MARK: Keri was supposed to be practicing her song! Then she heard and saw the fight.

KERI: I was practicing on the other side of the school. No one could see or hear me, but I could hear the ball players, and the bat hit the balls.

COACH BOB: Keri put her song practice second. She put Spikey first and took a stand! She and Mark chose positive peer pressure! They are positive role models and leaders! *(Coach Bob sits by Spikey. Spikey leans on him).*

MARK: Spikey and I were to meet and play catch. *(beat)* Spikey walked away from the other players to wait for me. Two kids were mean and took away his baseball and glove. I got there as Spikey was being bullied.

COACH BOB: Hero Mark stopped the fight as Keri texted and ran to me!

MARK: I held the kids back until Coach Bob got there. They said they were teasing not bullying. I asked Spikey if he thought it was funny. Of course Spikey said no. They did admit to hitting him. The girl was a bystander. Then she joined him! She stood and watched her brother hit Spikey by his eye! *(shakes his head)*

COACH BOB: She should have run for help, but made a bad choice. She chose to be a bully too. I heard their name calling.

ROBYN: Spikey, are you okay? *(Robyn enters running with ice pack) (She puts ice pack on Spikey).*

COACH BOB: Thanks Robyn. I had them text their parents. We all had a discussion. The kids apologized to Spikey. *(Robyn gives him thumbs up).* They were angry about other things, but there was no reason to take it out on Spikey. Mark got Spikey's ball and glove back. *(Spikey nods)* The parents took their son and his sister home. They told Spikey and I, there would be consequences for their behavior.

MARK: Kids <u>can</u> do mean things,

COACH BOB: It's not just kids!! Adults to! That's why we need to be proactive! We need to get into the game and help our friends and team! So lets all set good examples. Kids CAN be a strong influence!

ROBYN: Yes! We CAN change lives and attitudes! We CAN all do our part to help!

TIA: Hope so! Some need to change their anger and hurt inside. I've been bullied a lot. Bullies don't realize the damage they do. No one understands until <u>they've</u> been bullied.

KERI: I've been a bully and have been bullied. I see both sides.

BEN: Me too. Remember when I used Spikey's quill to try and poke holes in a convertible top?

KERI: And Jessica succeeded! But we're still friends. Jessica and I were bullied on Facebook, so we went to Twitter. It got worse.

SALLY: You two?! You're both smart, pretty... maybe that's why. I've seen your selfie photos.

KERI: I didn't tell my parents or any adults. No one knew. I used to skip school because I was scared to go. I couldn't sleep at night. I had horrible headaches and stomach aches.

TIA: Really! The bullies were jealous of you! That's the worst! It's hard to ignore meanies.

KERI: Exactly. But I chose NOT to read or listen to garbage. I tried to dump it, so it doesn't mess me up.

ROBYN: You rose above it. I remember you staying in the bathroom once, because you were scared to go out at lunch. Glad I found you, Keri! We went out together and the bullies stayed away from us. *(Keri nods).* Look how popular you are now! Now you believe in yourself and you make a point of being with a friend. Sometimes bad things happen to good people.

COACH BOB: Yeah, like to Spikey! When you know who you are though, it doesn't bother you, as much. You have to <u>stand up</u> to them. Sorry about the bullies, Spikey.

SPIKEY: Thanks for your help Coach Bob. You did an awesome job!
Today I'm giving Grammy away. That's scary enough.
Then I meet two kids half my size. But they were twice as tough!
My eye is sore. My feelings and bones are hurt.
I was thrown right in the dirt...
They said they were scared of me!
But their mean words, stung like a bee!
Today is supposed to be a happy day.
And now I just want to run away.

ROBYN: Spikey. we're your friends! We're here to help you!

SPIKEY: Thanks. You're the best friends! I sure hope <u>bullying,</u> someday ENDS!!!!

COACH BOB: We all do. I think you'll be okay Spikey. Just stay away from bullies. Sometimes they need a friend, and need to talk to a trusted adult or professional! Now, care about <u>you</u>!

ROBYN: Spikey, please take this ice pack home with you. *(Spikey nods his head, smiles at Robyn).* The innocent shouldn't be punished and bullied. Bullying destroys! That's a crime.

COACH BOB: You are so right, Robyn! It is. *(looks at Spikey)* It looks like the ice pack is helping you Spikey. Sure wish we could stop all bullying, hazing and cyber bullying! Well, gotta get ready for a double wedding, double fun!

ROBYN: We should all go! *(girls nod)* I hope mom has the Quill pen I got for her!! *(All exit SR, except Spikey & Misty. She's sitting beside him on the bench, holding the ice pack for him).*

MISTY: Just relax a few minutes, Spikey. We all know you're a good soul. You could hurt any bully back...but you choose not to! Why, one of your quills could injure them for life! Our quills are like little arrows. We could do major damage! Words are like that. Words can be very painful. Once thrown, they don't come back. The damage is done!

SPIKEY: Even if someone damages our joints – should we live quietly and carry strong points?!

MISTY: Yes, because kind souls are the winners in the end. We're not victims. Peace is inside us Spikey. We're at peace and we need to stay there. But bad things happen. We're supposed to tell an adult we trust. We need to be good examples to Punky and others at our new school.

SPIKEY: Wow – an example, I want to be. Role models, you and me!

MISTY: When we know and understand who we are, life is easier. We will always be bullied because we're different. We're walking talking porcupines! But we are good and pure. Anger in bullies can destroy them inside, and destroy their world around them. Wouldn't it be great if we could wave a magic wand, stop all the anger, fighting and pain, and put the whole world in peace?

SPIKEY: The world would be a better place. I can see the kindness in your face. *(Misty sings ** I Believe in You,** to Spikey.)* Together we can make, this world a better place! You've made me feel better! Ooops, my eye is getting wetter! *(They laugh as he removes ice pack, and sets it on bench).*

SPIKEY & MISTY: *(She helps Spikey stand up from bench).* Together we can make it!! *(They high five and sing (**World Are you Ready?**)) (Misty leads – Spikey joins in on chorus)*

MISTY: Well we better run! We've got a wedding, to get to!

(Together We Can Make It" Instrumental Music starts!) (Spikey exits SL, Misty follows, as "ushers" Coach Bob, Mark and Ben enter SR with their chairs.) (Spikey quickly re-enters SR wearing a bowtie, carrying his chair. Misty follows wearing a long pearl necklace, assisting on stage and carrying in her chair.) (Stage Manager ties white ribbon/bows on the benches) Guest Chairs are set up diagonally on either side of benches. Chorus enters carrying their own chairs.

Recorded Songs performed:

*(*Commit My Love,* * When you've got Love,* *Happily Ever After*)*

SCENE 8:

(Wedding Scene) *(All Cast, Chorus AND STAGE MANAGER are dressed for the Wedding) White bows, ribbons, with a (red) rose in the centre, are on both benches and all white plastic stacking chairs. (Spikey and Punky are wearing bow ties. If Punky is a girl, she could have a bow in her hair and wearing a pearl necklace, similar to the one worn by Misty).*

Both benches are moved in front of the rock, facing the audience. SR bench is for Grammy and Mr. T. SL bench for Sarah and Larry. Mark and Spikey move SR bench forward as Ben and Coach Bob move SL bench forward. There is a space wide enough in between benches for 4 chairs, for Punky, Spikey, the JP, and Keri. All face the audience.

Front LINE UP WILL BE: Bench: Mr. T, Grammy, CHAIRS: Spikey, Punky, JP, Keri, Bench: Sarah, Larry, CHAIRS: Mark, Ben. (SL bench: Inside of bench for Sarah, outside, for Larry. SR bench: Inside for Grammy, outside for Mr. T.)

Guest chairs angled on either side, facing bridal couples. Both benches face Audience, but separated.

(Mark exits SR) Ben turns the garbage can upside down, and puts it far SR. Mark re-enters carrying round white table cloth. Keri enters with 'Register' book, and quill pen. Mark puts table cloth over garbage can. Keri sets book and pen on top.

KERI: So mom's getting married today! I didn't think it was going to happen.

MARK: Yeah, same with Dad! He's been so busy, I didn't think he'd ever find time to get married. So glad he found someone who can cook!

BEN: Me too!! No more of Dad's surprises! *(Mark, Ben and Keri exit SR, as Ms Radcliffe runs in SL. She frantically sits in her chair and goes through her notes).*
Robyn, Tia and Sally Enter SR carrying in their chairs, set their chairs down as .
"Together We can Make It" music fades.

ROBYN: So our teacher, Ms Bell is getting married today!

SALLY: Yes, and your VP mom is marrying Ms Sarah Bell and Mr. Larry Law...

ROBYN: And Ms Sarah Bell's Father is marrying Mary...well, Grammy!

SALLY: Your mom can do it all! *(Enter Coach Bob. He ushers Misty to her chair).*

COACH BOB: *(to girls)* We need to take our seats now. *(ushers them in)*

MISTY: The wedding is about to start! *(sits)* Oh, this is so wonderful! What a beautiful day for a wedding!

TIA: A **Wacky** Wedding!! I've never been to a double wedding before! I'm so excited! *(sits)*

ROBYN: Shhhh! The ceremony is about to start! *(sighs)*
(All 4 girls, Chorus, Stage Manager, Misty then finally Coach Bob, take their seats).
(BEAT, Music starts! PROCESSIONAL Music) (Suggestion / Option "ARISO" played on flute and/or acoustic guitar).
Larry Enters first. Ben and Mark enter together and stand SR by Larry. All turn to face audience. Keri enters. She stands between two benches., and turns to face audience. Punky follows with 4 rings tied to his quills, on top of his head. He stands by Keri. Mark stands in front of the chair closest to where Larry', is sitting on the bench. Ben stands beside Mark. Keri stands in front of the chair by Sarah. Spikey will have a chair beside Grammy. The JP will be in-between Punky and Keri.
(Mark motions to Ben to get rid of his gum. Ben takes it out but doesn't know where to put it, so puts it on the back of the bench. Mark rolls his eyes). (Punky plays with rings and drops one. Keri reties it). (Sarah enters with Mr. T.) (GRAMMY follows, with Spikey). (Music ends when both couples are in front, facing audience).

MS RADCLIFFE: *(OFFICIANT)*
(To audience) Please be seated. *(Ariso or other processional music ends). (Mark, Ben, Keri and Punky sit on white chairs, near bridal couples). (Brides, grooms and Spikey remain standing).* Welcome Family and Friends. Welcome to our double wedding in the park! Today we celebrate two special loves. Larry Law and Sarah Bell. Also Joe Taylor and Mary Martens. *(Cheers)* Let's Begin. Who gives this woman Sarah, to be wed?

MR.T: Her father. Ummm. I do. *(Sarah & Mr. T kiss. Sarah moves to stand by Larry. They face audience).*

MS RADCLIFFE: Who gives this woman Mary... or Grammy...to be wed? *(pause)*

SPIKEY: Oh, I'm ready to ...! *(Loudly)* **I DO!** *(He sits. He's exhausted and slumps in his chair) (Duet with Larry & Misty) (or solo: MISTY and Chorus sing ** **Commit My Love** Chorus can include kids, Larry, Mr. T, Grammy and Sarah).*

MS RADCLIFFE: Thank you for the lovely singing. At this time, Larry and Sarah, Joe and Mary, wish to thank all of you, for joining them here today. You are invited to share this very special celebration with them. They hope you enjoy the inspirational words, they've chosen for their ceremony. You are part, of this joyous celebration! *(beat)* If anyone present can show just cause why these two couples, may not be lawfully joined together; you should declare it now, or hereafter hold your peace. *(pause)* There having been no impeachment, I mean impediment declared *(Spikey looks around nervously) (Mark drops his paper, but isn't aware).*

KERI: What happens if someone says NO!

ROBYN: Shhh! No one is going to say NO! *(Punky notices paper on floor, picks it up and makes airplane).*

KERI: But just what if? Has it ever happened?

ROBYN: Maybe in movies...I don't know! Shhh! Listen to my mom!

MS RADCLIFFE: *(Smiles at Robyn)* I will now ask Larry's oldest son Mark *(Mark panics and mouths NOW?!)* to read First Corinthians, Chapter 13, verses 4 to 8. *(Mark is caught off guard and is desperately looking for his paper, in his pants pocket, etc.)* Punky is still trying to make a paper airplane with Mark's notes. Mark takes it from Punky and unfolds it quickly. Mark rushes to the front).

MS RADCLIFFE: Mark Law will now be reading First Corinthians, Chapter 13, verses 4 to 8.

MARK: *(taking a deep breath)* "Love is patient, love is kind. It is not jealous or boastful. It is not inflated. It is not rude. It does not seek its own interests." *(angrily looks at Punky)* "It is not quick tempered. It does not brood over injury. It does not rejoice over wrongdoings, but rejoices with the truth. It bears all things, believes all things, hopes all things, endures all things. Love never fails." *(beat)* There will now be a poem by *(stumbles over word)* Kill Gibrin. *(Mark takes his seat).*

MS RADCLIFFE: Thank you Mark. The author is KAHIL GIBRAN. *(Mark smiles as he puts hands up).* Before we share the vows the couples have written together, both couples have chosen a favorite poem by Kahil Gibran. Kahil, pronounced Kahil was a Lebanese author, artist, prophet and philosopher who lived from 1883 – 1930. *(All kids look at each other and make a face).* He had this incredible spiritual power that was universal. He offered people gifts but possessed nothing! What a beautiful person. They have chosen Larry and Sarah's children to read their chosen poem, on Marriage. *(Applause as Keri, Mark and Ben step forward with paper, to read).*

KERI: "You were born together, and together you shall be forevermore."

MARK: "You shall be together when white wings of death scatter your days."

BEN: "You shall be together even in the silent memory of God."

KERI: "But let there be spaces in your togetherness,"

MARK: "And let the winds of the heavens dance between you."

BEN: "Love one another but make not a bond of love."

KERI: "Let it rather be a moving sea between the shores of your souls."

BEN/MARK: "Fill each others' cup but drink not from one cup."

TIA: Why not? Cuz of germs?

ROBYN: I dunno! Shhhh!

KERI: "Give one another of your bread but eat not from the same loaf."

BEN: "Sing and dance together and be joyous, but let each one of you be alone,"

MARK: "Even as the strings of a lute are alone though they"

KERI: "Quiver with the same music.."

TIA: What's a lute? Like a flute?

ROBYN: I dunno! Shhhh!

BEN: "Give your hearts, but not into each other's keeping."

MARK: "For only the hand of Life can contain your hearts."

KERI: "And stand together, yet not too near together:"

BEN: "For the pillars of the temple stand apart,"

MARK: "And the oak tree and the cypress grow not in each others' shadow."

MS RADCLIFFE:
>Thank you Keri, Ben and Mark for the readings. *(pause)* Ooops sorry...ummm, now what? I'm okay with being a vice principal but, I'm not used to this. *(to audience and people on stage). (Daughter Robyn is visably embarrassed, as she puts her head into her hands).* It's my first time as a JP, everyone, sorry, See, I was supposed to be a guest. The minister had a funeral, and I - Oh, right, the vows...And now I ask you - Larry & Sarah, and you Joe & Mary – to join your right hands. *(Couples do so, awkwardly)* I invite all of you, to join me in the reading of their vows. Larry, Joe, please repeat after me, I Larry and I Joe...

LARRY & MR.T: *(In unison)* I Larry and I Joe,

MS RADCLIFFE: No, not together. Larry, you say, I Larry and Joe, you say, I Joe. Let's try again. *(looks at Larry)* I Larry.

LARRY: I Larry

MS RADCLIFFE: *(looks at Mr. T)* I Joe

MR.T: I Joe

MS RADCLIFFE: *(points to Larry)* Take you Sarah,

LARRY: Take You Sarah,

MS RADCLIFFE: *(points to Mr. T)* Take you Mary, *(Punky leans on Keri. He/She is starting to get heavy eyed/sleepy).*

MR. T: Take You Mary

MS RADCLIFFE: *(points to both Larry and Joe)* Say this line together. To be my partner in life and my best friend.

LARRY & MR. T:*(confused)* To be my partner in life and my best friend. *(Punky's nodding off. He/She is not trying too hard to stay awake).*

MS RADCLIFFE: *(points to both Larry and Joe)* I respect your personal rights and views.

LARRY & MR. T: I respect your personal rights and views.

MS RADCLIFFE: And want to share equally with you.

LARRY & MR. T: And want to share equally with you.

MS RADCLIFFE: All that life has to offer.

LARRY & MR. T: All that life has to offer. *(beat)*

MS RADCLIFFE: Good! Now, Mary, Sarah, please repeat after me. I Mary, I Sarah – but not together!

SARAH: *(Ms R nods at Sarah)* I Sarah

GRAMMY: I Mary

MS RADCLIFFE: *(points to Sarah)* Take you Larry,

SARAH: Take You Larry,

MS RADCLIFFE: *(points to Grammy)* Take you Joe,

GRAMMY: Take you Joe.

MS RADCLIFFE: Now these lines, you can say together. To be my partner in life and my best friend.

SARAH & GRAMMY: To be my partner in life and my best friend.

MS RADCLIFFE: I respect your personal rights and views.

SARAH & GRAMMY: I respect your personal rights and views.

MS RADCLIFFE: And want to share equally with you.

SARAH & GRAMMY: And want to share equally with you.

MS RADCLIFFE: All that life has to offer.

SARAH & GRAMMY: All that life has to offer. *(beat)*

MS RADCLIFFE: Good! Now, Punky please step forward with the rings. *(Punky has fallen asleep).* PUNKY?! *(Keri wakes up Punky. He/She moves near Ms Radcliffe).*
The rings symbolize the wholeness of you as individuals
and of your love and commitment to one another.
(Ms Radcliffe takes rings from Punky and gives them to the Brides).
(Grammy drops her ring and has difficulty finding it. Spikey and kids giggle. Grammy finally finds it on the ground, then laughs as well).
As you place this ring on Larry's and Joe's finger, repeat after me.
I give you this ring as a symbol of my love and commitment.

SARAH & GRAMMY: I give you this ring as a symbol of my love and commitment.
(Sarah puts ring on Larry as Grammy puts ring on Mr. T.)

MS RADCLIFFE: *(She takes two remaining rings from Punky).*
Grooms – please take these rings and place them on your bride's fingers. As you place the ring on Sarah's and Mary's finger, repeat after me. I give you this ring as a symbol of my love & commitment.

LARRY & MR.T: I give you this ring as a symbol of my love and commitment.
(The grooms place the rings on the bride's fingers, with difficulty).

MS RADCLIFFE: You may now kiss the brides! *(Couples kiss - All clap).* At this time, we'd like to call upon Keri Bell, daughter of the bride, Sarah Bell and Grand-daughter of Mr. Joe Taylor. She will sing a song she wrote for the two couples. *(music cue for **WHEN YOU'VE GOT LOVE,** Keri sings as bridal couples sign the register. Kids can join in on Chorus.)*
(Keri steps forward / to the side as brides and grooms move towards 'garbage can' covered with white tablecloth, to sign Register. They sign with the 'quill' pen). (Music fades as couples stand together in line).

MS RADCLIFFE: Now the parents of Spikey, Punky, Keri, Mark and Ben, would like to sing a song to their children. *(music cue for **A PARENT'S LOVE**) (Full, original version)*
(Grammy, Sarah, Larry and Mr. T sing). (All applaud).

MS RADCLIFFE:

> "May the love which has brought you together, continue to grow and enrich your lives; bringing peace and inspiration to each of you.
> May you meet with courage the problems which arise to challenge you.
> May you meet with strength the troubles that beset you.
> May you always communicate openly and honestly with each other.
> May you continue to appreciate the individuality of each other.
> May your relationship remain one of love, trust and commitment.
> May your partnership be one of ever-growing depth, meaning, and respect –
> because of the sympathy, understanding, and love you give one another;
> in the life you share.
> May the happiness you share today, be with both couples always!" *(beat)*
> Family and friends, please stand as I present to you, our two, newly wed couples!...
> Sarah Bell and Larry Law *(applause)* AND Mary and Joe Taylor! *(applause) (all cheer as the newly weds face the audience)*

GRAMMY: *(yells out!)* Yay!!!! We did it!!!

SPIKEY: *(yells out!)* Hip Hiporay! Hip Hiporay! It's been a very wonderful day!!! *(All Cheer!)*

*(All on stage sing: ****<u>Happily Ever After!</u>****)*

GRAMMY: *(yells out!)* Reception Party at Grammy's! *(Kids, Spikey, Misty, Punky run out first)* And now for something completely different. I made Prickles! Pickles with a strong spicy bite to them! *(Impresses Larry, Sarah, Ms Radcliff, Bob. They give a thumbs up. Exit SL)*

MR.T: I'm sure they'll be great. Can hardly wait for the cheese balls with pretzels and Don't forget about my <u>spiked</u> drinks!

GRAMMY: Right! Of course! *(Grammy and Mr. T, pretend to 'clink glasses' Larry takes Sarah's hand. They smile at each other).*

SPIKEY: My wish for the bridal couples – may your happiness double! May any troubles soon cease. I wish you a lifetime of peace! *(All Cheer as they EXIT SL to backstage)*

MR.T: Cheers to a Happy Life!!

GRAMMY: And a great start to a new <u>beginning</u>!!! *(Mr. T kisses her on cheek, as they exit).*

BEN: And they all chose to live, 'Happily Ever After!' *(ALL EXIT SR, to Grammy's).*

THE END

Theme song plays 3 times – 1. Curtain Call   2. Cast SING   3. Cast Exit to foyer

INSTRUMENTAL Music Cue – "Together We Can Make It!" during
<u>C U R T A I N C A L L</u>:

ALL CAST SING THEME SONG, "Together We Can Make It" then Exit.
All Cast take Position On Stage. Take Bow when in place.

CURTAIN CALL:

<u>Chorus, Park Dancers:</u> *- enter SR*
<u>Punky,</u> *- enter SL*
<u>Coach Bob</u> *– enter SR*
<u>Ms Radcliffe</u> *- enter SL*
<u>Misty</u> *– enter SR*
<u>Sarah, Larry</u> *– enter SL*
<u>Grammy, Mr. T.</u> *– enter SR*
<u>Sally, Tia, Robyn,</u> *- enter SL*
<u>Keri</u> *- enter SR as* **<u>Ben and Mark</u>** *- enter SL*
    (Keri, Ben and Mark stand by Larry'.)

<u>Spikey</u> *is last, enters from Centre and breaks through*
    between two bridal couples, holding Grammy's and Sarah's hands.

After SPIKEY enters/bows - ALL CAST BOW TOGETHER.
Stage Assistant enters SR. Assistant Stage Mgr. enters SL.

Music fades. Reset: MUSIC CUE FOR "Together We Can Make It!"
CAST SING, then Exit through audience, to foyer.

READINGS / WEDDING SONG:
Wedding Vows / The Prophet, by Kahil Gibran – On MARRIAGE
Final Reading: May the Love, May the Happiness ...
Written/Used for the wedding of Eveleen Winter & Richard Cox, 1996

WEDDING SONG: 'Commit My Love'
Lyrics: Joy Winter-Schmidt. Music by Dave Schmidt,
Written for their wedding, July 1988
Also used: Scripture: 1 Corinthians Ch. 13: 4 – 8
ARISO by Bach

Set Design – Stage Info

Intros / Curtain Call:

STAGE SET: Artificial TREES/SHRUBS, Two Park Benches, Rock Prop *(CS Centre Stage)* Metal Garbage Can. OPTIONS: Picnic Table, Lawn Chair, Community Quill Newspaper.

PRIOR TO SHOW: *Some cast can be on stage, reading the "Community Quill," etc., prior to the show. They can be on a lawn chair or at the picnic table. (If there's a Chorus, they can join in with harmonies on all songs, or selected songs, determined by Choral Director. Some of the Chorus could be selected for singing and/or dancing.) Each Sequel Opens with: 1. Voiceover. 2. Theme Music from "Together We Can Make It," prior to cast Entering the Stage.*

MUSIC: Latin/Salsa Style on Recorded Instrumental.   Choreography: See DVD's

- **ALL four Sequels START with "Once Upon A Time" followed by brief theme music as on instrumental recording.**

(This Voiceover could also be read from sound booth or backstage, by a child.)
'Once Upon A Time' Voice Over, opens all Sequels.

"Once Upon A Time ... not that long ago, lived a walking, talking, singing porcupine, with mostly good points. His name was Spikey. His parents didn't make it across the road. Spikey barely made it. He lay injured on the side of the road. A dear old lady everyone called Grammy, found him and nurtured him back to health. He became a friend to many because he always tried to do the best he could. He lived, he loved, he laughed. He became a great example to follow ..." *brief theme music follows ... before or as cast enter.*

END OF SHOW: *Each Sequel Ends with a Black-Out, on the last line in the script. All Cast Exit. Theme Instrumental follows, while cast re-enter stage, with full house lights, for their CURTAIN CALL.*

- **ALL four Sequels END with CAST Singing Encore Theme Song: "Together We Can Make It," after Curtain Call**

Instrumental theme song music is repeated, while Cast immediately walk through audience, to foyer, to meet and greet with the 'mostly younger' audience! *(Theme Music plays 3X at the end of each sequel).*

Break A Leg!

All Lyrics for all sequels: Joy Winter-Schmidt. All Music/Recording by Paulo Bergantim (2003-'05) excluding Theme Song, "Together We Can Make It," and Wedding Song, "Commit My Love," by David Schmidt.

Sequel 1: WELCOME SPIKEY'S POINTS!

(FULL VERSIONS OF ALL SONGS)

Scene 1:   **Let's Make A Point:** *(Spikey, Sally, Lisa, Grammy)*

Scene 3:   **No Choices:** *(Keri's Solo. Spikey, Sally and Lisa join in on Chorus)*

Scene 4:   **Spikey Ballad:** *(Spikey, Keri and Grammy)*

Scene 6:   **World Are You Ready?:** *(Spikey, Keri, Grammy, Sally and Lisa)*

Scene 7:   **Look At Me** (Rap): Acapella or music/drum soundtrack *(Spikey) (Kids on Chorus)*

Clean Up Stomp (Country): *(All cast on stage, plus Larry, Mark, Ben, Sarah and Mr. T)*

Scene 8:   **A Parent's Love:** *(Full Version: Sarah, Larry, Mr. T and Grammy) (Kids, all on stage, on Chorus)*

Tribute To Grammy: (Reggae): *(Spikey's Solo)*

Scene 9:   **Celebrate Life!:** *(STAR's Solo) (Kids, all on stage, on Chorus)*

You Gotta Have A Dream! *(Featuring Sarah and all cast)*

Together We Can Make It: *(ALL CAST – After Curtain Call - Encore)*

Sequel 2: CATCH A FRIEND

(SHORT VERSIONS OF Several Songs)

Scene 1: **Let's Make A Point:** *(1 verse)*

Scene 3: **Catch A Friend:** *(Spikey, Sally, Tia, Ben and Mark)*

Scene 5: **Valuable Volunteers:** *(Spikey and Grammy)*

Hit Home With Your Heart: *(Spikey's Rap Solo)*

Scene 6: **World Are You Ready?:** *(1 verse, all on stage)*

Nobody's Perfect: *(Keri's Solo)*

Scene 8: **A Parent's Love:** *(**Short** Version – **1 verse**. Sarah, Larry) (Kids, all on stage, on Chorus)*

Attitude: *(Spikey, Larry, Sarah, Mr. T, and girls)*

Scene 9: **I Believe In You:** *(Larry and Sarah)*

Scene 10: **Pay It Forward:** *(All Cast) (**Short version**)*

Celebrate Life!: *(All Cast) (Dance feature – **1 Verse**, Short version)*

You Gotta Have A Dream!: *(**1 verse**, Featuring Sarah and all cast)*

Together We Can Make It: *(ALL CAST – After Curtain Call - Encore)*

Sequel 3: SPIKEY'S COOL SCHOOL

(SHORT VERSIONS OF Several Songs)

Scene 1:   **Let's Make A Point:** *(Spikey) (1 verse)*

   Friends: *(Verse 1) Spikey, Sally and Tia)*

Scene 2:   **Friends:** *(Verse 2) Spikey, Keri and Grammy)*

Scene 4:   **It Starts With Me:** *(Keri, Sally, Tia, Sarah, Ben, Mark, Bob and Larry)*

   Attitude: *(Sarah and all Students)*

Scene 6:   **When You've Got Love:** *(Keri's Solo, or with cast during chorus)*

Scene 7:   **You've Gotta Have A Dream:** *(Featuring Sarah, all cast on Chorus)*

   I Believe In You: *(Sarah, Larry, Mr. T and Grammy)*

Scene 8:   **Give – Don't Give Up:** *(Spikey. All on Stage except Ms Radcliff, join in on chorus)*

Scene 9:   **World Are You Ready?:** *(All on stage) (1 verse)*

   Together We Can Make It: *(ALL CAST – After Curtain Call - Encore)*

Sequel 4: HAPPILY EVER AFTER!

(FULL VERSIONS OF ALL SONGS)

Scene 1: **You Gotta Have A Dream:** *(Misty, Spikey, Grammy and Punky)*

Let's Make A Point: *(Spikey, Misty, Grammy and Punky)*

Scene 3: **Valuable Volunteers:** *(Spikey and Grammy)*

Tribute To Grammy: *(Spikey's Reggae Solo)*

Catch A Friend: *(All On Stage)*

Scene 6: **Attitude:** *(All on Stage)*

Scene 7: **I Believe In You:** *(Misty)*

World Are you Ready?: *(Misty, Spikey and all on stage)*

Scene 8: *Wedding Scene:*

Commit My Love: *(Larry and Misty, or solo) (All on Chorus)*

When You've Got Love: *(Keri's Solo, or with Ms Radcliffe/Sarah)*

A Parent's Love: *(FULL VERSION, from Sequel #1: Grammy, Sarah, Mr. T and Larry)*

Happily Ever After!: *(All Cast)*

Together We Can Make It: *(ALL CAST – After Curtain Call - Encore)*

LET'S MAKE A POINT!

Verse 1:
Hello world I'm Spikey. Here and as excited as I can be,
If I like you and if you like me, It's a wonderful world you'll see.
I love singing and a lot of dancing, so kick up your heels now,
And join me in prancing.
I like getting up in the morning, to see what a new day will bring.
I'm happy as a king.
You have to work, you need to play,
Chase all your troubles away.
Use a good attitude always, and make your way!

CHORUS:
Let's make a point, Let's make a difference!
And help someone along the way.
The good Lord put us on this earth,
And in His care, we'll always stay.
Yes make a point and take a stand
Put a big smile upon your face,
To everyone through out the land...
Extend your hand - and make their day!

Verse 2:
Life is full of change – but that can be good.
Problems can be challenging – just turn things around,
Do things you never thought you could.
A sunny outlook can be really helpful
Because cloudy thoughts can do no good -
when you're down – when you need to make changes, you should.
You can push and other times pull...
But life comes around just once,
so make the best of all things.
You can see the glass half full – you can give yourself some wings.
Don't hide inside your hood, look for the good!

Repeat Chorus: 2X

NO CHOICES

Verse 1:
I'm sittin' here in the back seat – I have to ride along.
I never get any choices – so how can I belong?
I'm just a little robot, a puppet on a string!
Sometimes I get the feelin' – my thoughts don't mean a thing!

CHORUS:

No Choices, No Choices – We need choices!
You know we kids have voices – voices, voices, voices!
We know those big decisions, can make things tough on you...
But we have feelings too!

Repeat 2X

Oh yeah, all right – so what about me? Okay I'm just a kid.
Why do I have to be so resilient? Believe me, I'm NOT stupid!
I SO don't want to move – and to leave my old life behind.
You grown-ups always make us kids adapt. I feel adults can be unkind.

Repeat Chorus

You really need to listen to us – our voices – we need choices!
Oh yes, and did I mention, that we need attention?
Ignoring us is not cool. I love you mom and dad, too – but I'm nobody's fool.

Repeat 2X

Repeat Chorus

During Instrumental, Keri weaves in and out of dance line. She improvizes, her speech.
She's loud and upset. She could cross her arms, 'walk and stomp.'

KERI: *"Why doesn't anyone ever listen to me? I just want to leave and go back home.*
Why do we have to move here? I'll miss my old friends!
Why doesn't anyone listen to me?!"

SPIKEY BALLAD

GRAMMY: *(to Keri)* Spikey, he scares people daily. It's something he doesn't mean to do. He's like to make a friend. He'd like to meet you!

KERI: *(to Spikey)* I'm Keri – and you're scary! So don't get too close, or I'll run.

I'm afraid of all your sharp points. I don't think porcupines are fun.

GRAMMY: *(to Keri)* Maybe he'll run and hide somewhere, 'cause people won't accept him.

But where can he go from here? Well, I will take care of him!

KERI: *(to Spikey)* I'm sorry, I hurt you. Guess I am, hurtin' too!

I'm frightened by change – and this new place. Not your quills or your face.

SPIKEY: *(to Keri)* Spikey – that's my name. Grammy, she's like my mom. She says I'm not to blame, if people think I'm dumb.

KERI: *(moving towards Spikey)* Oh how could we ever be friends? You're different, but you're OKAY! Yes, everyone would laugh at us. Could we face that every day?!

SPIKEY: *(to Keri, as he puts his hands in the air)* I'm Spikey – I just want to fit in!

KERI: I'm Keri – there's nothing wrong with me...

SPIKEY & KERI: We're both just a little different – but that's okay to be!

SPIKEY: Grammy says that CARE, takes time to grow, and that true love will laaaast.

SPIKEY & KERI: I really need a friend – and as friends, we'll be. And our friendship will last!

163

WORLD ARE YOU READY?
Suggested Dance: Jive during Chorus

Verse 1
I'm in this world now
And so there'll be, no turning back.
Wow – my Grammy held me in her arms
And truly loved me.
So now I'm ready to explore, all that's new
Discover who I am...
There's so much to see and do.

ALL on CHORUS:

So I say world are you ready
For a porcupine like me?
People will stare, it always seems
But I hold on to my hopes and dreams.
Sometimes I fear what's in the future
And what can be in store for me.
Cuz I'm a little funny looking
But I'm as friendly as can be!

REPEAT CHORUS 2X

Verse 2
I would like to be more like others,
And go, to school.
I have a goal to learn in the classroom,
but, This is the rule!
Still, I have good friends
And I will treasure, all the good times.
My dearest memories, I'll share with others-
In all my rhymes!

LOOK AT ME

(Spikey's RAP – Could feature Chorus /Tap Dancers) (Some stanzas could be changed to THIRD person, for cast to sing) (Example: 'Spikey' may look all prickly, 'HE' has good points to share, Give 'HIM' a chance.)

...2...3...4...COME ON EV'rybody – GATHer aROUND
I'm GONna do some RHYMin' to a BRAND new SOUND! 1...2...3...Hey!
LOOK here, LOOK at me, my POINTS can be SEEN.
I am DIFFerent – YES, I am, to LEARN, I am KEEN!
I NEED **you** to SEE what's beneath my LOOKS.
I like HOTdogs, BASEball, Nature and BOOKS!
I may LOOK all PRICKLY, but I've got GOOD points to SHARE.
GIVE me a CHANCE – let me SHOW you, I CARE!
My HEART beats strong, inSIDE of me, though at TIMES I FAIL.
I've an INt'restin' STOry – let me TELL you may TALE....1...2...3...Here's my story now...

I was ON the ROAD but I DIDn't get FAR.
GRAMmy found me AFTter I got hit by a bus or CAR.
She CARED so much and HELPED me survive.
I'm so THANKFUL to GRAMmy, who KEPT me aLIVE!
I ENDed up ON the road beside this PARK!
Right Over THERE, cut and BRUISed – in the DARK.
SOMEtimes I'm a TREMBlin' when I FIRST aWAKE
When I THINK of that NIGHTmare, well it MAKES me SHAKE!
But I am GRATEful to BE aLIVE –
In GRAMmy's love and CARE – I will SUREly survive! 1..2..1, 2, 3, 4...

I am learning to READ and WRITE.
Grammy's TEACHing ME, with ALL her MIGHT!
I love TRY'in new THINGS – I'd like to GO to SCHOOL.
SOMEday I could GET a job – THAT would be so COOL!

In EV'ry DAY I find SOMEthing to LOVE.
To CARE and share my LIFE, is a DREAM from aBOVE! 1...2...3.., Ev'rybody now...
LOOK here, LOOK at me, my POINTS can be SEEN.
I am DIFFerent – YES, I am – to LEARN, I am KEEN!
Look in – not OUT – to see inSIDE my HEART!
GIVE me a CHANCE – let's make a BRAND NEW START!
Oh Yeah....let's GO now! Let's make a BRAND NEW START!

CLEAN-UP STOMP
(SEQUEL # 1 only)

SUGGESTED MUSIC: Country Line-Dance/Two Step, Polka

Verse 1: <u>SPIKEY</u>: Howdy Partners, I'm Spikey. This messy park is a shame. Parks are for all to enjoy. Clean up can be a fun game. There is so much to clean...

<u>Selected CAST</u>: Who wants to clean alone? Mother Nature gave us trees and grass, So we could call it our home.

<u>ALL on CHORUS:</u>

Let's clean it up! The clean-up stomp! Let's make it clean, the clean-up stomp...
<u>Selected Cast & GRAMMY</u> *(harmony)*<u>:</u>
This park is here for all of us now to enjoy!

<u>ALL:</u> *Pick up a can! The clean-up stomp! Let's rake some leaves! The clean-up stomp...*
<u>Selected Cast & GRAMMY</u> *(Suggested 4 part harmony)*<u>:</u>
Respect the park you're in, and keep it looking clean!

Verse 2: <u>SPIKEY:</u> This is my first true home - Keep clean, for all to enjoy!

<u>MR. T & SARAH:</u> Make it safe both night and day, for every young girl and boy!

<u>GRAMMY & LARRY:</u> So grab a broom and have fun. This park needs <u>you,</u> can't you see?

<u>Cast & GRAMMY:</u> *(harmony)* Messy parks are such a shame. To clean up is a fun game!

<u>Repeat Chorus 3X!</u>

A PARENT'S LOVE

(Full version)

<u>VERSE **1:**</u> ***Grammy & Sarah:*** Being a mom is the most important job I've had. I try to pave the way and set some examples. I teach and nurture, listen and try to understand … and what they think of life, we can't ignore.

Mr. T & Larry: We try and teach them special things that we all know, so their knowledge of life will always grow. A child doesn't always know what's right or wrong … So our love and patience for them must be strong.

ALL ON CHORUS:
A Parent's Love Will, help you reach your dreams,
We know we'll both make some mistakes…
But we'll give you our unconditional love,
And we'll do whatever it takes! (2X)

<u>VERSE **2:**</u> ***Mr. T & Larry:*** I'll guide you but be careful of just what I say. Always with respect to your point of view. Needing us as parents to hold your hand and lead … to experience the world of something new.

Grammy & Sarah: I'll encourage some responsibility in you, as we kiss you goodnight with a tight hold. But when you kiss me on the cheek, I melt away … cuz you make my heart turn instantly to gold.

(ALL repeat Chorus 4X)

(Short version – Duet: Sarah and Larry) (Sequel 2 only: *Sing to Jessica***) (One verse with one chorus. No Chorus repeat)**

Verse For Sequel 2:

Parents try and teach special things that they all know, so that their child's knowledge of life will always grow. A child doesn't always know, what's right or wrong … So a parent's love and patience for them, must be strong.

They'll guide you and be careful of just what they say, always with respect to your point of view.

You need your parents to hold your hand and lead … To move, is to experience a world of something new.

TRIBUTE TO GRAMMY

Suggested Dance: Macarena/Limbo/Bachata

Verse 1:

This is where Grammy first found me.
A young and lonely, homeless porcupine.
I was lyin' by the side of the road.
I had no parents, so my life was on the line.

CAST ON CHORUS:

Lying' there, all alone – it made him want to cry.
He was cold and hungry – He was scared.
He could not imagine what tomorrow would bring,
Until Grammy came for him, and showed she cared.

Verse 2:

Grammy picked me up in the cold
My sad, prickly quills and all.
She taught me things like how to speak and sing.
And drink from a glass – and now I have some class.

Repeat Chorus

Verse 3:

I'm now a very "people" porcupine.
I use a knife and fork, and manners when I dine.
I kindly try to show only my good points too;
For all my new friends, Grammy and for you –oo-oo!

Repeat Chorus

CELEBRATE LIFE!

DANCE INTRO

Sing! Dance! Beat Your Own Drum!!
Keep your dancin' goin' there's no need to stop.
Feel the music – let your energy pop.
We all have a song to sing! Hop 'til you drop!

Verse 1:

Do you wanna
find out who you are now?
Just stop worryin' about tomorrow.
Do and be your best today!
So sing, dance - love,
laugh and celebrate life!

CHORUS:

Listenin' to good music, so good for ya!
In your heart and soul, celebrate life!
Find your purpose, fill a need!
Do what's meant for you.
Respect yourself and others.
Do what's right for you.
Live, laugh and celebrate life!

Verse 2:

There'll always be somethin' happ' nin'
But just say "we're not gonna get mad," now.
Follow life's good lessons – be glad!
Be you – just be yourself!
Live being true to your self!
Love, laugh and celebrate life! Celebrate life!

YOU GOTTA HAVE A DREAM!

Verse 1:

What do you want from this life you are living?

Where do you want to go?

What do you want to do?

What will your tomorrow bring?

Our good friend has a dream.

Something he's striving for,

Let's show him we're all on his team!

Spikey wants a chance to learn in school, with all his friends.

So we will be right here until his journey ends!

CHORUS

Everyone reach for the stars!
You gotta have a dream.
We have a chance at greatness, if we just believe.
Everyone reach for the stars!
You gotta have a dream.
Look in your heart and imagine, what you can achieve!

Verse 2:

We all need friends to help us on our way.
Anything's possible,
If you have a goal.
And a plan to get there someday.
Let no one knock you down.
Let no one make you frown.
Know in your heart it's okay.
To dream for something special, reach for the brightest star.
You friends are here to help you, though it seems so far.

Repeat Chorus

TOGETHER WE CAN MAKE IT!
THEME SONG:

Instrumental Intro, Scene changes and
Curtain Call Encore with Cast singing.

<u>Chorus:</u>

Together we can make it.
We can make it.
Together we can make it;
Cuz we can take, whatever comes our way.
We can make it, you and I.
I'm your friend and you are mine,
We'll give more than we take.
'Cuz life is what you make.
And together we can make -
This world a better place.
'Cuz life is not a race.
Sometimes it's a scary ride.
And it's so hard to hang on inside.
So just slow down, go your own pace,
And keep a smile upon your face – cuz,'

<u>Repeat Chorus.</u>

Lyrics: Joy Winter-Schmidt '1991, Music: David Schmidt '91,
Arranging/Recording: Paulo Bergantim 2003.

CATCH A FRIEND

Verse 1:

Go ahead, meet someone new.
Introduce yourself – I'm pleased to meet you!

Pre-Chorus:

First Base: Use your intuition.
Second Base: Show that you can listen.
Third Base: Keep appreciatin.'

CHORUS
Say a little bit about you!
Hear a little bit about them!
Some gonna lose – some gonna win.
See what you have in common!

Repeat Chorus

Verse 2:

If you want to make a friend,
Step up to the plate and lend a hand!

Pre-Chorus:

First Base: Use your intuition.
Second Base: Show that you can listen.
Third Base: Keep appreciatin.'

Repeat Chorus 2X

ENDING:

First Base: Use your intuition
Second Base: Show that you can listen
Third Base: Keep appreciatin.'
Do all this – and you will CATCH A FRIEND!

VALUABLE VOLUNTEERS

By taking time to help your neighbours and
friends in need, helping someone
with less than you, the homeless or hungry;
Your smile can bring happiness
and hope to someone whose lost their way.

Your kindness may be the only thing,
that brightens up their day.

If there's a job that needs to be done,
You can be the one to make a better day!

REPEAT 3X:

HIT HOME WITH YOUR HEART

Verse 1:

You may think you're batting zero
'Cuz you're stuck in the dugout.
Life is throwing lots of curve balls.
And you're often striking out... *But...*

CHORUS:

It's not over 'til it's over.
So get rid of all that doubt.
Just keep playing' the best you can!
And you'll have the victory shout!

Verse 2:

Winning isn't just the score.
It's making friends and so much more.
Steal a base, catch a smile.
You'll catch a friend, all the while ... *Cuz ...*

REPEAT CHORUS:

Verse 3:

Throw your pitch in celebration.
Play it fair and with team spirit.
Give your all, be a sensation!
Come on now, I wanna hear it!

HIT HOME WITH YOUR HEART - HIT HOME WITH YOUR HEART
HIT HOME WITH YOUR HEART
... Aw yeah ...

REPEAT CHORUS:

HIT HOME WITH YOUR HEART - HIT HOME WITH YOUR HEART
HIT HOME WITH YOUR HEART ...

NOBODY'S PERFECT

Verse 1:

Sometimes things don't go as planned
and we feel alone.
We feel weighed down and want to cry.
We try to hold on to our hopes and dreams,
And keep our head high. Believe in ourselves,
Wipe the tears from our eye, 'cause we're special.
There's lots of reasons why!
Keep a smile on our face!
Put a song in our heart!
Cuz we have so many good points.
Now that's a really good start!

CHORUS:

Nobody's Perfect! Everyone's different.
We're all created that way.
What's normal? What's different?
We're all perfect in our own way!

Verse 2

We try to fit in,
Find sunshine on a rainy day.
Find laughter when we're feeling sad and gray.
We all have some good points, we all have some bad.
Like ourselves anyway!
Nobody's perfect. Everyone is different.
Who gets to decide anyway?
We're all normal.
If we're different, we're all okay!

REPEAT CHORUS:

ATTITUDE

Intro...

<u>SPIKEY and/ or KERI:</u> *1st Narration:* I get down, I get up. I can cry like a little pup. People look at me and see, something they don't want to be. I'm trying to hear my call. I run, I lead, I fall...

*1st **Verse:*** *(Selected Soloist)* Life is hard. I do the best I can. I try but all I feel, is all alone...

Narration Response: Love is all around you. You're as strong as you can be. And we'll help you through it all!

ALL: Yeah! Yay!!

CHORUS:

We all have good points, and we all have bad points,
But we don't have to give up and lose. We'll find our way.
Let's be ready for change. And let's have a good attitude!
Sometimes life' s not as good as it should be,
But take the next moment to choose. Step up and say that,
"I'll try it a new way. I'll have a good attitude!"

<u>SPIKEY:</u> *2nd Narration:* Accept me 'cuz I've got to accept myself. I'm the one and only me! We're all different. We're all the same. We all have problems, but let's not lay blame.

*2nd **Verse:*** *(Selected Soloist)* I have dreams, to be the best I can. To dance and have some fun and make new friends.

Narration Response: It's nice to be important, but it's more important to be nice, in this game of life!

ALL: Yeah! Yay!! **REPEAT CHORUS**

<u>SPIKEY:</u> *3rd Narration:* I've got good points, and I've got bad. I get happy and I get sad. But we're all here for a reason. For everything there is a season. I'd still like to soften my quills. We can make it up those hills!

Narration Response: That's Right! Being ready to change gives us latitude! So let's get rid of that bad attitude!

ALL: Yeah! Yay!! **REPEAT CHORUS**

<u>Selected from Cast:</u> *4th Narration: / ENDING:* It doesn't matter who you are. Rich or poor, you are a star! We all have something we can give. It's when we give, we really live. Being different, gives us colour. God loves us all, sisters and brothers!

I BELIEVE IN YOU

<u>Mr. T:</u> I believe in you,
   <u>Grammy:</u> I believe in you,
   <u>Larry:</u> I see faith in your eyes.
      <u>Sarah:</u> You are stronger than you think.

<u>Mr. T:</u> I believe in you,
   <u>Grammy:</u> I believe in you,
   <u>Larry:</u> I'm so happy with you.
      <u>Sarah:</u> I can see how great you are.

<u>Mr. T:</u> I believe in you,
   <u>Grammy:</u> I believe in you,
   <u>Larry:</u> You always make me smile.
      <u>Sarah:</u> You're honest and you're true.

<u>Mr. T:</u> I believe in you,
   <u>Grammy:</u> I believe in you,
   <u>Larry:</u> Let me hold you in my arms.
      <u>Sarah:</u> And we'll always make it through.

(4 part harmony...)
<u>Mr. T:</u> I believe in you.
   <u>Grammy/Larry/Sarah:</u> That's why I believe in you.

<u>Misty's Solo:</u>

I believe in you, I see faith in your eyes.
You are stronger than you think.
I believe in you. I'm so happy with you.
I can see how great you are.
I believe in you. You always make me smile
You are honest and you're true.
I believe in you. Let me hold you in my arms.
And we'll always make it through.
I believe in you – I believe in you
That's why I believe in you.

PAY IT FORWARD

(same tune as Clean-Up Stomp, Sequel #1, only SHORTER version)

Verse 1:

Howdy Folks – we're changin'.
It's time to stand up for what's right.
We're not bystanders or fighters.
We're here to make a difference,
Every day and night!
Let's all try to clean up this world
And make it a safer home.

CHORUS:

Let's pay it forward – Pay it forward!
Life is here for all of us now, to enjoy!
Pass on a Smile – Pay it forward!
Let's lend a hand – Pay It forward!
Respect yourself and all,
And those less fortunate than you!

Verse 2:

Give as much as you can.
Take as little as you need.
Feeling sorry for ourselves
Doesn't get us anywhere.
Our anger at the world,
destroys the inside of us.
We can make a change,
With our friendly words.

Repeat Chorus

FRIENDS

Verse 1:

Friends care, friends share.
True friends are a light in the dark.
They make you laugh at home, at school,
And while playing in the park.
Friends are caring people you can trust.
They'll keep you safe from danger,
if they must.

CHORUS:

Friends care if you are happy,
Understand when you're blue.
Standing strong together.
Friends are powerful and true.
Be a friend to yourself.
Be a friend to each other.
By your side, through thick and thin,
A friend is like no other.

Verse 2:

A friend will listen to your dreams.
They'll stay forever near.
Miles may separate you,
But the memories stay dear.
A real friend stands by you
And keeps you strong.
They'll make you feel you're right,
where you belong.

REPEAT CHORUS:

Joy Winter-Schmidt

IT STARTS WITH ME

Verse 1:

Yes it does, it starts with me,
One small step can make a change today.
With what we say and what we do,
Our hearts and hands are sure to pave the way.

CHORUS:

It starts with me,
It starts with you,
Together there is so much we can do.
We can make a difference,
Together we are strong.
Soon we'll find together, is right where we belong!
If you want to help today
Take one step – come on now! - and say:

REPEAT CHORUS:

Ending

It starts with me,
It starts with you,
Together there is so much we can do!

WHEN YOU'VE GOT LOVE

Verse 1:
When you've got love, you've got it all.
Love catches the fall.
When you're feeling down, trust in your love,
It will calm your fears.

Pre-Chorus:

When there are hills and bills, love takes away tears.
Continue to hear love's call.

CHORUS:

When you've got love, you've got it all.
When you've got family ties, family comes first.
When you've got love, you got it all.
When you've got love, you got it all.

Verse 2:

Through your open heart,
may you always hear love's call.
Love is in your heart,
We see it in your eyes.

Repeat Pre – Chorus

Repeat CHORUS 2X

<u>GIVE – DON'T GIVE UP!</u>

<u>*Verse 1:*</u>

We won't let them crush our spirit.
We can change things, without a fight.
Our voices are strong, they can hear it.
We know in our hearts we are right.
In life there are folks who will challenge you.
Because they can't see your light.
Stay true to your friends. They have faith in you.
They'll help keep your goals in sight.

<u>CHORUS:</u>

Give. Don't Give Up! Let's take a stand!
We'll show them, the winning cards are in our hand.
Give, don't Give Up!
We know the way, to give all we've got,
and help our friends today.

<u>*Verse 2:*</u>

If you find yourself losing your nerve,
And can't see your dream to the end;
Keep giving 'til you get what you deserve.
And trust in the faith of a friend.
A new start can be a blessing.
But some folks are stuck in the past.
We just need to keep on pressing,
This struggle won't be our last!

COMMIT MY LOVE

*Lyrics: Joy Winter-Schmidt. Music composed by Dave
Schmidt for their Wedding, July 1988*

Verse 1:

Yesterday, you embraced me in your love.
Sharing feelings – believing in tomorrow.
And today as we stand here together
And recite our marriage vows.
I commit my love to you.
Your loyalty secures my trust in you.
Your gift of love, opened my heart.
You cared enough, to see through my faults.
And found the beauty inside.
I commit my Love to you.

CHORUS:

*I never needed anyone, the way that I need you.
I feel safe in the love that we share.
And should life become a struggle,
I will support you.
And God will meet all our needs.*

Verse 2:

I will love and respect you, my friend.
We will share our thoughts and compromise.
We will face reality with confidence.
We will work and stay together in love.
I commit my love to you.

REPEAT CHORUS

Yesterday, you embraced me in your love.
Sharing feelings – believing in tomorrow.
And today as we stand here together,
And recite our marriage vows.
I commit my love to you.

HAPPILY EVER AFTER!

Verse 1:

No one said life was gonna be easy.
But happiness is a frame of mind.
Attitude is enemy or friend.
Choose to be respectful and kind.
Open your eyes to see new things.
Do your best, be honest and true.
Love and do only good things,
And good things will come back to you!

CHORUS:

Believe in Happily Ever After.
By being happy wherever you're at.
Being grateful for all that you have.
Love others, give and you will receive.

Verse 1:

Grass is greener on the other side.
Happiness is not defined by things.
Keep your arms and heart, open wide.
Live, love, laugh, give more than you take.
A great relationship, you will make.
Understand where others come from.
May healing and forgiveness come.
Pain's part of life, things change and end.

LYRIC TITLES:

24 SPIKEY SONGS:

MUSIC: Paulo Bergantim: Composing/Recording/Arranging *(2003 - '05, 2016)*
Lyrics: Joy Winter-Schmidt *(1993, 2001 - 2015)*
Music: Dave Schmidt: Wedding Song *(1988)* Theme Song *(1993)*

- Let's Make A Point *(ALL CAST)*
- No Choices *(KERI)*
- Spikey Ballad *(Spikey / Keri / Grammy)*
- World Are You Ready? *(ALL)*
- Look At Me *(SPIKEY'S RAP)*
- The Clean Up Stomp *(ALL)*
- A Parent's Love *(Sarah / Grammy / Mr. T / Larry)*
- Tribute to Grammy *(SPIKEY)*
- Celebrate Life! *(STAR SOLO or with Spikey)*
- You Gotta Have A Dream *(SARAH & Cast)*
- Together We Can Make It *(Theme Encore: ALL)*
- Catch A Friend *(Spikey & Cast)*
- Valuable Volunteers *(Spikey & Grammy)*
- Hit Home With Your Heart *(ALL)*
- Nobody's Perfect *(KERI & Cast)*
- Attitude *(Selected Cast)*
- I Believe In You *(Sarah/Grammy/Mr. T/Larry) (Misty)*
- Pay It Forward *(Sarah and 'Leadership class')*
- Friends *(All) (Scenes 1 and 2)*
- It Starts With Me *(Selected Cast)*
- When You've Got Love *(Keri)*
- Give – Don't Give Up *(Selected Cast)*
- Commit My Love *(Selected Cast)*
- Happily Ever After! *(All)*

Set Photo / Properties

Properties for All Sequels:

- Large ROCK Prop, wooden base / solid enough for two to sit on. Suggestion: Covered with grey foam, painted for added effects. Metal garbage can visible but out of the way. *Other props include: Grammy's knitting bag, back packs, lunch kits, books, picnic basket, dance wear and tap dance shoes. (Sequel 1 only: non-perishable garbage, boxes, bottles, old shoes, etc, and recycling bin)*

- Two PARK BENCHES SR and SL. *(angled on stage).* Benches should be long enough for three to sit on. *Options: Small PICNIC TABLE, for SR, for Chorus, Kids/Tia's colouring book/crayons. Park Lawn Chair SL.*

- TREES / SHRUBS: 'Park appropriate' artificial trees, plants, flowers. *Options: Projected park image on big screen, behind set. Someone from Chorus reading Community Quill newspaper (with Spikey Cartoon).*

- Imitation CELL/ Blackberry. *(Sequel 2 only: baseball/gloves and sound system for Mark. Table/Chairs for Larry and Sarah's 'home scene.' Sequel 3: Judge robe, toy hammer, Sequel 4: White tablecloth, quill pen, wedding rings, ring bearer pillow).*

SPIKEY COLOURING PAGE

AVAILABLE TO ORDER:

Sheet Music & Recorded Music

(24 SONGS: Instrumental and Lyrics)
Used by Permission
from Composers Paulo Bergantim, David Schmidt & Lyric writer: Joy Winter-Schmidt

Sequels 1-4: **SONG ARRANGEMENTS: Robert MacLean**
Additional Arrangements: Somer Kenny, Dave Schmidt,
Marianne Crittenden, Rebecca Thiessen, Joy w-s.

Sheet Music / CDs: Contact Rebecca Thiessen:
rebeccathiessen@hotmail.comHYPERLINK
email: rebeccathiessen@hotmail.com

USB Flash Drives: Instrumental Music and with Cast
Contact: **Mark Hall:** email: mbhall1982@yahoo.ca

DVD's of Sequels 1-4:

(Live from the Gas Station Theatre! - Winnipeg MB, 2015 - 2018)
Contact: **Cody Zaporzan:** email: **czaporzan@gmail.com**
2nd videographer: Samantha Layer: layervideoimagery@gmail.com
DVD Spikey roles: 2015: Tyler Leighton 2016: Cameron Dubois...
Gas Station Arts Centre Technical Director / Stage Lighting: Todd Drader
Sound Technician: David Musso
All ACTORS listed on the DVD's!

Sterling Silver Spikey Pendants & Pins:
Contact: **Krista Reid: Velocity Jewellery**
Award Winning Silver Artist! www.uniquelymanitoba.ca
Velocity311@hotmail.com (204) **774-7478**

ROYALTY FREE!
Scripts / Lyrics / Recorded Music / Sheet Music
If used for SCHOOL: Drama / ESL / Literacy Programs,
CHURCH, CHARITY or NON-PROFIT Productions!

For Profit Productions, written permission must be obtained
from Composers Paulo Bergantim, David Schmidt & Lyric writer: Joy Winter-Schmidt
*For more info, email **jwinterschmidt@gmail.com** Winnipeg, Manitoba Canada*

PREMIER PERFORMANCE:
Western Manitoba Centennial Auditorium, June 1993
K- Gr. 6, Brandon School Division, Manitoba, Canada

Spikey - Derek Watson
Mother - Lisa Stadnyk, Daughter - Ann Ehnes

Butterflies: Emily Linklater, Nicole Rouire,
Erin May, Aynsley Hyndman

Animals in the forest:
Karen Loewen, Christine Victor,
Andrew Keachie, Melissa Mason, Kirsten Stovel,
Jennifer Perrin,
Kristi Brownlee, Margie Wolchuk,
Brittinee Long, Holly Wilson

Turtle - Cameron McPhail
Bee: Shara Molnar

All Cast Photos by Joy - with permission from the cast

2001

Spikey - River Ferreira

2002

Spikey - Dillon Spicer

Spikey - Kevin Schmidt

Spikey - Dillon Spicer

Spikey - Dillon Spicer

Spikey - Mike Dooley

2010

Spikey - Ted Kist

2011

Spikey - Ted Kist
Also Featuring Baby Porcupine - 'PUNKY'

Spikey's Points Musical 2014

Spikey - Dylan Hatcher

THANKS to ALL SPIKEY CASTS & CREWS!!!

And to Park Musicians,
Including Classical Guitarists: Randy Haley, Jon Bergen & Andrew Schmidt
Tannis Steiman (flute) & Allie Skwarchuk (harp)

Joy's 'Directing Spikey' ended in 2015.
She continues as Producer/Artistic Director/Consultant.
She's extremely grateful
for all the support from MANY over the years!

2015-2018: (Sequels 1-4, as recorded on DVD's & CD's)
DIRECTORS: Joy W-S, Mark Hall, Assistant: Kelley Hirst
CHORAL DIRECTORS: Dave Schmidt, Rebecca Thiessen
CHOREOGRAPHER: Erin J. McCallum
Additional Choreography:
Stephanie S. *(Bachata)* Joy W-S *(Jive)* Nikki H. *(Boot Scooting Boogie)*
Mark H., Jessica L., Rya K., Renelle T.
Sound Tech (Seq. 1-4): David Musso: smotts2002@gmail.com
Set Design (Seq. 2-4): Darryl Audette: www.darrylaudette.com

Spikey - Tyler Leighton

Welcome Spikey's Points
Sequel #1
(Cast Includes LISA & LADY LA LA)

2015/'16 + cast remain the same, with exception of Cameron Rey-Dubois as 'Spikey.' Kelley Hirst continues as 'Grammy,' Lawrence Hill as 'Mr. T,' Bethany Cook as 'Sarah,' Mark Hall as 'Larry,' Isabella & Ethan Neiser, as 'Keri' & 'Mark,' Hudson & Renelle Thiessen as 'Ben' & 'Tia', & Kayden Olson as 'Sally.'

Chorus included Rebecca Thiessen, community dancers & singers including Ariel Leo.

Sequel 2, 2016 new characters: Rya Keyes as 'Jessica,' Cameron Rey-Dubois as 'Spikey' Trevor Gatchell as 'Coach Bob,' and Jessica Lemanski as 'Misty.'

New Cast: Sequels 3/4 MS RADCLIFFE: Rebecca Thiessen,
ROBYN: Morgan Beveridge, **Punky:** Bijoux Giordmaina-Kubera

'BREAK A LEG!' all future Spikey CASTS! *from Winnipeg's non-profit community theatre group, 'Prickly Productions!'*

MR.T. with his grand-daughter KERI & his daughter SARAH

CATCH A FRIEND
WINNIPEG, MANITOBA
CANADA

Rebecca & Hudson

STAGE CREW
DAVID MUSSO
TAMMY PAUL

- D V D S -
Sequels 1-4
2015 - 2018

2017
Spikey's Cool
School

2018
Happily Ever
After

CAMERON REY-DUBOIS *as* SPIKEY!

ALL STAR CAST:

Back Row: **KERI:** Isabella Neiser, **SALLY:** Kayden Olson, **MARK:** Ethan Neiser,
LARRY & DIRECTOR: Mark Hall, **GRAMMY** & Assistant Director: Kelley Hirst,
Middle Row: **COACH BOB:** Trevor Gatchell, **SPIKEY:** Cameron Rey-Dubois,
MISTY: Jessica Lemanski,
Front Row: **JESSICA:** Rya Keyes, **TIA:** Renelle Thiessen

BEN: Hudson Thiessen, **MR. T:** Lawrence Hill, **SARAH:** Bethany Cook

CHORUS: Rebecca Thiessen, Jessica Lemanski, Nikki Harris,
Lara, Roxy & Aurora Gatchell, Gerald Adams-(trumpet)

MR. T & Grammy

New Characters & Cast added for Sequels 2-4, 2016 - 2018:
*TREVOR as **Coach Bob**, CAMERON as **Spikey**, RYA as **JESSICA** and*
*JESSICA as **MISTY** (2016)*

Best Wishes from Spikey Cast & Crew!

Break A Leg!...So Long...Farewell...

- T H E   E N D -

Printed in the United States
By Bookmasters